HER HALLOWEEN PARTY

B Mine Book 4

Brooklyn Ann

PRAISE FOR BROOKLYN ANN'S BOOKS

B-MINE SERIES

His Final Girl

"Brooklyn takes the reader on a rollercoaster ride through the horrors that lurk in the woods, yet keeps it light, before terror strikes. Full of pop culture references, horror, romance, enjoyable characters, and twists and turns to keep you wanting more, HIS FINAL GIRL has something for everyone. If Friday the 13th was a love story, this would be it." ~Anthony Northrup, Through the Black Hole

Gripping suspense, action, fabulous vivid scene descriptions, praise-worthy engaging characters and an awesome happy ending for the hero and the heroine. Enthralling page-turner that keeps you guessing who the ancient killer is. The author has done a fabulous job fusing horror and romance. Linnea and Wes are a perfect match; love them together. ~midniteink

Her Haunted Heart

"Another excellent, amazing read. I started today and finished it this morning because I couldn't put it down, it's that great, the ending will blow you away because it gives you a clue to another book this writer writes. Which I totally loved. Great characters and exceptional writing plus a lot of history that's fascinating. Highly recommend this book." ~Roxane

"This story was a cross between Supernatural *and* The Amityville Horror. *Creepy with a 1980's background it was a fun and interesting story."* ~Gina Johnson

His Scream Queen

"I really enjoyed the experience! It was so kitschy it was clever. It was delightful to temporarily travel back to the days of MTV, acid

washed jeans, feathered hair, and no cell phones. The book is full of stereotypes, but they are there for a reason, and without them, the book simply wouldn't have worked. So if you love your high school romances sweet and sentimental but also spiked with a heavy shot of evil, then be sure and grab this and see what it was like to be a kid in high school in the early '80s." ~Deana Aria

"This is the third book in the B Mine horror/romance series. I have to say Brooklyn found her comfort zone with this sub-genre and it really shows. This is my favorite so far. Set in the 80's there are plenty of references and Easter eggs in the story. Awesome story, solid prose, and great characters. I think fans of 80's slasher/supernatural and her best friend's exorcism will really enjoy this one!" ~Torrie04

HEARTS OF METAL SERIES

"Hearts of Metal is a rock series that is not to be missed." ~Kara's **Books**

Kissing Viciöus

"KISSING VICIÖUS is a sensual, rockin' romance with a hero to die for." ~Fresh Fiction

"This is not your usual rocker romance. I thank the author for creating strong characters and taking a different course from usual. We really need more strong characters like Kinley and Quinn in the romance genre." ~The Romance Reviews

With Vengeance

"I was hooked the minute I started reading!! This is a totally different rock star book, but that's not a bad thing at all!! It's refreshing to see a rock star not be all about the 'rock star' lifestyle. Klement and Katana's relationship is pure and genuine and I can't say enough good words about it!" ~B1tches N Books

"Plenty of kicking ass, hilarious moments, and one hell of a romance." ~Librarian by Day, Reader by Night

Rock God

"This story has the right mix of sex, sweet and romance. I fell in love with the characters from the very first page." ~Bramley, Emma, Obsessed Book Reviews

"Brooklyn Ann weaves us another amazing story fill with drama, angst, passion, and inspiration. Her characters are so realistic and written with so much depth... it's hard not to become emotionally attached to them all!" ~Rachel, Behind Closed Doors Book Reviews

Metal and Mistletoe

"Another winner. If you haven't read this author you're missing something." ~LuvLeeLorraine

"I will definitely read this one again when I want to feel warm, fuzzy and hopeful for my own happy ending." ~Fan Forever

Forbidden Song

"This is my favorite Bleeding Vengeance story. I was a little emotional as this story unfolded with happy tears at the end. I highly recommend this book and series." ~Christine Woinich

"Brooklyn Ann has created another great read in her Hearts of Metal series. Brooklyn writes in such a way as to show you the character development. Well worth reading." ~All Things Book

Tempting Beat

"The author is smart enough to keep the reader hooked - the characters are terrific, and even the secondary characters are well drawn. So read this book and slip into your Cinderella shoes - and fall in love with a young, handsome rock star who is more than he appears to be!" ~JennM

"I always look forward to a new book by Brooklyn Ann! I know I'm in for a treat and a fantastic read long into the night. I've read all her books, I've never been disappointed. This is book 6 in the Hearts of Metal series, but each book can definitely stand alone. Though you will want to go back and read about the other characters lives and how they came to be together. They are not typical romance books. There's something special about each one, making each one different. More than five stars!" ~ginger@thebeach

Heart Throb

"I don't want this series to end because I need more from all of the bands! I loved the way each character was not only depicted as skilled at what they did but also as imperfect, vulnerable, normal human beings. This was a fabulous read, with well-developed characters and a fascinating setting." ~BookLover

"Hot chemistry, romance, drama, and perceived betrayal make up this gripping rockstar romance. **Heart Throb** *is an entertaining read that moves at a good pace, thus keeping you entertained until the very end. Both Brand and Lexi are likable characters and are well developed. I really enjoyed this book and I am definitely going back to read the rest of the series."* ~AT_202

www.BOROUGHSPUBLISHINGGROUP.com

HER HALLOWEEN PARTY
Copyright © 2021 Brooklyn Ann

ISBN: 978-1-953810-83-0

To Karen Ann
(6-11-62 ~ 2-14-09)
Here's another horror movie I wish we could watch together.

And to Tony Northrup – thank you for being the biggest supporter of this series.
If not for your cheering me on, I may not have finished it.

ACKNOWLEDGMENTS

Huge thanks to everyone who made this book possible. To my developmental editor, John Trevillian, my publisher, Michelle, my agent, Nephele, my real-life romance hero, Kent, my amazing son, Micah, my best crit buddy, Layla (I'm glad you like your cameo), to my research buddies, Hans, David, and Marie, my sensitivity reader, Ana, and my sprinting partner, Donyae. To Juan Carlos Martinez for helping me keep sane at the hellacious day job. Extra thanks to the Horror Writers Association, and of course my readers.

AUTHOR'S NOTE

This book has been a daunting labor of love, as it pays homage to primarily two of my favorite horror films: *Night of the Demons* (the ultimate 80s B horror film) and *Rose Red* (my favorite evil house movie). *Her Halloween Party* also borrows the premise of *Hell Night* (a film I thought had a great concept, but flubbed the execution) to get my characters into the notoriously evil Raimi House. I've been teasing the Raimi House for a while in this series and hope it lives up to what you've anticipated. I also wanted to include a sad, but true, fact about North Idaho history.

The presence of the hate group Aryan Nations, who terrorized the region from the 1970s to the year 2000, when court cases and zoning changes made them lose their compound, lose the ability to throw their hateful parades, and imprisonment for their most violent members. Though Amteep is a fictional town, and though the hate group's presence has little to do with the story, I thought it would be wrong not to acknowledge their existence and the damage they did to people. Damage a demon, real or inner, could use to torment a person. I was lucky my only encounters with the Aryans were the hideous racist flyers left on my windshield, and the time I was fired from a local burger joint after my Native ancestry came to light. Other people were not so lucky.

On to happier subjects: I've included easter eggs from other books of mine that my big fans will recognize; I also did my best to put in all the details that will contribute to the Halloween spirit. So many books and movies set on Halloween don't have enough Halloween, y'know? That's another great aspect of *Night of the Demons*. The characters wore Halloween costumes. And though I didn't have as much of a chance to include as many '80s songs and fashions as I have in previous books, I put in a little, and then added more through my characters' costumes.

One last thing before this note becomes a ramble: since I started the B Mine series, I've had the joyous opportunity to meet so many new people in the horror community. I want to thank everyone who gave this romance writer a chance to fulfill her dream of writing in her first and most beloved genre.

HER HALLOWEEN PARTY

Chapter One

September 27, 1987

Amelia Craven was in hell. Well, technically not yet, since Hell Week was four weeks away. Tonight's hell was *another* frat party.

As the stereo blared Michael Jackson's *Bad* album for the hundredth time, Amelia reached into the ice-filled Rubbermaid tub for another wine cooler. The new album was okay, not as good as *Thriller*, and now less appealing since the Alpha Lambdas had played it way too loud every weekend at their parties. Her head ached and her throat hurt from having to yell over the music to have a conversation. The air reeked of spilled beer, cigarettes, Aqua Net, and the miasma of too many people packed in one place.

She didn't want to be here in the always chaotic, perpetually odorous Alpha Lambda house. She'd rather be back at the Omega Pi house, alone in the room she shared with her best friend Tiffany, studying—or even better—curled up with either *Cabal,* the newest Clive Barker novel, or *Mysteries of the Cursed Mine: An Unauthorized History of the Camp Natty Massacre.* Her opportunities to read for fun had been severely limited since the Ffall semester started five weeks ago.

She'd earned her associate's degree in English last spring from Amteep Community College and was pursuing her Master of Library Science here on the adjoining campus at North Idaho University. The coursework was heavier, but that didn't stop Tiffany from insisting that she and Amelia join the university's only sorority, the Omega Pis. Despite Amelia's fervent hopes otherwise, she and Tiffany were accepted as pledges. That meant instead of attending a few frat parties here and there, they had to go to *all* of them.

But Tiffany had been Amelia's best friend since junior year of high school. The popular blonde had been like a beautiful fairy princess, transforming Amelia from a wallflower to a member of the in crowd. Amelia owed Tiffany so much. She'd been so lonely before then, walking in a haze of grief from losing her mom in the eighth grade, her brown hair hanging in dull tangles, her clothes unkempt, losing herself in books about ghosts and monsters in fiction as well as the spooky real history of her hometown of Amteep. Then Tiffany, for reasons of pity, or perhaps desire for a challenge, took Amelia under her wing and became her friend. They did everything together. But lately, Amelia was beginning to chafe under Tiffany's perpetual leadership of their lives.

As if drawn by the thought, Amelia's roving gaze landed on one of hers and Tiffany's biggest subjects of contention: a man whose long, curly black hair framed an angular bronze face, deep brown eyes, and a smile to die for. Guillermo Romero, heir to Romero Construction, the most prominent building contractor in town, never failed to render Amelia breathless. He was a pledge for the Alpha Lambda fraternity and they'd been sharing their initiation woes. She'd met him in her first year at Amteep Community College, when they'd first had English and Intro to European History together. They'd also seen each other at metal concerts and parties, as well as on the campus, and struck up a tentative friendship over the last two years. Amelia had basked in the warmth of that friendship, free from pretenses or expectations, even as she harbored a secret crush on him since day one.

How could she not when, aside from his gorgeous face and physique, he was unfailingly kind, actually seemed to see her when he spoke to her, and had a husky, lullaby voice that haunted her dreams?

Every time they were both single and Amelia considered asking him out, Tiffany held her back. *"You should be with a guy of higher status. You don't want to be dating a fellow pledge. He probably wouldn't be interested in you anyway..."* and so on. After a lot of soul-searching, Amelia realized only the last argument held water.

Now Guillermo was single again—she couldn't suppress a wave of elation when she heard the nursing student he'd been dating split up with him over summer break—and now, as of last week, she was also unattached. So maybe...

Suddenly, the music stopped, making everyone curse and yell in protest.

Susan Acuff stood up on the keg and rang the cowbell reserved for announcements and waking up pledges, making a hush instantly fall over the crowded house. In spite of her petite stature and Goldilocks curls, as president of the Omega Pis—and girlfriend to Kirk Sorbo, the president of the Alpha Lambdas—she intimidated everybody. "It pains me to say this, but we have a rat in our midst. A filthy, dirty rat."

Kirk moved to stand beside her, a sentient Ken doll in a polo shirt with a sweater tied around his shoulders. He shoved his hands in the pockets of his Dockers and surveyed the crowd with a stern eye. "Someone revealed the location of the final initiation of our pledges."

Susan picked up where he left off, crossing her arms over her North Idaho University sweatshirt. "The rituals of our organizations are supposed to be sacred and secret."

"Where is the location?" Tiffany and a few others asked.

"Don't play innocent," Susan snapped. "There's a letter to the editor in both the *Amteep Press* and the university paper saying we shouldn't be allowed to rent the Raimi House. Someone had to have told. Or maybe one of *you* wrote that letter."

Holy shit. Amelia gasped. With her heavy course load, she hadn't had time to look at the newspaper since this semester started. "The *Raimi House?*"

Susan's anger momentarily dissipated as a triumphant smile lit her hazel eyes, making her look beautiful and sweet even though Amelia knew better. "Kirk and I managed to convince the owner to rent us the property for October and November. We get the keys and sign the paperwork on Tuesday the first." Her sour scowl returned. "It was *supposed* to be a surprise, but one of you spoiled it."

Despite her better judgment, Amelia spoke up again. "The rental agency probably gossiped. No one's occupied the Raimi House since 1962. The last person inside the house was an appraiser last year, and he died there. So, someone renting the place would be huge news. No way anyone in the agency would keep their mouth shut."

"That would be a relief *if* that's true," Susan said with a shark-like smile. "But how do I know *you* didn't say anything, pledge? Or maybe you're trying to protect your friend."

Nancy, Amelia and Tiffany's assigned mentor, countered the president in a firm voice. "I know it wasn't Amelia. Or Tiffany, for that matter. If their obvious shock isn't enough to convince you, I can attest that they've both been in sight every waking hour when we're not in class. Amelia's been buried with homework and studying all week. I haven't seen her look at either newspaper to see those editorials calling for us to cancel the party. And Tiffany—"

"The party?" Tiffany asked eagerly, making Amelia bite the insides of her cheeks to halt a chuckle. Tiff *loved* parties.

Susan sighed and attempted to thrust her hands in the pockets of her acid-washed jeans, but they were too tight. "We're going to have a Halloween party at the most notorious house in town."

Raucous cheers erupted around them while Amelia quivered with mingled excitement and trepidation. She'd been fascinated with creepy houses and local haunted landmarks ever since she saw her first ghost at a sleepover in one of the old Victorian houses downtown. Since then, the middle school librarian nurtured her interest, telling stories about the Raimi House to Amelia's sixth-grade class, but the idea of having a Halloween party with the final initiation taking place in the house where so many people had been killed or maimed scared her a little. Especially since what Kirk and Susan planned had to be *more* than a party. A party was supposed to be fun. Final initiations for pledges were *never* fun.

When the cheers died down, Kirk confirmed her thoughts. "After the party, all you pledges have to spend the night in the Raimi House alone together. If you eight survive the night, Guillermo, Mike, Chuck, and Dan will be inducted as active members of Alpha Lambda. And..." He paused while Susan whispered the girl pledges' names. "Tiffany, Amelia, Layla, and Tina will become full-fledged sisters of the Omega Pis."

Amelia's mouth went dry. Spend the night in the Raimi House? She looked back to Guillermo, who looked genuinely scared. As he should be. She may not believe in God or the devil, but she and everyone else familiar with the town of Amteep knew that place was pure evil. And yet, even knowing the horrific history of the haunted cliffside estate, Amelia squirmed with curiosity to see the subject of her obsession.

Suddenly, Layla Thomas, the only Black pledge, spoke up. "I guess I'm not going to be an Omega Pi then. Because there's no way in hell I'm going into that house."

With that, she strode out of the frat house. Amelia was torn between cheering Layla's bravery, envying her escape from the sorority, and being sad to see her go. Layla was one of the few people in the sorority house she liked, and the only girl who shared Amelia's love for heavy metal music.

"I'm not going there either," Dan Gatchel said. "I've heard the stories."

"Me too," Tina called behind Dan's shoulder. "I quit."

Susan stuck her nose in the air and made a prissy harrumph. "Fine. Then pack your bags. I want you out of the Omega Pi house tonight. Tell Layla she's out as well." She leaned over and whispered something to Kirk, then turned back to glare at everyone. "I can't believe the ingratitude I'm seeing. Kirk and I worked hard to gain access to this house and to give you pledges the most legendary initiation in history. One that you'll be able to tell your children and grandchildren about."

Guillermo made a derisive snort. "Yeah, if we survive to have children."

Kirk stepped forward and thrust out his chest like a rooster. "Any other chickens dropping out?"

The room fell silent. Amelia held her breath, wondering if Guillermo would be the next to walk out. Was it selfish to hope he stayed? Or was she an idiot to not walk out?

"Okay then." Kirk put his arm around Susan's waist. "After we get the keys on Tuesday, the ladies will clean the place up and the gentlemen will chop firewood, get supplies, and do any handyman work necessary to make sure the house is safe. All of you will ensure we have the best Halloween party in the history of our organizations. Now let's get back to the party."

Susan opened her mouth to say more, but Kirk gestured to the guy by the stereo. Michael Jackson's "Smooth Criminal" roared back at full volume, leaving her to pout at not having the last word.

Tiffany took Amelia's arm and led her away before opening her compact to inspect her perpetually flawless makeup. "You shouldn't have said anything about the rental agency gossiping about the

Raimi House. Going against Susan, especially in front of everyone, is going to incur her wrath."

"Everything incurs her wrath," Amelia grumbled.

Tiffany leaned in close, her breath smelling like vodka. "I'm going upstairs to spend a little time with Brandon. See what else he knows about the Raimi House initiation and make sure that tramp Valerie doesn't get her claws in him."

Amelia rolled her eyes as Tiffany walked away. Why did Tiff have to be so possessive over everyone in her sphere? Valerie barely ever spoke to Brandon. The sorority treasurer's only crime was being as beautiful as Tiff, with the cheekbones of a model and a voluminous permed mass of dark gold curls. At least Tiffany going upstairs with Brandon meant Amelia would be free of her bossiness for a while. Amelia wove her way through the crowd, refusing offers to dance. Her legs throbbed from the lunges Susan had made the pledges do that afternoon. Amelia was used to staying in shape, a habit from being on the dance team in high school, but Susan treated exercise as punishment and a way to shame and torment anyone who wasn't as thin as her. She constantly mocked Amelia's thighs to the point where she was ashamed of them.

Amelia found Guillermo lounging on a sofa in the corner, farthest from the speakers and the masses. Miraculously, the place beside him was empty. She met his dark obsidian eyes and gave him a questioning look. With how rude her best friend was to him, he had every right to refuse Amelia's company.

When he nodded, she sat by him. Her heartbeat accelerated at being next to him, feeling the heat of his muscular legs only inches from hers, admiring the way the band shirts he wore—Dokken tonight—stretched across his broad chest and accentuated his brown biceps and his forearms… *Goddamn.* She subjected herself to this sweet torment every chance she got. Which wasn't very often, since Tiffany interrupted every time she spotted them talking.

But Tiff's disdain wouldn't stop Amelia from talking to him, though it did embarrass her enough to keep her distance when her friend was around.

"How's your week been going?" It was a lame question, but she had to start somewhere.

"Awful," Guillermo answered, though his white teeth flashed in a heart-melting smile. "They made us eat spoiled food from the fridge. And now they're gonna make us try to steal your pledge pins."

Amelia immediately removed her pin and handed it to him. "Here. Tell them you stole mine."

His brows drew together with touching concern. "Won't you get some sort of punishment for losing yours?"

"Maybe." Amelia shrugged, feeling brave now that she was with him. "Or maybe I can take Layla's or Tina's pins since they're dropping out."

"I'm thinking of dropping out," Guillermo said so quietly she almost didn't hear him over the music.

"Me too," Amelia replied hesitantly, taking a moment to imagine being brave enough to ask him to run away with her, out of this frat house and into each other's arms and Tiffany be damned.

A reflexive pang of guilt for the thoughts she'd been having about her best friend gnawed at her, albeit lighter than usual.

Guillermo's eyes widened. "You don't want to join the Omega Pis?"

"Not really."

"Let me guess." Guillermo gave her a knowing look. "You're here because your friend wants to join."

Damn it, so it was that obvious. She tried not to sound defensive. "I don't want to do *everything* Tiffany does."

She hadn't wanted to try out for the cheerleading squad back in high school, which had been Tiff's original aim, and they only settled on the much more fun dance team when they hadn't made the cut.

Then there were the little ways Tiffany tried to control her. Every time Amelia was rocking out to Helloween in their room on her cassette player, Tiffany popped the tape out and put Madonna on. When Amelia wanted to wear black velvet and leather or band t-shirts, Tiffany wheedled her until she put on something trendy instead. Tiff was always disparaging her for having her nose in a book or watching comedy films.

Guillermo brought her attention back to the present. "I heard you and Cameron broke up last week."

"That's right." Cameron Dane, best friend of Tiffany's boyfriend, Brandon Schmidt, was the latest of a long string of guys Tiffany set her up with. Back in high school, it seemed convenient, and sometimes a little romantic, for her to be with the close friend of Tiffany's current flavor. The double dates worked well and the two girls could better understand each other when venting or celebrating the relationship ups and downs. But as an adult, Amelia had soured on the experience of having dates arranged for her. And Cameron was the worst. All he'd wanted to do was try to get into Amelia's pants. He'd finally succeeded last week, when Amelia had been passed out drunk, leading her to a pregnancy and STD scare. That's when Amelia had enough. She broke up with him the next morning.

Tiffany was still mad at her about breaking up with Cameron. Amelia's story about what Cam had done only made Tiff shrug and say that was how guys were. Her lack of empathy felt like a knife through the heart.

"He seems to have moved on pretty fast." Guillermo pointed at Amelia's ex, who sat on a recliner over by the coolers, plying drinks on Laura Hayward, one of the few sorority sisters who was actually sorta nice. Amelia made a mental note to keep an eye on Laura in case Cameron tried to take advantage of her as well.

She turned back to Guillermo, who seemed to be watching her reaction to the sight of her ex with another girl. Her heart did a little skip. Did his observation mean he'd ask her out now?

She tried not to sound too hopeful. "I'm the one who broke up with him because he's an asshole."

After a long pause, Guillermo nodded. His expression was frustratingly unreadable. "So, are you going to drop out of the sorority?"

Amelia's heart sank at the change in subject. "I'd been seriously considering it all week.

But I can't help being curious about the Raimi House. I've had a thing for creepy places since I was little."

And now something else that Kirk had said about the initiation struck her with a chord of excitement. If she and Guillermo went through with it, they'd be spending the night together. The Raimi House was huge, with a lot of places where they could be alone. A lot of *bedrooms*.

A fresh and powerful resolve filled her. It was past time to break loose from Tiffany's control. For starters, Tiffany wouldn't have any more say over who Amelia dated. Now she would to find a way to date Guillermo.

The problem was that since Tiffany always assigned boyfriends to her, she had no idea how to even flirt with a guy, much less ask him out. Even worse was the terror that filled her at the thought of Guillermo rejecting her and losing the safe haven of his friendship.

Then Amelia had an idea.

Chapter Two

Guillermo drank in Amelia Craven's beauty while she was looking down at her hands. If she caught him looking at her like he was now, he wondered what she'd do. He'd harbored a serious fascination with her since the first time they'd met in Euro history back at the community college. Aside from her being drop-dead gorgeous, with her long wavy brown hair, hourglass figure, and eyes so bright and pale blue they reminded him of icicles on a winter morning, Amelia was kind, smart, and mysterious. Too bad she had a boyfriend then, and he'd had a long-distance girlfriend who was accepted to an Ivy League school.

Instead, Guillermo and Amelia struck up a friendship in the classes they'd shared, and at the various parties they'd encountered each other, when he'd seen she was kind of a wallflower. Unfortunately, they'd never been single at the same time. Until now.

Just as he opened his mouth to ask her out for dinner next weekend, Amelia spoke. "What do *you* think about our final initiation being at the Raimi House?"

"I think it's a terrible idea." Relief flowed through him to be able to say something that was guaranteed to get him laughed at by anyone else. "Everyone who's grown up in this town should know better."

"Maybe that's the problem. Half our classmates moved here from other states, so they *didn't* grow up here." Amelia gave him that little knowing smile that only locals exchanged. "I know both Susan and Kirk came from LA a few years ago. They think the Raimi House is a novelty and don't believe it's really haunted. No doubt they're gonna rig up some pranks to try to scare us."

Guillermo nodded, remembering when Kirk cheerfully told him his family had moved to Idaho to "get away from all those Mexicans." When Guillermo had pointed out that he was Mexican, Kirk had blustered some nonsense about assuming Guillermo was Italian and then reassured him he wasn't one of *those* Mexicans because he spoke good English. Guillermo already couldn't stand the frat house president before he said that shit, but that doubled his desire to leave. This idiotic and dangerous plan to finish the initiation at the Raimi House had Guillermo making up his mind to turn in his pin and quit the fraternity. To hell with fulfilling a family tradition and being the third Romero to belong to Alpha Lambda.

But with the way Amelia was talking…

"You're not seriously thinking of spending the night in that place, are you?" Guillermo gave her what he hoped was a stern look. "Don't you know how many people died there?"

"Hundreds," Amelia answered, unaffected. "No one knows the true number. But I have a survival plan."

Even though Guillermo had planned on dropping out of the fraternity and not going anywhere near the Raimi House, he couldn't help but be intrigued. "Survival plan?"

Amelia nodded. "I have a few books that are either about the Raimi House, or about haunted places in general, so we can do some research. Find out if there are any patterns that indicate which rooms, if any, are safe. We also need to learn about who's survived the house and if there's a common thread as to why. And then…" She faltered, cheeks turning pink. "We should also research spiritual and magical means of protection."

Guillermo fell silent, thinking of all his grandma's superstitious rituals, like lighting special candles, keeping aloe vera plants in every room where they'd survive, burning herbs for good luck, and doing various things with eggs when Guillermo or his brother or sister were sick. They'd believed every one of these until their father slowly chipped away the magic of childhood in his attempt to make them proper realists. But Guillermo remembered Grandma's rituals helping him more than any prayers, beads, and other trappings of his Catholic upbringing did. Likely it was Grandma's love that was powerful. And yet… "Do you think any of that stuff works?"

"I do," Amelia said with utter confidence that he envied. "After all, if there are forces of evil in the Raimi House and other places, why wouldn't there be equal and opposing forces for good?"

That made some sense. "Okay, but knowing our luck, Kirk and Susan will do something to mess with us if we try to protect ourselves."

"I know they will. Those two take such pleasure in tormenting pledges and anyone else they consider to be beneath them. They're sadistic assholes, through and through." She leaned closer to him. "But I have an idea on how we can keep our research and off-campus ventures secret."

"Oh?" His mouth went dry at her nearness. He could smell her faint perfume, something floral with a hint of bergamot.

"We can pretend to be dating." Amelia's blush returned. "Then all the time we spend together off campus and behind closed doors will make sense."

Why not date for real? Guillermo wanted to ask. Why didn't Amelia have any interest in him beyond friendship? He wasn't a vain guy, but he wasn't blind to the reactions many women had to his looks, especially when he was shirtless on a job site. Did she still have feelings for Cameron? From her reaction to seeing him flirt with another sorority girl, that probably wasn't it. Maybe it was because she agreed with what he overheard her friend saying and didn't think he was good enough for her. After all, one of her nicknames on campus was the ice princess.

But maybe it wasn't personal. Maybe she just thought of him as a friend. No matter the reason, this opportunity to spend more time with her gave him the chance to change her mind.

The silence between them grew uncomfortable before he managed to answer. "Okay, let's do this. We could go to the bookstore tomorrow to look up stuff about the town history and then have dinner and a movie."

Amelia looked up at him and her eyes brightened. "And like I said, I have some books about Amteep's history at home. I also have an autobiography by Helen Raimi, the last survivor of the Raimi dynasty and the last person to live in the house. It's full of lots of spooky stuff. But I'm always looking for more."

"Wow." Guillermo had no idea Amelia was into haunted houses until tonight. But he knew she loved history, especially the local legends. "I know my grandfather and his crew worked on one of the many renovations of the house. My father might have worked on them as well. I can ask my grandma when I have Sunday dinner with the family. And if you're not doing anything, you could come with me."

"I'd love to." Her exclamation carried over the music, making some people turn to stare.

Was her enthusiasm at the prospect of spending more time with him, or for getting more stories about the Raimi House? Guillermo wished he knew, then decided not to care because she looked so passionate and alive.

"Great, so we're on for dates tomorrow and Sunday," he said. "And as the bookstore closes at five, I'll pick you up at three. Maybe we can grab dinner somewhere after." He faltered. "You know…to keep up the dating illusion."

"Okay." She looked away and something in her eyes dimmed. Then her mouth curled into a scowl. "Oh shit. I gotta rescue Laura before Cameron takes advantage."

A mixture of rage and protective concern tightened Guillermo's chest. Had Cameron done that to Amelia? Remembering the way the guy talked about boozing up the hot chicks he hooked up with at these parties and how Guillermo often saw said girls swaying, he figured Cam had to have done so. His fists clenched with the urge to strangle the pig. "I'll help you."

Together, they rose from the couch and wove their way through the dancers to the stairway where Cameron was struggling to guide the clearly wasted girl up the stairs.

"Laura," Amelia exclaimed in an artificial cheery voice. "You made me promise to take you home by midnight, remember? And it's half past."

Laura mumbled incoherently but allowed Amelia to thread her arm around her waist as she released Cameron.

"Hey," Cam growled, straightening his white sport coat like a preening bird. "We were just going up to my room to have a little fun."

Amelia glared up at him. "She can't have fun when she's barely conscious. Besides, you can't imagine the hell she'll put me through if I break my promise to get her home."

"Why don't you ask her what she wants?" Cameron sneered.

"Fine." Amelia tapped Laura's cheek as the girl almost dozed off. "Do you want to go home, Laura?"

"Home," Laura repeated with a lopsided nod, and then hiccupped. "Wanna go sleep."

Guillermo was unable to hide his disgust for a guy who'd have sex with a girl in this drunken state. "There you have it. Come on, Amelia. I'll walk you two home."

Cameron turned his thwarted anger to Guillermo. "What are you doing? Horning in on my action, pledge?"

"There is no action. I'm helping our Greek sisters get home safely. We all clearly heard Laura's wanting to go home and Amelia's promise to take her there."

Although Cameron wasn't usually one to bully or even pull rank on the pledges, he straightened his stance and lifted up on his toes in an attempt to loom over Guillermo. "After I have my say with Kirk, you'll be spending tomorrow scrubbing up tonight's vomit with a toothbrush, pledge."

Guillermo shrugged, beyond tired of the inane displays of dominance. "And I'll have my say with the standards officer, since all I'm doing is adhering to the Alpha Lambda oath on chivalry. Maybe you should reread the rule book."

With that, he and Amelia practically carried Laura out of the frat house. The second they were out in the crisp, late September air, Amelia groaned with frustration. "God, Cameron's such an asshole. I can't believe he's trying to have you punished for helping me stop him from raping a coed."

"He was going to rape me?" Laura spoke in a squeak. The fresh air must have sobered her up somewhat because she looked more alert.

"Yeah." Amelia sounded tired, but sympathetic. "Why do you think he was taking you upstairs?"

Laura gagged and tugged away from Amelia's and Guillermo's grips. "Excuse me. I need to throw up."

She staggered to the bushes lining the frat house and immediately hurled. Amelia held Laura's crimped blonde hair and steadied her. She was no ice princess. It looked like those guys were full of shit. Just upset that she didn't want to fuck them or something. Because a woman who looked out for others and took care of someone in need was anything but icy.

After Laura was done purging, Amelia and Guillermo helped her walk down the sidewalk. The Omega Pi house was only a block and a half away, the two houses separated by one coed dorm house for the wealthier students who either didn't qualify for an organization or had no interest. After that house was a little park, where students studied when the weather was nice. The Pi house was around the corner from that, a huge Victorian like the Lambda house, but in much better shape.

Guillermo held the door after Amelia unlocked it and helped her guide Laura up the stairs to her room. He remained in the hall and found himself wondering what Amelia's room looked like. Did she have posters of male actors or rock stars she liked? Or did she have unique artwork? A little over two years of knowing her and yet he felt like he barely knew her at all.

"Do you want a cup of coffee or a pop?" Amelia said as she returned.

"Coffee sounds perfect after tonight. I didn't overdo it on the booze, but I didn't underdo it either."

Her light laugh gave him a ripple of euphoria. "Me too."

He followed her into the kitchen, which had a little breakfast nook that was much better than the pitiful three-legged Formica table in the Lambdas' kitchen. The Pi kitchen was a lot cleaner too, despite housing what—thirteen or fourteen people?

Amelia put the coffee on and rummaged through the cream-painted cupboard for mugs. The one she selected for him was Einstein sticking out his tongue. Cute. Hers had a Persian cat with messed-up fur and the caption "Bad Hair Day."

As Guillermo sat at the table and watched Amelia pace impatiently in front of the coffeemaker, he asked, "How long have you been interested in haunted houses?"

She hesitated a moment before joy suffused her features. "Ever since I was eight years old and saw my first ghost." She poured their mugs full of coffee and set them on the table, along with a sugar dispenser and a container of nondairy creamer before taking a seat across from him. "I had a sleepover with a girl who lived in one of these old houses downtown. There was an old woman who sat in a rocking chair in the corner of the living room, knitting. But you could see through her. The girl told me it was the ghost of her great-grandma and that I was the only other person who'd seen her. A few years later, I dug into the town's history and local legends about haunted places in Amteep. There are a lot. I also dated Jason Shaye for two months in high school, while Tiffany was together with one of his friends. His older sister inherited the Sazerac House."

Guillermo shoved down the irrational pang of jealousy over Amelia mentioning dating another guy. Especially since her stories were fascinating. He'd heard all sorts of stuff about the Sazerac House, like how one of the Sazerac women had been thrown through the attic window even though the room had been locked from the inside. And another woman had vanished on her wedding day. Her skeleton had been found in an overgrown well on the property back in '81. "No shit?"

"Uh-huh." Amelia nodded with a grin that made him smile back. "That place was as full of ghosts as I'd expected, but wanna know something crazy?"

"What?"

"Despite all the tragedies that happened under the roof of that place, when I was there, it didn't feel evil or scary." Amelia took a sip of her coffee and her blush returned. "This might sound crazy but I think it was because Jason's sister—"

The front door opened and a gaggle of noisy girls stumbled into the house. They were led by Tiffany, who strode into the kitchen on unsteady legs, like a person on the deck of a ship in a storm. She was Guillermo's roommate's girlfriend, and also the person most often glued to Amelia's side. "Why the hell did you leave without telling me?"

Guillermo noted Tiffany's tousled hair and bee-stung lips.

Amelia blinked at her friend. "You were upstairs with Brandon. What the hell was I supposed to do? Interrupt?"

Tiffany made a silly huffing sound and glared at Amelia like a stern parent. "No, but you could have passed on a message or something. And don't swear. I told you it makes you sound like a truck driver."

Amelia shrugged off her friend's petulant words. "Cameron made enough of a spectacle about Guillermo and me helping Laura home that there's no way you didn't hear about it when you came back downstairs."

Another sorority girl chimed in. "Yeah, Cam was pissed that he didn't get a chance to prey on another one of us. Good job rescuing Laura."

Susan made a disapproving sound. "It's not a good idea to anger members of our partner fraternity."

Guillermo rose from the table. "It would have pissed Cam off more if the girl had puked all over him. Besides, I'll take the heat for thwarting his attempt to bring her upstairs, even though Amelia was only fulfilling a promise to take her sorority sister home before midnight."

"She's not her sister yet, since she's just a pledge, like you." Susan tried to look down her nose at him, but since he was taller, she only managed to look cross-eyed. "Speaking of, that means Amelia hasn't earned the right to have a man in this house, so you need to leave."

"Fine." Guillermo gritted his teeth in a forced smile. There was no pleasing this bitch, who took visible pleasure out of tormenting Amelia and others. No wonder she and Kirk were together. They were cut from the same unyielding cloth.

Amelia got up from the table and came to stand at his side like an ally in battle. "I'll walk you out."

Her long, graceful fingers gripped his upper arm, making his body jolt with heat. At first, he was surprised at her touch, but then he remembered their agreement to pretend to be dating.

When they were back out on the covered porch in the chilly quiet, the nearly full moon shining down like a spotlight, Guillermo turned to say something to Amelia. He didn't know what, and then noticed a bunch of sorority girls crowding the windows, peering at them.

"Man, they're really on your ass. I thought I had it bad with the Alpha Lambs." He turned his gaze back to her moonlit beauty. "What persuaded you to go along with your friend and join up with a sorority in the first place? No offense, but you don't seem like the type."

"Offense?" Amelia laughed. "I'm flattered. As for why I listened to Tiff, that's a long story that can wait for later."

"Okay." He shoved his hands in his pockets, not thrilled to leave her in this nest of harpies. Not that his house was any safer. "So, picking you up at three for the bookstore, right?"

"Three sounds great."

Guillermo turned to leave, but Amelia grasped his forearm and pulled him back. "Since we have witnesses, we might as well start up our pretense."

He glanced at the girls watching from the windows and frowned. "What do you mean?"

"Kiss me."

Was it his imagination, or did her voice tremble with excitement at those words? Guillermo didn't need any further encouragement. He'd been dreaming of kissing Amelia Craven ever since their first class together.

He slid one arm around her waist, flattening his palm over her lower back, trying not to sigh at the heat of her body underneath the fabric of her cashmere sweater. His other hand plunged into her hair that somehow managed to be soft even with hairspray.

Her wide-eyed expression and lips parted in surprise encouraged him as he dipped her down old movie-style and captured her full lips with his. At the soft yielding, his knees went weak, but he managed to hold her up. Her subtle scent filled his senses, making him dizzy with bliss. He didn't think she wanted to go as far as French kissing for this act, so instead, his lips gently glided over hers, exploring, while he enjoyed the frissons of pleasure racing down his spine.

When he released her, she took a wobbly step back and gasped for breath. Pride warmed his chest at being able to affect her like that, even as the rest of him felt cold at not having her in his arms anymore.

"Good night, Amelia."

"Good night, Guillermo."

When he got back to the frat house, almost everyone was thankfully passed out. Even better, his side of the room was unmolested from the party. His roommate, Brandon Schmidt, on the other hand, lay sprawled on his bed still in his clothes, beer cans littering the floor and nightstand. A used condom was draped over the wastebasket, making Guillermo grateful that he had his own small garbage can by his little desk.

Guillermo was far from being a neat freak, but his grandmother was, and now that he was experiencing the chaos and squalor of this frat house, he'd been horrified. Still was. After taking a quick shower, knowing from experience that in the mornings, others fought over the bathrooms and used all the hot water, he went to bed.

Sleep didn't come easy, as memories of kissing Amelia alternated with the realization that they'd be spending Halloween night in the creepiest place in town.

I'm going to do it, Guillermo realized, opening his eyes to stare blankly at a shaft of moonlight across his bedspread. Despite how close he'd been to leaving the fraternity tonight, it wasn't only the dangerous prospect of entering the Raimi House that had prompted his almost-decision to do so. It was the stupidity of this so-called Greek Life in general. He didn't like getting yelled at by the likes of Kirk and Simon and all the other guys who were born with silver spoons in their mouths and obsessed with the meaningless ranking system of the fraternity. He despised the degrading initiation rituals, which consisted of things like slave labor, paddling, gross-out challenges, and often dares to do shitty things to women. And since Guillermo refused to do the latter, he was subjected to twice the former as the other pledges.

He never wanted to join the fraternity in the first place, but family pressure to follow in the footsteps of his father and grandfather crumbled his resistance. Furthermore, moving into the frat house was a slightly better option than staying at home. Dad's dominating attitude drove Guillermo crazy, but he missed his mom and grandma. He even missed his younger brother, Antonio, and his sister, Maria.

The Raimi House was supposed to be the straw that broke the camel's back. He'd already been anticipating having homecooked meals every night and listening to his grandma play her mandolin.

Then Amelia came to him, offering the one thing he couldn't resist: a chance to be with her.

As Guillermo closed his eyes and again relived that first kiss, his priorities were firmly established: win Amelia's heart and survive the Raimi House.

The problem was, he wasn't sure he could accomplish either.

Chapter Three

September 28, 1987

Amelia's stomach fluttered as she rode in Guillermo's adorable blue Toyota pickup. Metal Church played from the stereo. Another love they shared. Her legs were inches from his. Once more, she marveled at how powerfully his presence impacted her. Now that he'd kissed her, she couldn't look at his lips without flames licking up and down her body. That kiss and this time with him made the latest argument with Tiffany worth enduring. Still, Amelia's stomach churned in a discomfiting combination of sorrow and elation at her further break from her friend.

As soon as she'd gone back into the sorority house, still reeling from Guillermo's kiss, Tiffany had grabbed Amelia's hand and practically dragged her up the stairs to their shared room.

"What do you think you're doing? That guy is in *construction*." Tiffany's nose had crinkled like she'd said a dirty word. "I know things didn't work out with you and Cam, but you could take your pick of much better guys at this school. A future doctor, a soon-to-be lawyer, or maybe even a businessman."

Amelia had trembled a little at her friend's disappointment, then straightened her shoulders because the intimidation was a reflex, left over from back when she was a cast-adrift ninth-grade loser. Now she was on a course to her goals and knew what she wanted. "Guillermo *is* a business major. But that's not even the point."

"And what is?" Tiffany had asked with an ugly sneer.

"He's the guy I want." Amelia had kicked off her shoes and turned her back to take off her clothes for bed, knowing how it pissed Tiff off to not be given full attention. "You've been arranging my dates since eleventh grade. I think I'm capable of picking my own now."

Just like Amelia had to put her foot down about her choice to major in library science with hopes to become a librarian. Tiffany had bullied and pestered her to major in advertising like Tiffany. Tiff still held out on her dream of both of them moving to a chic city like LA or New York, but it sounded more and more distasteful to Amelia every day.

She wanted to stay in Amteep. The years of parties and hanging out at the mall with Tiff had taught Amelia that she hated crowds, and instead loved mountains and trees.

She couldn't deny it any longer: she and Tiff were growing apart.

Tiffany started on her again this afternoon while Amelia got ready for her outing with Guillermo. By the time Amelia had finished standing her ground and putting on her makeup, she'd forgotten how she was only pretending to date Guillermo. Now, sitting beside him, she wished for the hundredth time since he'd left last night that he'd kissed her because he wanted to, and not for the sake of putting on a show.

The touch of sadness vanished when he parked in front of Maturin Books. Amelia loved the store, with its scent of old and new books with a hint of wood polish used to keep the shelves gleaming. And of course, the store's namesake, a giant turtle, carved out of some green stone, always positioned on guard beside the cash register. The owner, Tony Beam, was working today and grinned broadly when they walked in.

"Amelia. I'm so glad you stopped by. I have a surprise…" Tony trailed off when he noticed Guillermo. "Oh wow. Hey, Guillermo. I didn't expect to see you here with her."

Amelia blinked at Tony's abrupt awkwardness and responded before Guillermo. "We're friends on a mission. What's the surprise?"

Tony's face turned a deep shade of red and he looked back at Guillermo. "Please don't be mad at me, man. Amelia's been first in line for these for a while now." Then he reached behind the counter and pulled out a large paperback with a beloved name in gold lettering.

Amelia forgot all about the weirdness with Guillermo and gasped. "*Holy shit.* Is that the advance reviewer copy of Stephen King's next book?"

Tony grinned at her. "It is. Our store scored two and I saved this one for you."

Guillermo finally spoke. "Hey, why does she get an ARC?"

The bookstore owner looked abashed. "Because Amelia and I started talking about King before you and I did."

"And she's prettier than me," Guillermo said with a teasing smile. "I thought you weren't supposed to sell advanced copies."

"I don't sell them to her. I give them to her with her purchases here. Wait." Tony stuck his finger in the air. "I have something that you might like, Guillermo."

Tony disappeared behind his counter and then emerged with another advance copy. *Koko* by Peter Straub. "This one comes out next spring, and I was thrilled to get review copies so soon."

"Awesome." Guillermo's eyes seemed to glitter with delight. "I can't thank you enough for turning me on to Straub." He cleared his throat. "Anyway, Amelia and I are looking for books on…well, the occult. It's, um, for school."

Amelia nodded. "And I'm still looking for anything on local hauntings. Especially the Raimi House."

Tony guided them to the New Age section. Most of the books were hippie-dippy volumes on meditation and self-discovery. Nothing that would be helpful in a house that possibly ate people and worse. They did find a couple of books that might prove useful: one on protective talismans and amulets around the world that looked fairly well-researched; another two focused on spells and charms.

The cream of the crop was the find Tony had reserved for her: *The Diary of Claudia Raimi.* The volume was locally printed, transcribed, and published by Claudia's descendent, Helen Raimi. Amelia had seen the diary referenced in Helen's autobiography and had asked every bookstore in town to try to track it down for her. Now, after three years of searching, Tony had found the diary. Since soon she'd be setting foot inside the Raimi House, Amelia saw it as an omen. Hopefully it was a good one.

By the time they left the store with their haul of books, Amelia's stomach was growling with hunger, but she was elated with their finds.

Guillermo alternated between watching the road and turning to grin at her. "I can't believe you managed to score a review copy of *The Tommyknockers*."

"And I can't believe you're also a Stephen King fan." If she'd known before, she could have had more excuses to seek him out and talk to him.

"Not quite his *number one fan*, though." They both laughed at his reference to the last book, *Misery*. "What's this new one about?"

She pulled the advanced copy out of her bag and read the description on the back: "Aliens. Not my preferred topic, but I like King's writing, so I'll check it out."

"Can I borrow it when you're done?"

"Of course." Her stomach growled again, making her face burn in humiliation. "Sorry."

"Don't worry. I'm starving too. I was thinking we could go to Bava's."

"Bava's?" Amelia blinked, not sure if she heard him right. "Isn't that a little...pricey for what we're doing?"

An intense but unreadable look flew across his features before they settled into a devil-may-care smile that made her stomach flutter. "You look so good today that it would be a shame not to take you somewhere nice. Besides, what better way to cement the idea of us being a couple than being seen at one of the best restaurants in town?"

Amelia's face heated again as she inwardly cursed herself for suggesting they pretend to date. She was already being punished by Tiffany for this scheme; now it seemed Guillermo would unwittingly taunt her too by showing her what she couldn't have.

All those worries fled at dinner, however, when they enjoyed the orgasmic food and talked for over an hour about their favorite Stephen King novels. The movie after was excellent too. *Hellraiser* blew their minds, even though Amelia found it difficult to focus on the plot with Guillermo sitting beside her in the dark, their hands occasionally brushing in the popcorn tub.

"Was it just me," Guillermo asked as they drove back to campus, "or did those spooky creatures from hell seem like the good guys?"

"They really did. Antiheroes at the very least."

The more she and Guillermo talked, the more bittersweet she felt. He was such a good listener and they had a lot more in common than she ever could have dreamed. A candle of hope lit the dark, lonely place inside her. Maybe he would want to be with her for real. That is, if he didn't think she was stupid for proposing they pretend to date. Or if he flat-out wasn't interested.

For the rest of the ride back home, Amelia warred with herself. How the hell would she extricate herself from this lie about only wanting to pretend to date? And could she even come clean to Guillermo about her real interest in being more than friends? She'd created a mess. Maybe that's why she'd allowed Tiffany to pick her boyfriends before this. Because it was easier than risking her heart and fragile self-esteem on a guy she *actually* wanted to be with. The dating game was a lot scarier when there were real stakes.

When they arrived at the sorority house and Guillermo gave her a thorough kiss good night that almost made her knees buckle, Amelia forgot all about her anxieties and melted in his arms. After she went into the house, she had to fight back the urge to sigh and twirl around like a Disney character. Even Tiffany couldn't ruin her mood, but Susan made her best attempt, ordering both pledges to sit on the kitchen floor on top of plastic garbage bags while she and the other sorority sisters poured maple syrup over their heads. The excuse was that it was another initiation ritual, but Amelia suspected the motive was revenge for being talked back to at last night's party. Tiffany and Valerie—who didn't even need a shower—used up all the hot water before Amelia had a turn to shower. She'd wrapped her hair in a warm wet towel beforehand, so when she had to wash under the chilly spray, it didn't take long to get her hair clean. Still, when she got out of the shower, her teeth chattered. It was a good thing summer was over so Guillermo wouldn't see that she didn't shave her legs this time.

Back in her room, Tiffany was already in bed, facing the wall. Amelia could tell by Tiff's breathing that she was still awake, but purposefully avoiding her. Probably punishing her for getting them all punished, or for putting her foot down on her dating choices, or both.

A little over a year ago, Amelia would have been rife with guilt and turning herself inside out to gain her friend's forgiveness. Now, she was relieved not to have to talk to Tiff. Not after a perfect first date and not with two exciting books calling to her from the Maturin Books shopping bag under the bed. Temptation to peek at the advance King book sang to her, but the diary was more important. Amelia turned off the main light and flicked on the reading lamp beside her bed before reaching under the bed and grabbing the book.

The first entry was dated June 2nd, 1890. Claudia Raimi wrote that she'd just returned from her honeymoon and this was her first night spent in hers and her husband's newly constructed house.

"The manor my dear Adam had built for me is as beautiful as it is daunting," Claudia wrote. *"The countless turrets bring to mind a fairytale castle. I should fall in love with this place...and yet—"* The entry broke off. The next entry was dated four days later.

Amelia finished the likely thought. *And yet something is wrong.*

In the June 6th entry Claudia had discovered a frightening truth: The land her new home was built upon had been an infamous army base where hundreds of soldiers had vanished thirty years prior. Claudia's husband, Adam Raimi, had been proud of the low price the army had asked.

Claudia had been distraught. *"Every step I take in this house is treading upon the dead. The very air seems heavy, and always with a chill. I feel like I'm breathing in a curse."*

"No fucking way," Amelia whispered, momentarily stopping reading.

In the book *Amteep Legends*, Amelia had read that back in the 1850s, there had been an army base built on top of a Salish burial ground, belonging to either the Coeur d'Alene or Kootenai tribe. Then, in 1864, every soldier and officer on the base disappeared, without even the slightest evidence of struggle or bloodshed. Amelia had read the story at least four times over the years, but she'd never guessed that the Raimi House was built on *that* land. The knowledge made her realize the house was even more cursed than she initially realized.

With shaky fingers, she turned to the next entry in the diary only to discover even more horrors.

Chapter Four

The next evening, Guillermo fidgeted with nervousness as he drove Amelia to his parents' house. His mom and grandma remained very connected to their Mexican heritage. Dad, on the other hand, did his best to divorce himself from his roots, just like Grandpa. He'd been against Guillermo and his siblings learning Spanish, wanting the Romeros to fully assimilate into American culture. But Mom believed that to be American was to embrace the melting pot of cultures and remember where your family came from, so she put her foot down with Grandma's support, and together they taught Guillermo, Maria, and Antonio the language. As a result, both English and Spanish were spoken in the home, though they did try to stick to English when guests were around. Would Amelia look down on his family's culture?

Then there were Grandma's superstitions, which embarrassed Dad. Crazy how those superstitions might be helpful in surviving their night at the Raimi House.

As if reading his mind, Amelia talked about what she'd read in Claudia Raimi's diary. The fact that the place was built on native burial ground that was stolen by the US Army, who then vanished like the Donner Party, was edifying as to why the house was cursed. However, Guillermo couldn't manage to feel sorry for the soldiers, who'd driven the local tribes from their sacred lands, even though the story was chilling.

Amelia continued outlining horrors. "On their second night in the house, Claudia awoke to see a figure floating above her. She tried to scream, but she was paralyzed. She sketched the thing's face in the diary and I think it's going to give me nightmares."

Yet again, Guillermo wondered if he should insist that they ditch this crazy plan and go on a real date instead for Halloween. But two things kept him from voicing common sense. The first was that the stories about the house made him curious to see the place where so many terrible things happened. Secondly, he *liked* being teamed up with Amelia. The feeling that they could face down evil together was potent in its lure.

When he parked in front of the large two-story colonial revival house that Grandpa had built himself back in the forties, Guillermo turned to Amelia. "I'm going to introduce you as a friend, otherwise my grandmother will go crazy over you and immediately begin sizing up your virtues as a wife."

Her blush was adorable. "Okay."

"She and my mom might be embarrassing as it is. If you're uncomfortable, nudge me and I'll make an excuse for us to leave."

Amelia chuckled. "I'm sure that unless they blatantly hate me, I'll be fine. Nothing could be as bad as dinners at my dad's house." She looked away at the mention of her father.

Mingled curiosity and sympathy welled within him at her words, along with the hurt and bitterness in her voice. Guillermo didn't always get along with his father, but he couldn't imagine *hating* spending time with him. He was tempted to ask her more about her family, but they'd already been sitting in the car too long and he saw the curtain lift in the kitchen window and Grandma's face peeking out.

"Well, let's do this. I'm starving." Guillermo got out of the truck and resisted the urge to go around to open Amelia's door for her. They weren't pretend-dating today.

Amelia got out and joined him on the flagstone walkway. "I can smell the food from here and it's heavenly. What did you say your grandma was cooking again?"

"Chicken mole." Anticipation and pride curved his lips. "You're in for a treat. Mom and Grandma work all day on the sauce. Since it takes so long, they usually only make it for special occasions. But since I moved into the frat house, they've been making my favorites for Sunday dinner."

"That sounds wonderful."

As soon as they walked through the blue-painted front door with a little octagonal window, Guillermo was immediately mobbed by

Mom and Grandma while Dad hovered at the edge of the living room, trying to look nonchalant while his eyes blazed with unspoken questions. His brother, Antonio, and sister, Maria, looked away from the TV, gave Guillermo casual waves, then stared at Amelia.

Dad extended his hand first. "I'm Alejandro. Welcome to our home. This is my wife, Ana, my mother, Flora, and the kids glued to the TV are Maria and Antonio."

"We're not kids," Maria and Antonio protested, abandoning the TV as they got up from the dark green shag carpet floor that Mom always complained about wanting to upgrade. "I'm in college too, and Tony's a senior at Amteep High." The blatant appreciation in Antonio's eyes made Guillermo glare at him until he looked away. Sure, Amelia looked like a goddess, but that didn't mean it was okay to leer at her.

Amelia smiled at them all and shook hands. The reserved demeanor Guillermo had often observed in her had returned, but now he saw past it. She wasn't cold at all; she was shy. How had he not seen that before?

When they sat down to eat in the wood-paneled dining room with decorative plates and scenic paintings on the walls, the rest of Guillermo's trepidation about how she'd react to his family vanished. She sat quietly and observed the etiquette, making sure to follow whatever Guillermo did. Other times when he had brought a friend or girlfriend over, they had often either sneered or smirked in amusement or scorn at either Grandma's prayer, the custom of waiting until the host took the first bite before everyone else started eating, or the specific uses of each utensil. Not Amelia. Instead, a delightful mixture of respect and fascination glittered in her pale blue eyes.

The conversation was cheery at first, with Amelia praising Mom and Grandma for their cooking, complimenting Dad on the house he was building in the new development by the high school, offering advice to Maria on her classes at the community college, and commiserating with Antonio on how much of a pain high school was.

Unfortunately, Dad decided to embarrass them when he gave Amelia an appraising look across the table. "I don't recall my son mentioning you being his friend before."

Mom spoke before he could answer. "Yes, he has. He told us about her when he first started college. They've had classes together ever since. She's joining the Omega Pi sorority."

"I must have forgotten." But something in his tone was off. "The only girl I remember him telling me about was an ice princess he had his eye on."

Guillermo almost choked on his rice as his eyes darted to Amelia in a panic. Would she put two and two together?

As her lips curved into a smile that looked forced, he dreaded the worst.

"Wait, did you have a thing for Tiffany?" Did she sound jealous, or was that wishful thinking on his part?

"God no," he said so vehemently that he immediately regretted it, despite his relief that she didn't figure out she was the ice princess in question. "I mean, um. I know she's your friend and all, but no offense, she's not my type."

"None taken." In fact, she looked pleased.

Grandma scolded him quietly in Spanish about taking the Lord's name in vain and Guillermo was again able to take delight in Amelia's visible enjoyment of the meal.

Peacefulness returned to the meal until Dad brought the conversation back to the fraternity. His eyes sparkled with nostalgia as he asked Guillermo and Amelia about the hazing and initiations they'd endured so far. He actually bragged about how the Alpha Lambdas had buried him alive for his final initiation.

Amelia gasped. "Are these initiations always so morbid?"

He turned his avid gaze to her. "Why do you ask? Do you know what yours will be yet?"

Guillermo forced a nonchalant tone despite his irritation with his father liking all the childish and degrading stuff involved in Greek life. "We're sworn to secrecy in regards to the final initiation. You know that, Dad."

As soon as the meal was finished, Guillermo escaped further talk about the fraternity by insisting Mom relax while he helped Grandma clean up in the kitchen. Amelia offered to help too, but Grandma ordered her to sit at the little green Formica table where the family ate breakfast. "You're a guest. Would you like a glass of *horchata*?"

"What is it?"

"Rice milk with cinnamon and sugar."

Amelia's smile made Guillermo's heart accelerate. "That sounds wonderful."

"*Abuela*?" Guillermo addressed Grandma with her Spanish title since it pleased her. "I've been wanting to ask you about the Raimi House."

At the name of the house, Grandma crossed herself. "Evil place."

"Yeah." And he was learning just how evil it was. "*Abuelo* worked on the last renovation the previous owner did on the house. And wasn't *Papá* there as well?"

"Yes." She darted a wary glance at Amelia. "Terrible things happened. I am not sure this is suitable for company."

"We're doing a project together for history class. Since it will be due the last week of October, the topic is spooky historical sites. Amelia and I thought the Raimi House would be a perfect subject for our paper." It wasn't a total lie. They did have history together again and there was mention of an upcoming paper assignment on the syllabus.

Grandma regarded them both with a grim smile. "Perhaps too spooky."

"Please, tell us what happened on the job site." He gave her his most imploring look that never failed to sway her.

She sighed and handed Guillermo a dish to wash and stepped back from the sink, making it clear he would pay for making her tell this unpleasant story. After taking the *horchata* pitcher out of the fridge and taking a seat across from Amelia, she poured two glasses and began. "The Raimi renovation was the worst contract your *abuelo* ever worked on. Enrique told me he could feel the evil in the air. Every single man on his crew would see shadows, and sometimes *people*, out of the corners of their eyes. Ladders were often pushed by unseen forces, and tools and building materials fell and struck the poor workers. Many crewmembers walked off the site, claiming they saw the faces of monsters peering through the windows at them. The loss of workers made the job take longer. Enrique was frightened every morning when he left for work and had nightmares at night. Your father did too, though he tried to pretend he wasn't afraid. We went to every Mass during that time instead of only on Sundays, and Enrique would stay after to have the priest bless him."

She sighed and took a deep drink from her glass. "Then, one man's harness was untied and he fell from the roof and broke his back. He was fortunate to survive, but he was paralyzed for life. He said he watched the harness untie itself. Thankfully, the company insurance paid the settlement, but we had to pay a higher premium for many years."

"Wow." Guillermo rubbed the goosebumps that had rose up on his arms. "Did *Abuelo* see any of the monsters the other workers talked about?"

Grandma crossed herself. "He saw—"

Mom's voice cut her off, sounding furious as she strode into the kitchen. "Guillermo, when you take over the business, I want you to promise me that you'll *never* take a contract to work on that house."

"I swear it." An easy promise to make even as guilt and discomfort filled him for not only neglecting to tell her he'd be spending Halloween night in that house, but also that he didn't want to take over the construction business.

In that moment, Guillermo realized that even though he thought he'd resigned himself to putting that yoke on his shoulders, with majoring in business to following in his father's and grandfather's footsteps in joining the fraternity, part of him was still looking for a way out.

On the way home, he and Amelia discussed their game plan for the rest of the week. The growing mountain of schoolwork didn't allow them much time for pretend dates until the weekend, but at least on top of studying together, they could also continue their research on the house and protective measures they could take.

He wove his truck around a granny's Buick and took a moment to admire the oranges and golds of the fall leaves that made a canopy over this particular street. "I'll go to the next Sunday dinner on my own and try to get my grandma alone so I can see if she'll tell me about any charms or talismans that she had my dad and grandpa carry when they were working on the place. She won't talk about that sort of thing in front of an outsider."

"Good idea." Suddenly, Amelia changed the subject. "So, who *was* the ice princess you had a crush on?"

He tilted his head down to hide his hot cheeks with his hair. "I… um. It's kind of a silly story since I turned out to be wrong about her. I'll tell you later. We're almost back to Frat Row."

He chanced a glance at her. She looked like she wanted to press the issue, then her lips curved into an enigmatic smile before she turned her head to look out the window.

What if she was interested in him back? If so, he'd be an idiot not to tell her that he'd fallen for her back in the first class they'd had together. But if she didn't reciprocate his feelings, all this time he got to spend with her would end.

He pulled in front of the Omega Pi house, gratified that a couple girls were peeking out the windows at them. Another excuse to kiss her again.

When Guillermo savored the feel of Amelia in his arms and the taste of her lips, a fresh determination filled him. He would make this pretend relationship real and keep them safe from the Raimi House.

Chapter Five

October 14, 1987

Amelia watched with amusement as Tiffany lashed out at someone else for a change.

"Wait, what?" Tiffany blinked at Susan in horror. "You mean we're not waiting until Halloween to go the Raimi House?"

Susan rolled her eyes and popped her gum. "Were you not paying attention when Kirk said you'd be cleaning the place to get it ready for the party? God, I swear the pledges get dumber every year."

Although Tiffany was usually good at keeping her head down and not talking back to Susan, the thought of manual labor of this magnitude broke her silence. "There's no way only two of us can get that house clean. Not with our classes and homework, the parties, and the other initiation stuff."

Instead of being angry, Susan seemed amused. She gestured to Mary, the new member educator, to speak. Since Layla and Tina had left, Mary's role had become superfluous given that Amelia and Tiffany already had Nancy as a mentor.

Mary favored Amelia and Tiffany with reassuring smiles. "Relax, Tiff. The Alpha Lambda pledges will be helping too. Also, we're only cleaning part of the main floor…and the bedrooms you two and the three Alpha Lambda pledges will be spending the night in. I hope nothing happens that will make your Brandon jealous."

Amelia's shoulders relaxed with relief, not at more hands sharing the labor, but at hearing that Guillermo would be there. Between heavy schoolwork and torture by the Lambdas and the Pis, she and Guillermo barely spent any time together. Four study-dates and two actual dates was all. Not enough time to enjoy his kisses, find out what would be the key to gaining real romantic interest from him and—

Not enough time. The words repeated in her head with a foreboding tone that was somehow also scolding. Hers and Guillermo's top priority wasn't romance, much as she wished it could be. They needed to do more research, gather more materials that could possibly keep them safe from the house's evil.

Simon Chamberlain's fake wood-paneled van pulled up in front of the sorority house. Simon was the fraternity's dean of pledges, the same job as Mary, but with a fancier title. Amelia spotted Kirk Sorbo in the front passenger seat. Guillermo must be in the back with Mike and Chuck. The horn honked, prompting Susan, Mary, and Rebecca, the sorority standards officer, to gather bags of cleaning supplies from the breakfast nook table and usher the pledges outside. Amelia suppressed a groan of dread at Rebecca's presence. The standards officer was militantly strict to everyone except those few who met her snobby ideals of worth. She was worse than Tiffany when it came to judging a person by how much money their family had.

Six people was a tight squeeze, but Amelia didn't mind since that meant she was pressed up against Guillermo. Unlike most of the frat guys, he didn't douse himself in cologne, but instead had a nice clean scent that made her wish she could ask what kind of soap he used. There was also a remnant of freshly cut wood emanating from his jacket, since yesterday he'd had to miss a research session to go help his father on a job site.

His dark eyes met hers, glinting with nervousness at going to the house before they were ready. She wished they could talk about it, but they didn't dare reveal their preparations.

The van's shocks were in bad shape, resulting in bumps that jarred her hips and back and made the view out the back window of the red and gold leafy trees lining the streets blurry. Giving up on the limited sightseeing for the ride, she vacillated between savoring the warmth of Guillermo's solid frame beside her and sifting through all the eerie things she'd read in Claudia Raimi's diary, huddled under her blanket with a flashlight like a kid up past her bedtime so she didn't wake up Tiffany.

What had been the most fucked-up thing to read was that Claudia's husband, Adam Raimi, didn't believe her about the shadows constantly darting in and out of view or the demons hovering over her at night. He'd called a doctor, who'd promptly diagnosed Claudia with hysteria and she spent the majority of her pregnancy locked in the attic. Probably the reason why her firstborn child, Linus, had come out so listless and sickly. Claudia's early years in the Raimi House were often interrupted with frequent confines to the attic, until her husband's suicide.

As the van wove on the winding road around the lake, Mike broke through Amelia's chilling reverie, pointing out the back window at a stretch of beach and a rotting dock on Lake Skeetshue. "Hey. That's the Raimis' private beach. A body was found there in the spring of eighty-four. Did you guys hear about that?"

Amelia and a few others nodded. "I didn't know it was *this* beach, though."

Kirk shrugged as he made a left. "Wasn't that also the year that crazy high school senior killed off almost all her rivals for prom queen?"

"Creepy coincidence," Guillermo muttered, making everyone around him nod.

The van trundled up the steep road to the cliffside houses, a row of luxurious mansions overlooking the lake with private docks below. Soon, they pulled in front of the impossibly tall wrought-iron gates that Amelia could barely see between the heads and shoulders of the others in the van.

Kirk pulled a large key from his pocket, then got out of the van and strode to the gate entrance . He unlocked the gate and they saw him wince, at first thinking it was from the rusty shriek of the hinges. But when he got back in the van and Simon began to pull in, Amelia noticed with unease that he'd somehow cut himself on the gate. Blood seeped from his hand, making Kirk grimace and Susan talk about rushing him to the hospital for a tetanus shot.

"I'll be fine, babe. I had my shot before the semester started." Kirk rolled his eyes. "Don't embarrass me. There's a first aid kit under the front passenger seat."

When they passed through the gate, Amelia shivered at the sight of the sharp spikes on top of every bar and how the bars were too close together to squeeze through. Once upon a time, there had been a reason to make it difficult for one to leave the grounds. While Simon guided the van up the long, cracked flagstone drive, Susan got out the first aid kit and fussed over Kirk with more tenderness than Amelia had seen in the sorority president ever.

After parking, Simon let them out of the back of the van, leaving the two presidents behind. "Everybody out, we're wasting daylight. The caretaker says no one should be here after dark."

Some of the guys made fake ghost noises.

"What about the caretaker?" Tiffany asked.

"He doesn't stay here. He's got one of those little beach bungalows we passed near Bava's restaurant."

The Raimi House loomed over them, a gray brick monstrosity with multiple turrets, chimneys, and parapets. Arched windows on the upper floors twinkled in the sunlight like suspicious eyes, while the lower windows, boarded up, conveyed a sense of gloom. Multiple wings of the house sprawled on the grounds like a hulking beast, defying logistics. Tops of trees that were part of a small forest behind the house could be seen between the turrets. The overgrown chaos of the garden lay downhill to the south, near the guesthouse. To the northwest, where the cliffside ended and the gate began, was a little cemetery that had been originally intended to be a family plot, but had been turned into a cemetery for Amteep's elite back in 1920, when the Raimi family had lost their first fortune. The first to be buried was Adam Raimi, who killed himself after going bankrupt. Amelia wondered what it was like for the descendants of others buried here to not be able to visit their ancestors' graves. Not without risking their lives.

And yet, here she was, risking hers, not to join a sorority she had no interest in, but to have the chance to spend the night with Guillermo. If she was being honest with herself, she also had a combination of irresistible curiosity about the house and arrogance in believing she could protect herself from its evil.

Guillermo interrupted her musings. "I've been on these roads to jobsites in the neighboring lake houses and there's no way this property should be able to hold a house of this size, much less everything else. The parcel should be broken up by the back roads at the base of the mountains, or the cliff above the lake road, yet somehow, here the property sprawls: Five acres of land on what should be one acre. There is something seriously wrong with this place."

Tiffany overheard them and sneered at Guillermo. "Figures that you're a chicken."

He shrugged. "Only fools mistake caution for cowardice."

Her jaw dropped at his comeback. "Are you calling me a fool?"

"Of course not," he said mildly. "You're Amelia's friend, so she *must* have told you about all the deaths and disappearances, which means you would have known before me that this place isn't right."

Amelia bit the insides of her cheeks to hold back a grin. How Guillermo could sound so sincere after Tiffany had been so bitchy, she'd never know.

Tiff's face turned strawberry-red as she visibly struggled for a response. At last, her features screwed up in an expression of awkwardness and anger. "*Duh.* But that doesn't mean I—"

Susan cut her off. "Enough chitchatting, pledges. Time to get to work. Unless you want to be stuck here after dark. That's when most of the bad things have happened here, right, Spook-brain? I mean, Amelia."

"Right." Amelia gritted her teeth and forced a smile. She wished Susan would encounter a ghost or something that would turn her smarmy voice into a scream.

Immediately, the pledges were loaded up with the bags of cleaning supplies.

When they made their way up the cracked brick steps, Susan took the keys from Kirk to unlock the door. Her hand trembled. Perhaps she was afraid she'd get a mysterious cut to match her boyfriend's.

The ornately carved front door opened with a wailing creak. Amelia stared at the worn carvings of roses in the oak until she was pushed forward. After they crossed the threshold, Kirk cursed under his breath. Blood soaked from his bandage and dripped on the white marble floor of the foyer.

"That's it." Susan tugged on his arm. "I'm taking you to get stitches."

"Babe, the cut isn't that deep."

She ignored Kirk, wheedled the van keys from Simon, and they both left. Since no one else was rushing forward to clean up the blood, Amelia pulled a cloth and spray bottle from the bag she carried. But when she bent down to clean the spot, the blood had vanished into the black and white marble floor as if the house had drunk it up.

Creepy.

She thought of asking the others if they'd noticed, but Rebecca and Simon were already barking orders. She turned to tell Guillermo, yet sadly he was occupied too. Her attention shifted to the inside of the house that had captured her fascination since she was a kid.

Romanesque statues lined the foyer, though Amelia doubted they were made from real marble unlike the blood-drinking floor. This extended as far as the foyer, then the floors became a dark, scuffed hardwood. As they walked farther inside, they came into a great room with a huge fireplace, faded sofas, loveseats, overstuffed chairs, and plush rugs. A dusty grandfather clock stood in a corner, cobwebs covering the curlicues around the face and extending down to the floor in gossamer strands.

Amelia looked back at the foyer statues and then turned to the grandfather clock. Those things would sell for a fortune at any of the antique stores in town. Why had they and the other old furnishings been left behind?

Rebecca's imperious voice echoed in the cavernous space. "Come on, pledges, it's time to stop gawking and start cleaning."

"We don't even get a tour?" Amelia asked while hauling her bag of cleaning supplies.

Simon shook his head with a deep scowl on his narrow face. "Nope. I don't know my way around and the caretaker isn't here today."

Amelia hoped with Susan and Kirk gone things would be more pleasant, but Simon and Rebecca seemed to want to make up for the absence. They separated the sorority and fraternity pledges, making the women clean the kitchen and the men clean the bathrooms while they hovered around, barking orders to scrub harder or clean faster. Only Mary was polite in directing them, but she didn't dare countermand Rebecca.

Mary stood beside Amelia, watching her scrub the stove that probably wouldn't even be used. "Why did Susan call you 'Spook-brain'?"

Amelia eyed Mary closely, looking for a hint of mockery. When she found none, she answered. "I have a bit of a hobby-horse over haunted places and this is one of my biggest subjects of interest."

"Oh wow. So you probably know more about the freaky stuff that happened here than most of us. Can you tell us a few stories?"

Tiffany huffed from over in the corner, then immediately sneezed as she inhaled a cloud of dust from the cupboard she was cleaning. "I don't wanna hear any of that creepy stuff while we're in here. Or ever, really."

"Well, we do," Rebecca said, looking up from the law textbook she was studying. "Give us the dirty details, Amelia."

Amelia's face grew hot as she felt all eyes on her. This was the first time any of the sorority sisters wanted her to talk about something that wasn't about why she should be allowed to join their ranks. She didn't want to tell them about the demons Claudia Raimi had written about in her diary because no one would believe her. Instead, she remembered something from Helen Raimi's autobiography. "Did either of you hear about the last thing that happened that made the Raimi family give up and leave the house?"

"No," Tiffany and Rebecca said in unison.

"Well, Helen Raimi—she was the last member of the family to live in the house—had been furious at the house for taking one of her children and driving away her husband. Anyway, she first called in a priest, and while he saw enough demonic phenomena to justify action, his superiors refused to believe him. So, Helen moved on to other denominations that professed to believe in demons. A fringe sect of Pentecostals believed her and scheduled an exorcism. They brought their minister, their top evangelists, and other special members to attempt to cast the devil out of the house. It didn't go well."

Amelia paused and felt a twinge of pleasure as both women pleaded with her to continue. "Okay, but give Tiff and me some of those pops out of that cooler I saw you and Simon bring in. This is thirsty work."

Rebecca relented and dragged in the cooler. Amelia helped herself to a can of Slice, scorning the Pepsi she and Tiffany used to drink together. Another break from Tiff's control, since Amelia never even liked Pepsi that much and only drank it because Tiff had always paid for them. Amelia leaned against the counter she'd cleaned and took a deep drink before continuing her tale. "From Helen's account, the Pentecostal minister took the devil into himself. He became possessed and massacred his fellow church members.

First with the fire poker, then with the superhuman strength of his own hands. He twisted one evangelist's head backwards. Helen also claims the bodies in the embalming room came alive, but the police never found any disturbances of the corpses."

"Wait," Tiffany interrupted with a squeak that gave Amelia petty delight. "Embalming room? Here?"

"Yeah." Amelia suppressed a shiver as she realized how close she was to said room. From what she'd read, the funeral parlor section of the house was through a hallway right outside the door at the back of the kitchen. Clients had a separate entrance on the north side of the house. "The Raimi family used part of the house as a funeral home. First in the early nineteen hundreds, which was also when they opened up some of the land as a cemetery for the rich, then again in the fifties."

"What did the family do between those times?" Rebecca asked.

"They used the south wing as an insane asylum for the wealthy." Amelia wondered if there was anything left over from those days. Padded rooms? Straitjackets? Lobotomy tools? "But deaths and disappearances of the patients made the family close off that part of the house and revert to only taking in dead people."

Tiffany met Amelia's gaze, her blue eyes brimming with morbid curiosity. "Do you think they still have coffins here?"

Rebecca laughed in a way that told Amelia she knew *something*. "You'll get the chance to find out on Halloween."

Since the kitchen was so filthy, the guys had to come in to help, breaking up Amelia's story time. But she didn't mind one bit since Guillermo joined her in scrubbing some unknown stain on the cracked tile checkered floor beside the island. His presence electrified her senses, overwhelming her with excitement and bliss just to be near him.

"I don't think we're going to make it to the bedrooms today." He blushed as people giggled at his words. "I mean, it's going to be dark in an hour."

Amelia glanced up at the window, seeing the dimming light streaming in. Someone walked past the doorway in the corner of her vision. She looked around and saw that everyone was still in the kitchen.

The hairs on the back of her neck stood up. They weren't alone here. Before she could say something, Guillermo leaned in close, the scent of his skin making things tighten low in her body.

"I was thinking," he whispered, "when we come back to clean the living room and bedrooms, we could stash some of our protective stuff, like the aloe plants my grandma told me about."

Amelia remembered Guillermo coming home from his Sunday family dinner, practically quivering with excitement as he'd listed some of the protective charms and rituals his grandma had told him about. She'd also had an unreasonable wistful pang of sadness that she hadn't been invited back to share another meal with that warm, vibrant family. A foolish feeling, since their pretend-dating didn't extend to Guillermo's relatives, so it would have looked suspicious if he brought her to every Sunday dinner.

All those cold, lonely suppers of canned or boxed meals alone while Dad worked had made her whimsical, wanting something she'd never had. And since Tiffany stopped inviting her to eat with her family when Amelia started dating Guillermo, many of Amelia's weekend meals had been alone.

She *really* needed to stop thinking about that. Especially now, when she'd very likely seen her first ghost in this place. What was important was that Guillermo was getting very useful research done on how to keep them safe here. He was finding possible protection methods that weren't in any of the books Amelia had come across. Now Amelia wondered what various other cultures used for spiritual protection. After all, the trappings of Anglo-Christianity hadn't been effective in this house, but, just in case, Guillermo had stolen some holy water when he attended Mass with his family earlier in the week.

She grinned at Guillermo, deciding to not tell him about the possible ghost she'd seen until she was sure. "Stashing our stuff in advance is a brilliant idea. I also want to talk to Mark Aripa. He's a member of the Coeur d'Alene tribe, who is part of a tribal organization to resurrect the Salish language and customs. The university gave him a research grant, so he has an office on campus. He might know more about the burial ground this place was built on, and maybe even the sort of curse that was put on it."

Last year, Amelia had read a book by Aripa released by the university's press. She admired his work even as she was disappointed that he never mentioned the horrors he'd endured in the summer camp massacre of '78 except to say the land was cursed. Amelia was dying to know what he'd meant by that. The newspapers had reported that the killings had been done by a madman, but what if there was something more to it?

There she was again, getting off track.

Guillermo brought her wandering mind back to focus. "That's an excellent idea. And then we could—" He broke off and stared wide-eyed at something over her shoulder. "I saw something."

"You too? What was it?"

Before he could answer, they heard the front door open and Susan's shrill voice echoing from the cavernous foyer. Their worst tormenters had returned from Urgent Care. Rebecca and Simon lurched up from the kitchen table and charged out, accusing the couple of going to the clinic to avoid having to babysit the pledges, while Mary sat in the kitchen and rolled her eyes.

"The cut was really bad," Susan argued.

"No, it wasn't..." Kirk's voice broke mid-protest. "Oh shit."

Amelia and Guillermo headed out of the kitchen in time to see a crimson blossom spread through Kirk's fresh bandage. Susan snapped at them to put away the cleaning supplies and head back to the van. Kirk went out to the front porch to have a cigarette with Simon.

On the ride back, Amelia whispered to Guillermo, "Did you notice that Kirk bled heavier every time he entered the house?"

"I did. That was spooky as hell." His breath against her ear and neck made her skin tingle pleasurably despite the ominous subject matter.

They huddled together for the rest of the ride, the chatter of the others distant as Amelia took advantage of the pretend dating scenario and rested her head against Guillermo's chest. His arms enclosed her in a warm cocoon of safety; his heartbeat a soothing promise that everything would turn out okay.

When they got back to the frat house, the beat of the music was loud enough to be heard outside. Another party was in full swing. The women, including Susan, grumbled about having to shower and change first.

As Guillermo helped Amelia out of the back of the van, he bent and spoke quietly. "As soon as you get back here, come up to my room."

Her heart skipped a beat. Did he want to make things real between them?

His next words dashed her tentative hopes. "I don't think I can handle partying tonight. Maybe we can take inventory of our supplies and hang out and just…talk."

"Sure." She tried to hide her disappointment. On her way back to the Omega Pi house, Amelia scolded herself. How could she be agonizing about the mess she'd made with this fake relationship with Guillermo when earlier today, she'd not only been inside the Raimi House, but she'd also seen it drink blood?

Chapter Six

Guillermo paced back and forth in his room. Amelia and the other girls who'd been on the cleaning mission should be arriving any minute. The noise of the party downstairs amplified his nervousness. Amelia hadn't seemed thrilled with the idea of being alone with him in his room. Did she think he'd try to sleep with her? Sure, he wanted to, but was her long silence an indication that she didn't feel anything for him all those times they'd kissed and held each other to keep up their fake dating act? He pinched the bridge of his nose. Should he even be worrying about that when their main priority was to not die in two weeks?

The soft knock made him jump.

He opened the door to see Amelia looking as frazzled as he was, though he couldn't tell if it was because she was worried about his motives, or if she was still shaken by the spookiness of the Raimi House. For a moment he was again stunned silent by her beauty. Her hair was still damp from her shower, glistening in obsidian waves. Her pale blue eyes glittered like icicles in an early December evening. She wore a long-sleeved black velvet dress that was cut in a vee, revealing her mouthwatering cleavage. The dress came to her knees, showing off her shapely calves before her suede half-boots covered the rest.

Amelia usually didn't dress up this much for parties. Had she done so to please him, or to torment him? Both were working.

Before he did something to spook her, he turned away and grabbed a notebook from his backpack. "I made a list of the things we have so far, and started a list of things we still need to get."

When he handed her the list, Amelia sat on his bed and read the items from the first page. "Squirt guns, holy water, communion wafers, salt, basil, sage, saint candles, and two rosaries. And we still need to get garlic, evil eye pendants, and some of those protective bracelets from the international market in Spokane that I told you about. I also think we're going to need a lot more salt. Do you have a pen?"

They worked on the list together, while Guillermo struggled to concentrate while silently reveling and suffering at the press of her warm thigh against his leg and her hair sometimes brushing his cheek when she bent to add something else to the list. Finally, he took the notebook from her and set it on the nightstand. "Do you mind if we call it a night for that part? I want to get that house out of my head before I go to sleep."

"Sure. Should I go?" Amelia started to get off the bed.

"No." He gently grasped her wrist. "I meant that we can talk about other stuff. I've been thinking that even after knowing you for two years, there's a lot I don't know about you."

She lay back on his bed with her legs dangling off the side. "What do you want to know?"

"Why are you friends with Tiffany?" He hoped she wouldn't resent him prying, but he was curious about their strange dynamic.

Amelia's pained sigh made him regret asking. "My mom died when I was thirteen, an age where I really, really needed her, and my dad… Well, let's just say parenthood wasn't his thing. I mean, I can't blame his neglect and lack of interest on him completely. He had to work long hours to feed me and keep a roof over my head, so it's no wonder he didn't have any energy left over to play with me, or ask how my day was. Also, I look a lot like my mom and he said it was painful to look at me."

Guillermo shivered at the thought of growing up in such a household. The antithesis of the warm, if somewhat overheated, atmosphere of his own. And though it wasn't his place to say anything, it hurt him deep inside to hear Amelia make excuses for her father's treatment of her. It sounded like he was punishing Amelia for her mother's death. But Guillermo hadn't asked about her terrible father. He'd asked about her awful friend.

He lay down beside her. "You must have been lonely."

"I was. And I think my desperation was obvious because the more I tried to make friends, the more I was ostracized. So, by the time Tiffany came into the picture, I was blind to her controlling tendencies. She was like a fairy godmother, transforming me into one of the popular, beautiful people, while at the same time being the sister I never had." Her wistful tone broke his heart. "It's embarrassing to admit that Tiffany has kept me on a short leash for years and I'm only now coming to realize it. She can be sweet and all, and she w—*is* my best friend, but I don't think we should have to do *everything* together."

For a long time, Guillermo was stunned silent, digesting the heartbreaking logic of her words. He'd seen Tiffany's recent coldness toward Amelia. Was it because Amelia was no longer following her whims? He'd also seen a similar dynamic with some of the guys in the fraternity. Hell, the fraternity itself had a culture of conformity he found chafing. Amelia probably wouldn't appreciate him analyzing her relationship with her friend this soon, so instead he moved to the happier subject of dating her. "Wow. I knew she had some hold on you, but I had no idea it was something so insidious."

Amelia tilted her head so her cheek leaned against his shoulder. "Now it's my turn to pry into your business. It might have been my imagination, but did I detect some awkwardness between you and your dad?"

He opened his mouth to tell the reflexive lie he fed to all his other friends: that everything was fine. But for some reason, he couldn't bring himself to lie to Amelia. Had he ever done so? He didn't think so.

Guillermo took a deep breath and began. "I don't know if you've ever noticed, but people with my background aren't exactly well-received in this part of Idaho, well, probably the whole state. When my grandfather moved up here, the Aryans spray-painted slurs on the side of his house and left pamphlets warning about a Mexican invasion on the windshields of every car in the neighborhood."

"That's fucked up."

He nodded. "But that only made him more determined to put down roots and establish a successful business here. Which he did. According to Dad, Grandpa Juan fully assimilated into the community. He raised my father and aunts to speak English as their primary language and to never say or do anything in public that sounded too 'foreign.' However, Dad must have some bit of love for his heritage left, or at least he didn't hate it enough, since he married my mom. The names of his children and the food we eat at home speak to that as well. But Dad was originally against Mom teaching me and my siblings to speak Spanish, and he's hostile to Grandma telling us her stories about her family and life in Mexico, talking about her superstitions, and honoring most of our special holidays. On top of that, he wants me to follow in his footsteps and do everything he does, from joining this stupid fraternity to getting the same degree he has, and to eventually taking over the family business." He sighed. "I'm not even sure I want to take over the business." He paused as that admission sank in. "Oh my God, that's the first time I've said that out loud. I mean, I like building houses. I love watching bags of concrete, rebar, wood boards, and sheetrock become homes where people can eat, sleep, play, and build their dreams. But I don't live for the business side of it. I don't enjoy giving orders to workers, negotiating contracts with property owners, ordering materials, counting the nickels and dimes… My sister loves all that stuff, though. Too bad she isn't the firstborn." *And a man.*

When Guillermo fell silent, he noticed how quiet it had gotten downstairs. No more loud music or shouts, just level talking. "The party must be wrapping up. I better walk you back to the Pi house before my roommate comes up here and makes an ass out of himself."

When they went downstairs, the frat brothers cheered and held up their hands for high-fives, making clear what they assumed he and Amelia had been doing in his room. Guillermo and Amelia escaped as fast as they could.

The crisp October air felt good on his burning cheeks. The scent of dying leaves was strong and somehow melancholy. Maybe because the sight and smell of those red and orange leaves meant that summer, his favorite season, was over.

Amelia broke the silence, but instead of saying something about the crass way the guys had acted, she surprised him. "I used to love jumping in those big piles of leaves."

"Me too." Guillermo couldn't stop smiling at her guileless enthusiasm. "I don't think I've done that since elementary school."

She took his hand. "What are we waiting for?"

They ran together and leapt into the biggest pile left by the street-sweeper, laughing at the soft, yet crunchy sensation of the leaves beneath and around them, and the fleeting return to carefree youth. At the moment, the leaves no longer smelled melancholy. Instead, they carried the heady perfume of childhood and imagination.

After scrambling up from the pile, they laughed even more as they pulled leaves out of each other's hair.

When they reached the front door of the sorority house, Amelia threaded her arms around his neck and pulled him down to give him a kiss that drove away any dreams about the Raimi House.

***

The final weeks leading up to Halloween seemed to move at warp speed. Guillermo and Amelia took a road trip to the international market in Spokane to get the rest of the herbs on their list as well, along with some evil eye pendants. Then it was off to a garden store for some aloe plants, and a New Age store for various stones that were supposed to be good for protection. He tried to work in as much romance as he could, with romantic dinners, a chilly walk on Lake Skeetshue's boardwalk, and a visit to Carver Farms for some pumpkins to carve. But the rest of their time was reserved for studying occult books and Amelia's copies of books about the Raimi House and family.

To hinder their research and romancing even further, both schoolwork and torture by the fraternity and sorority ramped up, culminating in Hell Week, the traditional seven days where the pledges were subjected to the worst series of physical and mental torments.

Amelia and Guillermo swapped stories that almost made the horrors of the Raimi House seem tame.

In the sorority, Amelia and Tiffany had endured sleep deprivation from several nights of being woken at odd hours by the others before being ordered by Heidi to exercise or by Rebecca to clean something. Then Susan subjected them to sensory deprivation by having to do ridiculous things blindfolded and wearing silencing earmuffs meant for the shooting range. And yesterday, the pledges had endured the humiliating ritual of being paddled, which Susan and Rebecca seemed to get off on.

Guillermo and his fellow pledges had also been paddled, sleep deprived, and branded, thankfully not bad enough to scar. Plus, Mike, the one pledge who cried out during the branding, was pissed on by Paul, the fraternity vice president. The only thing that kept Guillermo from walking out of the frat house was the fear that if he put a stop to his and Amelia's secret mission, he'd lose her.

Sometimes, he'd lie awake in his bed, resolved to confess his real feelings to Amelia. Yet the day after those vows, he found himself tongue-tied before her pale blue eyes. So he shoved down his lovestruck inclinations and dedicated himself to their mutual goals.

They had three more cleaning ventures at the house. When they got to clean the bedroom they'd be sharing for the big night, Amelia and Guillermo stashed their boxes of protective items under the bed and burnt some sage in the room.

Maybe it was a placebo effect, but the room did feel less sinister after the sage burning. Guillermo's optimism grew with each trip to the house. Sure, he spotted a few more ghosts, the creepiest being an old woman in one of those dressing gowns from the turn of the century with spooky blue-glazed cataracts.

But if ghost sightings were all they'd experience, Guillermo would count them lucky.

The encounter with Mr. Hill, the caretaker, on their third cleaning trip reminded him to remain on guard. The man himself had been creepy, so thin and knobby he appeared to be made of sticks. He'd nodded in reluctant approval at how clean the kitchen, dining area, great room, and some of the bedrooms were. Then he gave everyone a reluctant tour, pointing out which wings of the house were to be avoided. The short-lived asylum was up the stairs one floor and to the right in the south wing, while the funeral parlor and embalming room were on the main floor to the north. The caretaker didn't show them those areas, sternly warning them to stay away. Susan had asked why, and did not accept Mr. Hill's vague explanation that bad things happened there. "We paid good money to rent this house and we can go where we want."

"Then you'd be wise to remember you signed papers stating that the property owner is not liable for any injuries, deaths, or psychological harm that could occur with you or anyone you bring onto the premises." The caretaker had looked like he was going to continue his tirade, but then his gaze strayed to the windows and the dimming light outside. "It's nearly dark. Get out now."

They'd been so stunned with the guy's abrupt shift in mood that they'd immediately obeyed.

The fourth trip had been the best. Instead of cleaning, all the pledges got to decorate the great room and dining room for the party. Amelia's unabashed delight Halloween decorating had made her practically glow. Her good mood had been infectious. Hanging up skeletons, spiders, and bits of black lace in an ancient mansion was such fun that everyone mostly forgot about the house's evil reputation for a few hours.

The night before Halloween, Guillermo's worries about the Raimi House barely touched on the possible ghostly encounters and inevitable pranks that Kirk and Susan were sure to have set up. His biggest concern was what would happen with his and Amelia's relationship afterward. When the initiation was complete, they had no further reason to pretend to be dating. Furthermore, if she dropped out of the Omega Pis instead of completing the swearing-in ceremony the night after Halloween, he had no idea where she'd go. Another dorm on campus, or back to her cold father's house? Guillermo had fully intended on leaving the Alpha Lambdas, but now he found himself willing to wait and see what Amelia would do first. Wait, no. To hell with waiting and seeing.

In these four weeks, Amelia had not only become his best friend, he'd also fallen for her. He had to know if she felt the same.

I'll ask her, he vowed to himself as he listened to Kirk and another frat brother bragging about how scared the pledges would be tomorrow. *As soon as we get to the house, I'll ask if she wants to be with me for real.*

The problem was, the prospect of losing Amelia scared him worse than anything the Raimi House could throw at him.

Chapter Seven

Halloween

Amelia twirled in front of the mirror, admiring the way the full skirt of white wedding gown floated around her legs. Her Halloween costume was perfect, even though her hair had taken forever.

Now it was time to head to the Raimi House for the big night. A fresh wave of nervousness washed over her. Would any of the stuff they'd researched and gathered actually work on the evil entities in the house? Or would something terrible happen?

She wished she'd gotten more time to talk with Mark Aripa like she'd planned. The days of sick torture had not only made assignments and studying impossible, but it had also prevented Amelia from being able to have a proper meeting with him. When she finally found Mr. Aripa, he was on his way off campus to the reservation for a vacation. She'd followed him to his car, clumsily inquiring about methods to combat evil, but his only advice was: "Don't go to the Raimi House." Even worse than the demoralizing failure to get more helpful knowledge was that Guillermo and Amelia barely got to spend any time together, much less do further research.

At least she'd have all night with Guillermo.. Her entire being quivered with anticipation to be in his arms again. She hadn't had a religious upbringing, but all the same, she whispered a small prayer that they'd be safe tonight.

Loud rapping on the bathroom door tore her gaze from the mirror.

Susan's voice was muffled through the wood. "Hurry up in there. I need to do my makeup."

Amelia opened the door and walked out of the bathroom. Susan gave the wedding gown a once-over and smirked. "Only children dress as brides."

"It's not a bride costume, it's—" She broke off with a sigh. Every sorority sister except for Tiffany assumed that Amelia's costume was a generic bride outfit, even though the way she'd done her hair should have been a dead giveaway.

Susan ignored her, went into the bathroom with her giant makeup case, and slammed the door.

In only a few minutes, they'd load up in cars and vans and head to the Raimi House. It would be the fourth time she'd been in the evil place, but the first time she'd be there after dark. Tiffany looked nervous as well, pacing by the front door and checking her makeup. She was dressed as Madonna, with a black bustier almost hidden by multiple necklaces, a lacy black mid-length skirt, black lace gloves, dangly earrings, and a thick black ribbon tied in her crimped blonde hair. Amelia had to admit that her former friend looked awesome and felt a stab of regret, missing the Halloweens where they'd helped each other with their costumes. Of course, Tiffany had never let Amelia choose what to wear.

Amelia paused on the stairs, not knowing if she should try to talk to her former best friend. Tiffany had been giving her the silent treatment ever since their first visit to the Raimi House, only breaking it when she didn't have anyone else to complain to about the juggling of schoolwork and sorority activities. Amelia listened to her patiently, and offered sympathy as she always did when it came to her friend's plights, but then Tiffany's face would shift back to a cold mask and she'd go back to ignoring her. As if sensing Amelia's presence, Tiffany turned from the door. "So this is it. The final initiation. I can't believe that there are only two of us left to join the sorority. Layla and Tina were crazy to leave."

Amelia gave a noncommittal nod. As she continued on down the stairs, she wondered if Layla and Tina had been the smartest of the pledges.

Tiffany approached her and lowered her voice to a whisper, "Maybe since they need us to keep up their membership numbers, they'll take it easy on us tonight."

"I wouldn't be so sure."

Yesterday, some of the Omega Pis and Alpha Lambdas went on another trip to the house, this time not taking any pledges. Guillermo and Amelia knew the fraternity brothers and sorority sisters were setting up traps and pranks to scare them. Amelia hoped they hadn't gotten into the stash of protective items she and Guillermo had hidden in what was to be their bedroom for the night.

At the sound of Guillermo's truck pulling up outside, Amelia shouldered her backpack containing her coat, books, more containers of salt, and other potential protective items.

For a moment, Tiffany and Amelia looked at each other and Amelia felt a pang of regret at the loss of a five-year-long friendship. At first, the same wistful sentiment reflected in Tiff's blue eyes, but then her features hardened and she left the door to go talk to Rebecca.

With a sigh, Amelia headed to the kitchen and gathered up the pair of jack-o-lanterns she'd carved. A fond smile curved her lips as she remembered carving the first one with Guillermo and roasting the seeds. The second one had been done at the sorority house where only she, Nancy, and Miranda had bothered to carve pumpkins, though Susan had brought a few uncarved ones and placed them on the snack table during their previous decorating trip.

As Amelia carefully worked the front door open without dropping the pumpkins, she worried about what Guillermo would think about her costume. They'd decided to keep their costumes secret and surprise each other. It had been a fun plan until now, when doubt churned in her stomach like a cement mixer.

When she met Guillermo outside, his eyes widened in appreciation and surprised delight. "Princess Vespa."

Amelia's heart leapt with joy that he recognized her costume. "*Spaceballs* is one of my all-time favorite movies."

"Mine too." The enthusiastic agreement was almost as wonderful as his costume.

Guillermo had dressed as Gomez Addams from the old black and white TV show. Amelia adored those reruns. And what a handsome Gomez he made. Even better-looking than John Astin. The pinstripe suit accentuated his muscled form, and his long black curls looked almost as good slicked back as they did when they were free and flowing around her shoulders. Now she understood why he'd grown out a thin mustache.

Amelia set down her backpack and the jack-o-lanterns, then held out her hand in her best Morticia impression. "*Mon cher.*"

"'Tish, you spoke French." Guillermo took her hand and kissed his way up from her wrist to her shoulder, making her tremble with desire. "I'm so glad you recognized my costume. So many of the guys thought I was dressed as a gangster from the thirties."

"I know how you feel." She laughed. "The girls think I'm a generic bride."

"Even with the braid buns?" Guillermo shook his head and put his arm around her. "We're surrounded by fools who have no taste. Anyway, are you ready to go? I figured we'd take my truck so that if we need to get the hell out, we can."

They loaded their backpacks and her jack-o-lanterns in the bed of the pickup alongside the pumpkin he'd carved and joined the small convoy of vehicles ready for the party. Guillermo and Amelia both frowned at the keg and coolers loaded up in Kevin Daugharty's truck. Kevin was the chief standards officer and was supposed to enforce the fraternity's rules, but seemed to encourage breaking them instead.

Amelia sighed. "One good thing about us spending the night is that at least we won't be drunk driving. As much as I can't stand most of these people, I don't want them to die in an accident after they leave us alone in a deadly house."

"They also hired Gilbert Curtis to sell drugs and bootleg music." Disgust laced his voice. "But I don't plan on even getting drunk in that place, much less do any drugs."

"Yeah. Somehow, I don't think the experience would be as pleasant as the time I got stoned at the Sazerac House." Amelia giggled. "Only the good ghosts were around at the time and their mischief had me giggling."

"There are good ghosts?"

Amelia nodded. "But probably not in the Raimi House."

They grew quiet as they followed the convoy from the levee road that surrounded the university and the community college, overlooking the Amteep River. The water reflected pinks and oranges from the setting sun. A full moon was visible in the gradually darkening sky. When they emerged onto Wright Avenue, Amteep's main downtown road, Amelia spotted trick-or-treaters walking hand in hand with their parents, carrying pillowcases or plastic pumpkin buckets as they begged for Halloween candy from the expensive shops meant for tourists. Childlike giddiness filled her at the sight of their bright smiles and colorful costumes. She'd loved trick-or-treating as a child. For a moment, the joy of Halloween suffused her being, calming her worries about the evil she was going to face.

Guillermo's voice broke through her nostalgia. "You really love Halloween, don't you?"

"It's my favorite holiday." Amelia couldn't hide her excitement. "I have a lot of memories of my mom taking me trick-or-treating before she passed away. Then I went with my best grade-school friend, Suzanne, who'd moved away in seventh-grade. We went to the rich neighborhoods, where we got full-size candy bars and sometimes quarters and dollar bills from the people who'd forgotten to buy candy. The decorations on those big houses were the best."

"I love Halloween too." He glanced over at the trick-or-treaters before turning his attention back to the road. "Grandma does not. She believes evil spirits roam on this night. And where we're going, that's probably true. She's upset with me that I'll be gone for most of All Saints' Day tomorrow. But Dad is excited for my final initiation and being inducted into the fraternity soon."

The distaste in his voice mirrored her thoughts on being sworn in as a member of the Omega Pis. "I'm glad my dad isn't the one pushing me into the sorority."

"Being pressured by someone who's supposed to be your best friend is bad too."

Amelia nodded, embarrassment still flooding her being at admitting how she'd let another person control her so completely. Even more embarrassing were her feelings of being cast adrift in an endless dark sea of uncertainty and fear, with no one to hold on to and shine a light. What was that psychology term? Codependency?

When the truck turned onto the road that wound around the lake, Guillermo glanced over at her, his dark eyes full of concern. "You're quiet. Did I upset you by bringing up your rift with your friend, or are you nervous about tonight?"

"No, I'm nervous." What she didn't tell him was how worried she was that she'd screw things up with their relationship.

What if she already had? After tonight, the dating ruse would end. She'd have to come clean about wanting to be with him for real.

What if he wasn't interested in her in a romantic sense at all? What if he grew angry with her for her ruse and stopped being her friend?

She wished she hadn't made such a mess of things. Amelia had never dated a guy she'd chosen on her own, a guy she wanted to be with. And even though her friendship with Tiffany was probably toast, she wished she had a friend to confide in, to give her advice on not screwing this up.

If Guillermo hadn't been the guy she'd fallen for, she would have been comfortable coming to him for advice. And that was the best thing about him. That she was *comfortable* around him. Amelia realized she'd never been so at ease around anyone besides Mom. Unlike with Dad, Guillermo didn't make her feel like an inconvenience or a burden. And unlike with Tiffany, she never got the feeling that Guillermo would mock her for anything she said, or try to make her do things she didn't want to. Previous boyfriends had made her feel like an object, an ornament to be on their arms in public, and a bragging point about what she did with them in private.

His deep, soothing voice broke through her inner lashings of self-doubt. "We'll make it through this." Her breath caught. It was as if he'd read her mind. "We won't let anything in that house get us as long as we're together."

Amelia's heart warmed at his solemn assurances he'd face all potential evils at her side. Such fervent words gave her hope they could work out...and they'd live long enough for that to happen.

Guillermo drove through the open gates of the Raimi House and parked beside Brandon Teller's car. Amelia got out and looked up at the monstrous mansion. In the red and purple light from the sunset, the house looked festive for the occasion. The slate roof burned crimson, and red light reflected in the window panes that weren't broken or boarded up. Shadows lengthened down the eaves and across the overgrown lawn. It was the epitome of a haunted house.

Words from Helen Raimi's autobiography whispered in her mind. *"People mistake the house as being haunted. It is something different altogether."*

Guillermo's fingers slipped between hers. He gripped her hand and squeezed it, warming her chilled skin. "Let's do this."

They unloaded their stuff and entered the house. The party was already getting going, with a guy dressed as Darth Vader playing music from a DJ station set up in the great room. The dining room table was loaded with snacks and multiple coolers were under the table. But the coolers weren't the only things containing beer. Someone had dragged a coffin from the funeral parlor wing out to the dining room and filled it with ice and booze.

Guillermo noticed the coffin too. "Damn, that would be a practical repurpose if it weren't for the satin lining."

"Yeah. It's perfect for the Halloween spirit." She admired how fitting the coffin looked amidst all the other decorations.

Amelia detected the pungent odor of marijuana and saw a man dressed like Clint Eastwood in a spaghetti Western. This must be the infamous Gilbert Curtis, the man who could get anything. He had set himself up in the round, turreted parlor between the great room and the dining room and covered the table with his notorious bootleg cassettes, t-shirts, snacks, and various novelty items. The drugs weren't in view, possibly obscured by a jack-o-lantern on his table of goods, but from the covert way Paul Gibson was whispering to him, Amelia knew Gilbert had them. She chuckled when she realized the gun in his holster was a plastic squirt gun. Why hadn't she and Guillermo thought of getting toy holsters for their holy water squirt guns? They'd come in handy since her Princess Vespa gown had no pockets.

It was tempting to go see some of Gilbert's legal wares, but she decided to wait until later. She put the pumpkins she'd carved on top of the elaborate stone hearth above the fireplace and lit candles inside them. A few cheers and whoops echoed behind her from the costumed dancers. Guillermo placed his pumpkin on the snack table. In mutual, silent accord, Amelia and Guillermo went upstairs to the bedroom they'd chosen and put their backpacks with the last of their supplies in the enormous closet, then made sure that the boxes containing the stuff they'd stashed were still safe under the bed.

Amelia turned toward the door to head back down to the party when Guillermo stopped her.

He paced in front of the bed, looking nervous. "Wait. There's something I need to talk to you about before we rejoin the fray."

She stepped closer to him, her heartbeat quickening at the growing proximity and the intent look in his dark eyes. "Yes?"

Guillermo stopped pacing and for a moment silently regarded her with intent dark eyes before he softly replied in a husky tone. "Who says we have to pretend?"

Elation made her light-headed even as her face burned as she answered the question that she'd been building the courage to ask *him*. "I—I thought you wouldn't be interested."

"Me? Not interested?" He blinked at her in visible disbelief. "I mean, I know we've never run in the same crowds, but why would you think I wouldn't be interested? You're..." He trailed off and made a wide sweeping gesture at her. "Gorgeous, smart, and fun to talk to."

Amelia's face burned and her hands fidgeted with the skirt of her dress. "I dunno. I never got that vibe from you before last month, and we've never talked much about that sort of thing...so..."

"That's because when you weren't already dating someone, I was. And then you were almost always surrounded by your friends, so you weren't exactly approachable at the right place and time for me to work up the nerve to tell you how I feel. Remember when my dad mentioned that I had thing for an ice princess?"

"He was referring to *me*?" Her eyes widened, then narrowed on him. "You thought I was an ice princess? Even after we've been friends for two years?"

Guillermo's cheeks darkened. "Tiffany sticks her nose up in the air every time you two encountered me. And you wouldn't talk to me when you were with her. Only when you were alone was I worthy of your attention."

"I'm sorry." For once, she didn't curse Tiffany for trying to keep her away from Guillermo. She cursed herself for not being brave enough to go after what she truly wanted.

He reached out and brushed his knuckles along her cheek, the gentle touch easing her trembling. "So, do you want to make this thing between us real?"

"Yes." She lifted her chin and looked up at him with her lips parted in invitation.

Guillermo lowered his head and claimed those lips in the first kiss that wasn't a performance. He pulled her into his arms, crushed her to him. Amelia kissed him back and gave in to the hunger she'd had since the first time she laid eyes on him.

A low moan escaped her lips and she let her fingers slide up the back of his neck in a light, caressing motion before her hand plunged into his hair. Even with the gel he'd used to slick it back, his curls felt soft. Guillermo deepened the kiss and stroked her back, filling her with sensations of warmth.

That first real kiss only increased her hunger for more. Amelia held him tight, refusing to let him go. Thankfully, he seemed to have no desire to leave. She continued to kiss him back as fervently, her tongue teasing his and her hands exploring his back, his hair, and the nape of his neck. The intense way his body responded surprised and delighted her.

As if needing to affect her as intently, Guillermo trailed kisses across her cheek and up and down her neck until he found a place right above her shoulder that made her gasp and tremble. Amelia clung to him, rising up on her toes to grind her hips against his erection. She nipped at his earlobe, and his husky groan brought another surge of erotic sensation.

He shifted from nibbling her neck to claiming her lips again. His tongue tangled with hers, mimicking other movements she wanted to do with him. The way he moved against her revealed that his desire was just as potent as hers.

By the time he broke the kiss, they were both panting and Amelia was so aroused that she ached. Her dazed look from his kiss made his chest swell with primal satisfaction.

"Should I lock the door?" His brown eyes seemed to glow with their own inner fire, as well as the knowledge that he was asking about more than the door.

"Yes." Her voice trembled.

The click of the lock had a weight to it. A sound of finality, taking a step that neither could walk back from.

Guillermo sat on the bed and shrugged out of his suit jacket, then unbuttoned his shirt. When he took it off, revealing a muscular chest, broad shoulders, and a flat stomach, Amelia licked her lips.

"Wow," Amelia breathed, unable to hide her admiration. "Construction work really pays off."

His pleased grin morphed into an open-mouthed look of awe when she carefully removed her dress. Standing in front of the bed in nothing but her shoes and a matching black bra and panties, Amelia reveled in the blatant appreciation in his eyes.

Tentatively, he reached out and placed his hands on her waist. Her palms were hot against her skin. Amelia crouched to kiss him before she sat beside him on the bed. When she bent to take off her shoes, it was all she could do not to peek as she heard him taking off his pants and shoes.

Soon, they were stretched out on the bed together, kissing and exploring each other's bodies. When he slid his finger under the waistband of her panties and his finger grazed her clit, she bit back a gasp. Then she reached into his boxers and closed her fingers around his shaft, making him suck in his breath. She writhed at his touch, in awe how he touched like an expert musician handled his instrument. Never before had a guy taken so much time to give her pleasure before the main act. Somewhere in their mutual fondling, their underwear vanished.

Guillermo paused long enough to get a condom from his discarded pants. As he rolled it on, he looked down at her with reverence.

"Please," she whispered, gripping his upper arms and pulling him down to cover her body with his. When he slid into her wet heat, neither were able to suppress groans of pleasure. God, he felt so good.

She arched her back beneath him and shifted her hips to take him in deeper, intensifying the pleasure. They found a rhythm that morphed the heady sensations to pure, intoxicating ecstasy. Together, they climbed the peak of passion, their pleasure building and mounting until they both flew over the precipice. Amelia's climax hit like a bolt of lightning that electrified her further as Guillermo trembled and spasmed inside her. He kissed her and held her until her tremors subsided.

After cleaning up, they reluctantly dressed, neither eager to go downstairs and join the party, but knowing if they stayed in here, Kirk and Susan would unleash more torture.

They made their way back downstairs to the snack table and loaded up paper plates with cheese, sliced summer sausage, and Planters Cheez Balls, then found a few empty chairs and settled down to eat and watch the festivities. Amelia admired the costumes she saw. Even Susan was in the spirit, though she had to be freezing in her cheerleader outfit despite the heat from the fireplace. Kirk wore a football player uniform to match her. The colors of both outfits made Amelia wonder if those were genuine uniforms from when they were in high school at Lake Valley High, Amteep High's biggest rival. Tiffany's boyfriend, Brandon, was Vegas Elvis. Other costumes included cats, a pirate, the Wicked Witch of the West, and many others.

After they finished eating, Guillermo asked Amelia to dance. Twirling in his arms to "A Tale That Wasn't Right" by Helloween made Amelia feel like all evil was banished from this room. The combination of dancing for the first time in years and being in the arms of the man who'd just finished making love to her made her almost dizzy with joy, despite the song being about a breakup. The next song was Heart's "Alone," which was more fitting. After that was Dokken's "Into the Fire."

After Dokken faded away, Darth Vader pointed at Amelia and Tiffany, and spoke with Dave Garris's voice. "I remember you on the dance team back at Amteep High. You two should do a dance for us. This area's big enough."

"Yeah." Miranda Cohen nodded, adjusting the brim of her pointed witch hat. "I'd love to see that."

"I don't know," Tiffany said, tossing her crimped hair.

But Brandon along with most of the sorority members all implored for Tiffany and Amelia to dance.

Guillermo echoed the sentiment, giving Amelia an encouraging smile that made her want to show him her talent. Even though it was one she hardly used anymore.

Amelia and Tiffany looked at each other, tangible awkwardness radiating between them. Finally, they nodded and approached Darth Dave.

"Do you have 'Superfreak'?" they asked in tandem. That was the song that they'd choreographed together, nearly got them in trouble, and won them the state championship in their senior year of high school.

Dave lifted his Vader helmet and grinned. "I'd be a failure of a DJ if I didn't."

The others backed up to give Amelia and Tiffany space and made a big circle around them. The music started and Amelia joined her former best friend in the steps they'd created together. The skirt of her Princess Vespa gown floated around Amelia as they spun. At first, they focused to execute the motions right, but soon they smiled at each other, and the weeks of separation and all the angst between them vanished. For the duration of the song, they were best friends again, moving together as a synchronized unit.

Applause rang out when the song finished and Tiffany and Amelia joined hands and took a bow.

Tiffany met Amelia's eyes and suddenly looked more serious than she ever had. "I'm sorry I was such a bitch these past few weeks. I was—"

Susan cut them off. "I think it's time for some party games."

There was a mixture of groans of dread and enthusiastic noises. The sorority president ignored them all and gestured for everyone to follow her into the dining room.

"I swear," Guillermo whispered to Amelia, "if they make us put our hands in bowls of cold spaghetti and peeled grapes like at a kids' party, I will not be amused."

But Susan's idea was even dumber than juvenile gross-out tricks. She had everyone sit at the long dining room table. Rebecca, Valerie, and Nancy brought out candles in elaborate silver holders. Nancy was dressed as Wonder Woman, Valerie was a nurse, and Rebecca wore one of the same skirt-suits she wore to her law classes. Amelia wasn't surprised that the sorority chief standards officer was too stuck up to wear a costume. Susan's three lackeys arranged the candles on the table, and lit them before turning the lights off, leaving only candlelight and the fireplace to illuminate the austere room.

Susan emerged from the parlor with what looked like either a board game or a jigsaw puzzle. But Amelia knew it had to be something worse.

Sure enough, Laura Hayward, one of the sorority sisters sitting on the other end of the table, close enough to read the box by candlelight, shook her head so vigorously that the tiara she wore as part of her Cinderella costume fell off. "Oh hell no. Not in this place."

"Yeah." Deb crossed her arms over the front of her skimpy Vegas showgirl outfit. "A Ouija board is a bad idea."

The second the board was identified, chairs scraped back from the table as everyone objected. Even Kirk. "Babe, let's not tempt fate."

"Oh, c'mon," Susan huffed, bouncing on her heels like a kid begging for a treat. "I can't believe I'm surrounded by such wimps. It's just a silly game. I wanted the pledges in a proper spooked-out mood before we leave them alone for the night."

Guillermo cleared his throat. "With all due respect, being in this house has us spooked enough as it is."

"I can't believe so many of you actually *believe* all those ridiculous stories." Susan rolled her eyes. "Much less that you're gullible enough to believe playing with a Parker Brothers board game will actually summon evil spirits. There's no such thing." With that, she threw back her head, raised her hands in the air, and shouted, "Spirits in this house, I dare you to come out and prove to me you're real."

"Please, *don't*," Amelia found herself pleading. When nothing happened and Susan lowered her arms and smirked, she relaxed somewhat.

Then a loud pounding sound came from beneath their feet. *Oh shit.*

Tiffany made a disgusted sound. "I suppose this thumping was supposed to come when we had the Ouija board going?"

Guillermo took Amelia's hand and nodded. "We know you guys are bound to have some scares planned for us, but you can chalk this one up to a failure."

"Yeah." Chuck, one of the other pledges, nodded at Guillermo and finished his beer in one large gulp. He wore a Superman costume. "Can we turn the music on and get back to partying?"

Kirk nodded. "That sounds like a good plan. This beer isn't going to drink itself and—" He broke off and rubbed his arms. "Did someone open a window?"

A cold wind blew through the room, making Amelia shiver. But the breeze disappeared as fast as it came.

"Another party guest must have shown up late," Betty said, sounding like she was trying to reassure herself as she fidgeted in her Sandy from *Grease* costume. Suddenly, her nose wrinkled. "Ewww, what's that smell?"

A putrid odor wafted through the area, making everyone gag and cover their mouths and noses. The fireplace flared brightly and crackled, making them jump.

Susan shrugged and uncovered her face. "Whatever it was, it's gone. I told you, there's no such thing as evil spirits."

Then a gray cloud formed in the center of the makeshift circle everyone had made around the long table. Amelia stared at the thing, captivated. She opened her mouth to ask if anyone knew what the hell it was, then closed it as she watched the diaphanous shape fly into Susan's mouth and disappear.

"Oh fuck," Amelia and Guillermo whispered at the same time.

Susan fell to her knees, her long blonde hair tumbling down to cover her face. Kirk knelt beside her and placed his hand on her shoulder. "Babe? Are you okay? *Babe?*"

Everyone held their breath, watching the sorority president trembling on the floor. Slowly, she rose to her feet and lifted her head. Amelia jumped back. Susan's face was now mottled gray with red splotches and hideous greenish boils. Her once-beautiful blue eyes were now a blazing yellowish orange. A deep-throated growl poured from her lips, which parted to reveal a mouth full of jagged, glistening sharp teeth like a shark's.

"What the hell?" Kirk yelped when he saw Susan's face.

He turned to run away, but Susan's discolored, clawed hands grabbed his head and pulled it off with a sickening sound that was both meaty and crunchy. Blood poured from Kirk's neck and his body collapsed like a dropped toy.

Chapter Eight

Guillermo blinked at Kirk's still-twitching corpse and the spreading puddle of blood on the hardwood floor, frozen in horrified disbelief. Was this really happening? Before he could process this insanity any further, screams nearly deafened him and a stampede of terrified coeds charged out of the dining room to the foyer, racing to get to the front door.

Through the dining room's wide doorway, he watched a girl wearing mouse ears trip over nothing and fall to the white marble floor, where fleeing partygoers trampled her. By the time the girl was back in view, blood trickled from her nose and mouth. The crimson liquid flowed heavier when she sat up with a groan that morphed into a gurgled cry of agony that turned to a wheeze. She must have a punctured lung, probably from broken ribs, and Guillermo had done nothing to help her. With deepening terror and guilt, he saw a round hole in her cheek. For a moment, he was perplexed as to what could have made the hole, then with dawning horror, he realized it came from the stiletto heel of one of her sorority sisters' shoes.

He moved forward to try to do something for the poor woman when Amelia pulled him back. Then he saw the thing that used to be Susan shambling into the foyer after the shrieking mob, who remained oblivious, fixated on trying to escape.

"It won't open," someone cried out from the front door.

"Move out of the way!" The crowd swelled and surged like a chaotic anthill.

"We can't. We're trapped!"

A few people realized trying to get out through the front door was futile and turned around in time to see the Susan-thing. They were able to dodge her, since she wasn't very fast. The thing lunged at a straggler, then turned back to those still crammed against the door for easier prey.

Guillermo didn't wait to see who she'd kill next. He and Amelia gestured for those who'd fled from the foyer to follow them through another doorway in the dining room. They'd try the back door, even though he had a sinking feeling that it would be stuck too.

After making their way down a long corridor, getting lost in a couple rooms, then finally finding another hall that led to the back door, he was proved right. It felt like there was no door at all, only a doorknob screwed into the wall as a joke. If there were more time, he would have tried prying the boards free from the windows, but from the sounds of the demonic growls behind them, more people had been transformed into whatever Susan was.

"Our bedroom," Amelia said. "We can hide in there. We have some protective things that might keep us safe."

"To hell with that," Simon said. "I'm gonna look for another way out. Who's with me?"

"I don't think the house will let us out." Considering the circumstances, Amelia seemed calm.

"Bullshit." Simon's eyes darted around wildly, showing too much white. The stethoscope he wore over his doctor costume seemed to vibrate with his shaking. "I said, who is with me?"

Paul, Deb, Valerie, Steve, and Cheryl raised shaky hands. That was over half the group who'd followed Amelia and Guillermo to the frozen back door.

Guillermo shook his head. "Splitting up is a very bad idea. And I think Amelia's right. Those doors aren't stuck in any natural way."

"You're wrong, pledge." With that, Simon ran off, his new followers chasing to keep up.

The remaining coeds—Tiffany, Miranda, Mary, Brandon, and Chuck—followed Guillermo and Amelia back to the first staircase that led up to the floor where the bedrooms were. He hoped most of the others who'd been crushed against the front door had escaped Susan. When they got all the way up the stairs, he decided to look. From the second-floor railing, they saw the carnage in the foyer below. Susan had torn Dave's throat out, and Rebecca had become another monster. Blood dripped from her mottled face, staining her pastel pink blouse beneath her blue suit jacket.

"Are they zombies?" Mary asked in a quiet voice that was almost a whimper. She clung to the tail pinned to her cat costume.

"I don't think so," Amelia answered even more quietly. "I think they're demons."

Even though Guillermo had been done with church as soon as he was old enough to refuse to go, he crossed himself. "We need to move before they see us."

They backed away from the banister and crept down the hall until they reached the room where Guillermo and Amelia stored their arsenal against evil.

Amelia pulled one of the boxes out from under the bed and took out a container of salt. She made a circle of salt around the room while Guillermo pulled out the unhappy aloe plants with red string carefully tied around the thick leaves.

"This isn't real," Tiffany said in a hysterical tone. "Susan and Kirk faked the whole thing to scare us as part of our initiation."

"No," Amelia told her firmly. "Even if they managed to get hold of Hollywood-quality makeup and prosthetics, there's no way Susan could have applied them that fast. And neither she nor Kirk could fake a decapitation. In the movies, they use dummies. Kirk was visible the whole time, so he couldn't have been swapped out for a dummy."

Brandon nodded and rubbed Tiffany's shoulders. "She's right, sweetheart. There's something seriously evil about this house and it's taken over Susan and Rebecca. If nothing in here will stop them, we're gonna be dead or turned into one of those things."

For the longest time, Tiffany stood there, frozen and silent. Then she squeaked, "Real?"

"Real," everyone else huddling in the room echoed.

Tiffany nodded. "Real." With that, she rushed into the adjoining bathroom and they soon heard her retching, followed by the splash of vomit hitting the toilet bowl. Brandon waited outside the door, ready to comfort her when she was done.

Mary approached Amelia and Guillermo. "Is there anything I can do to help?"

Amelia nodded. "You can—"

The sharp sound of breaking glass came from the bathroom. Brandon cried out Tiffany's name and rammed his shoulder into the door, forcing it open. Aside from the broken mirror over the sink, nothing looked out of sorts.

Tiffany walked out of the bathroom, clutching her handbag. An oddly serene smile played across her lips, which were obscured by the mess she'd made of her lipstick. Bright pink surrounded her mouth, going outside her lips like clown paint and spreading out in thick lines all the way across her cheeks to her ears. Her eye makeup—if you could call it that—looked more like face paint at a football game. Blue eyeshadow was streaked in wide swathes over her eyelids and up her forehead. Her eyeliner was scribbled in various curlicues beneath her eyes.

There were also white, powdery splotches all over her face that Guillermo at first worried was cocaine, then he saw an ancient silver compact and powderpuff on the bathroom floor with a mess of powder everywhere.

Brandon reached for Tiffany, his eyes wide with a mixture of shock and disgust at her appearance. "Tiffy-baby, why did you do this to yourself?

Tiffany giggled and ignored him. "I love makeup. Don't you, Amelia?"

Amelia edged closer to Guillermo. The others backed away from Tiffany too. All but Brandon.

"I love it so much I could just eat it up." Tiffany reached into her handbag, pulled out a lipstick tube, and popped it into her mouth.

The sound of crushing plastic made Guillermo cringe.

Brandon gasped and tried to grab the bag. "Tiffany, stop!"

Tiffany growled and shoved him with one hand with astonishing strength. Brandon flew backward, barely missed Amelia, and crashed into the mahogany frame of the bed.

Her eyes glowed yellow as she pulled out different makeup implements from her bag and ate them. When she put her compact in her mouth, the glass mirror broke and the shards cut up her gums. Blood flowed from her mouth and her teeth grew long and sharp. She ate a mascara tube, an eyeshadow palette, and another compact, cutting her mouth on more glass.

When she'd devoured all the makeup, Tiffany turned to Amelia. "And now I'll eat you."

Guillermo pulled a squirt gun from the pocket of his suit jacket and sprayed Tiffany with holy water. Nothing happened.

"She broke the salt circle." Amelia nudged them toward the bedroom door. "We need to get out of here."

Tiffany walked toward Amelia, shambling like a drunk person. Mary, Miranda, and Chuck scrambled away. Brandon regained his footing and rushed to Tiffany, seeming not to see her monstrous face.

Her arms slipped around his waist and for a moment, it looked like she was embracing him like everything was normal. Her voice even sounded like hers when she lifted her chin and pleaded, "Kiss me, Brandon."

"No," Amelia shouted. "Get away from her."

But Brandon didn't appear to hear her or anyone else shouting warnings. As if in a trance, Brandon lowered his head to kiss the monster. Another demonic growl emanated from Tiffany before her sharp teeth sank into his lips and tore them off like a strip of meat, leaving behind exposed bone and mutilated gums. Blood sprayed all over Tiffany's face and chest and her grin broadened.

Guillermo had seen enough. He made it to the bedroom door and opened it, ushering Amelia and everyone else out. The last thing he saw was Tiffany reaching for one of the aloe plants to smash it. She shrieked in pain and her hand sizzled and smoked.

So, something *did* work. Too bad he couldn't get past her to grab some of the plants. Amelia tugged on his arm and he ran with her down the hall to catch up with Mary, Miranda, and Chuck. The three disappeared around a corner as the door to the room they'd fled opened. Tiffany's growl sounded. Guillermo reached for the closest bedroom door and pulled Amelia inside.

The room was mostly dark, except for a bright beam of moonlight streaming in the window. This room hadn't been selected by the pledges for staying the night and contained just a stripped-bare dusty mattress, a wardrobe, and two end tables. The furnishings were covered with sheets, and the whole area reeked of staleness and mothballs.

After locking the door, Guillermo dove under the bed and Amelia followed. He willed his breathing to slow and tried to listen over his pounding heart for sounds of approaching demons.

Amelia gripped his hand tightly as they heard a growl and footsteps outside the door. When the growling and footsteps faded, they remained still for a tense eternity before Guillermo's shoulders relaxed. He wasn't ready to come out from under the bed. He could barely make out Amelia's features in the darkness, but what little he could see made it clear she was terrified.

She squeezed his hand and scooted closer to him. "I'm so sorry, Guillermo. This is all my fault."

"What the hell are you talking about?" he whispered, wondering if she was losing her sanity after what happened to her former best friend. "You didn't decide to have a Halloween party in the most notoriously evil house in town, and you sure as hell didn't invite demons to join the festivities."

"Yes, but I have a confession to make." Amelia took a deep breath. "The reason I didn't drop out of the sorority and say no to this initiation wasn't only because of my fascination with the Raimi House. It was because I would have the chance to spend the night with you. If I hadn't come up with that stupid pretend dating scheme, you'd be at home safe with your family."

"And you?"

A bitter-sounding laugh escaped her. "I probably still would have been helpless against the temptation to get inside this house. But still, I at least could have come clean about my feelings for you before we ended up here. Then we'd both be safe and I'd be content with the earlier visits to this place. I am so sorry I put us in danger and—"

Guillermo silenced her by pressing his finger to her lips. "Although I had no interest in the creepiest house in town and was about to bail as soon as I learned we were going there, I too decided to stay because of the chance to spend the night with you. And the chance to convince you to date me for real. And did it occur to you that I also feel guilty for not telling you about how I feel until tonight?"

"No, but you shouldn't."

"Well, I do. Especially since I'm not sure that I would have tried to stop us from coming here tonight. Not after we worked so hard on researching ways to fight the evil in this place. What can I say? I got cocky."

She tilted her head against his. "I wish the stuff we got worked better."

"But some of it *did* work," Guillermo told her. "The aloe plant burned Tiffany and the salt circle may be effective as long as no one breaks our next one. And we have plenty of other things to try."

"Okay." Amelia released his hand and started scooting out from under the bed. "That means instead of hiding here, waiting to be found, we should probably find the others and see if there's a way to fight these things. Strength in numbers, you know?"

Reluctantly, Guillermo agreed. They tiptoed across the room and he unlocked the door and opened it as quietly as possible. A quick peek verified that the hall outside was empty. Though he was tempted to return to the room where they'd stashed the protective gear and the aloe plants, he remembered that he'd only heard one demon passing their door when they'd hid. That meant the other could still be in the room.

Following the direction that Miranda, Chuck, and Mary had run, they paused at each door, listening for sounds of demons and non-possessed people. After rounding a corner and passing a third door, Guillermo heard muffled voices coming from one of the bedrooms. "It sounds like other people are in here."

Amelia tugged on his sleeve. "How can we know if they're like Tiffany and going to turn into one of those things?"

Guillermo shook his head. "We don't. But maybe Tiffany got possessed because she used something that belonged to the house. There was an antique compact and powder puff on the bathroom floor behind her and her face was blotted with powder. But I do agree with you that we should be cautious and watch for signs of anyone acting weird."

Tentatively, he knocked on the door. The muffled voices were discernable this time. Someone in the room loudly whispered, "Oh shit, what if it's one of them?"

"I don't think they knock," a voice that sounded like Alvin Schwartz, the frat treasurer, replied. "You saw how dumb they were."

Guillermo raised his voice enough to be heard. "We're not one of them."

The door opened to reveal Alvin, dressed as a pirate. "Inside, quick."

Amelia and Guillermo rushed inside the roomand took inventory of the survivors in the furnished room that was reserved for one of the pledges. As well as Alvin Schwartz, he saw Nancy, the pledge mentor for the sorority, Kevin Daugharty in a fitting cop costume, fellow pledges Chuck and Mike, Betty, Laura, Miranda, Mary, and, disappointingly, Cameron, looking ridiculous in a Macho Man Randy Savage costume. Not that Guillermo wanted the guy to be dead, but it would be nicer if Amelia's rapist ex had survived somewhere away from them.

Alvin interrupted Guillermo's silent count. Sometime since the shit hit the fan, he'd lost the fake sword and eyepatch from his pirate costume. "What brought you guys out of hiding?"

Guillermo explained what happened to Tiffany. "I think she got possessed from using that antique face powder. I hope none of you guys have used anything from this house."

"Yeah, Miranda told us what happened with Tiffany and Brandon. But is that what you think they are?" Nancy fiddled with her Wonder Woman headband. "Possessed?"

Amelia answered. "It lines up with Helen Raimi's account of what happened with the Pentecostals."

She retold the story about how the Pentecostals who'd tried to exorcise the demons from the house had gotten massacred when their leader became possessed.

Alvin shook his head. "Too bad we don't have any holy water."

A bitter laugh escaped Guillermo. "Actually, we do. It had no effect on Tiffany. But the aloe plants Amelia and I smuggled in burned her hand."

"Aloe?" Betty echoed, smoothing her pink '50s poodle skirt. "Why would that work?"

"Wait." Laura held up a pale blue gloved hand. "You two smuggled in protective stuff? Why didn't you tell us?"

"Because we figured Kirk or Susan wouldn't have let us," Guillermo said. "I don't know if you've noticed, but both seemed big on cruelty for cruelty's sake. We also thought they'd planned some sort of prank to scare us."

"They did," Cameron admitted sullenly. "I don't know exactly what they were setting up, but there are probably some fake-outs planted in this place."

Mike took off his cowboy hat and squeezed the brim. His voice shook, like he was barely holding himself together. "Why does it matter? We're staying in here, aren't we?"

"I think that's a bad idea." Guillermo met everyone's eyes as he spoke. "Didn't you see how strong those things are? They could break down this door easily and have us cornered. The only reason why Amelia, the others, and I got out of the room we were in was because Tiffany was occupied with killing Brandon, then she was burned by the aloe plants. We don't have anything like that in this room."

Alvin cleared his throat. "They might not find us in here, though. The demon-things are slow and clumsy and seem to have trouble hearing and seeing."

"That makes sense," Miranda said softly. "Their bodies are probably like puppets for the demons that they have to operate.

Guillermo shuddered at the description. "There are twelve of us crammed into this room. There has got to be a better place we can hide. Especially if these demons aren't going to go away any time soon."

Betty hugged her knees and rocked on the edge of the bed. "How long do you think they'll be around? And what made them come in the first place? Aside from that story Amelia told, none of the other legends about this place mention something like this happening."

Amelia didn't speak up, which worried Guillermo. Not only because she was their expert on this house of horrors, but also because he couldn't stand to see her hurting. She'd lost her best friend tonight. A toxic friend, but a close connection nonetheless. He hoped he'd have a chance to comfort her and prayed they'd both survive so he could be there for her while she processed her grief.

He slipped an arm around Amelia's shoulders and pulled her against his side as he speculated aloud. "When we were here the previous two times cleaning, the caretaker yelled at us to get away before dark, so maybe these demons can manifest only at night. But it's also Halloween, and many old superstitions believe this is the one night of the year that spirits can roam free."

Amelia finally spoke. "Do you think the people who were possessed will go back to normal in the morning?"

"I don't know." Tiffany had swallowed a lot of plastic, glass, and God only knew what chemicals were in the makeup she ate. He didn't say that out loud because he didn't want to kill Amelia's hope.

Mary leaned against the wall, then cringed as cobwebs stuck to her shoulder. "I wish we could get those aloe plants and the rest of the stuff you had in the other room."

"Maybe we can." Guillermo gave her a grateful look. "If all twelve of us stick close together and we find some sort of weapon, we can knock any demons we encounter over the balcony and rush to our room, grab the stuff, and find somewhere to hole up until dawn."

"Wouldn't knocking them over the balcony kill them, though?" Nancy helped Mary get the cobwebs off her cat costume. "If they're going to change back to normal, I don't want to murder anyone."

Amelia nodded and clung to Guillermo's arm. "Maybe we can knock them out or restrain them instead?"

"Okay. Let's see what we can do for weapons."

The room was practically empty, but Guillermo, Alvin, and Cameron managed to muscle the long wood posts off the bed. Amelia and Betty took the two tall lamps from either side of the bed, and Nancy took a wooden hanging rod out of the closet.

With those with weapons in front, they cautiously made their way out of the bedroom.

The hallway was demon-free, but something else was wrong. When they turned the corner, Guillermo froze and stared at the ugly cabbage-rose wallpaper on *both* walls. The balcony that overlooked the ground floor was gone; so were the groupings of doors that lined the second floor, and the vacuumed blue carpet was now a bare wood floor coated with a thick layer of dust. Cobwebs hung from the low ceiling and the air smelled stale.

"What the hell?" Guillermo whispered.

Amelia leaned against him and he felt the fine tremble of her body countering the strong tone of her voice. "The house is messing with us. It did this to many members of the Raimi family. And one time, back when they were using the north wing as a funeral home, a man attending a funeral disappeared for three days. When he was found in the ballroom, he was hysterical and babbling. Eventually, authorities got an explanation out of him. He'd tried to go outside for a smoke, but when he opened the door that was supposed to be an exit, he ended up in the library, then when he tried to go back to the funeral parlor, the door then led to the abandoned asylum wing. For three days he wandered around the house, sometimes hearing people, but he could never get to them."

The implications of her words filled him with icy jets of fear. How could they fight in a house that was constantly changing around them? He grabbed Amelia's hand, seeking the same comfort she sought from him. "That means we have more to worry about than demons."

Chapter Nine

Amelia clung to Guillermo's hand and wielded her lamp with the other. Even though the weapon was a thin brass pole with a delicate light fixture, the weight seemed to increase as they made their way through whatever part of the house they'd been transported to. The cabbage roses on the wallpaper were faded and distorted. They looked like mocking faces. Wall sconces with those old pointed bulbs that replaced candles provided sporadic illumination since most were burnt out. Eventually, the long dusty hall gave way to a staircase that went both up and down. The bare wood steps made her wonder if this was a path meant for the servants.

Cameron paused and looked back at him. "Should we go up or down?"

"Down." Guillermo's tone sounded perplexed. Probably wondering why the frat brother who'd been making his life hell for the past few weeks was now looking to him to call the shots. "Then we should at least be on the main floor. We can get food and drinks there and maybe find the way to the stairs that lead to the room that has our stuff."

His plan dampened some of Amelia's fear. "And we might find Simon and his group and talk sense into them about finding safety in numbers."

"Unless they're dead, possessed, or found a way outside," Miranda said grimly. Somewhere in the chaos, she'd lost her witch hat.

Her point was sobering. "Let's hope it was the latter."

When they got downstairs, the group found themselves in the ballroom. Every wall was covered with floor-to-ceiling mirrors. The dust muffled their footsteps on the wood floor and distorted their reflections in the mirrors. The ginormous chandelier in the center of the raised ceiling was unlit. If it weren't for the mirrors reflecting light from the three doorways around the room, they'd be in complete darkness. As it was, Amelia had a tough time seeing past all the dark spots in the room.

Betty bumped into Amelia, making them both jump. "This place is so creepy."

Amelia nodded, even though her fear was buried beneath other emotions. Guilt crushed her soul like she was buried under an avalanche of sharp rocks. It was *her* fault Tiffany was possessed and possibly dead. No matter what he'd said to assure her, it *was* her fault Guillermo was in danger. If she'd listened to her brain and not her stupid heart, Guillermo would have dropped out of the fraternity and would be at home, safe with his loving family, celebrating All Saints' Day. She should have dropped out of the initiation and found a way to convince Tiff to stay home too. Hell, maybe she could have even convinced all the pledges to rebel so that Susan and Kirk were forced to drop the idea. Then she could have found another way to be with Guillermo.

Something appeared in her line of sight, damming her inner flood of guilt. When it moved closer, she saw that it was the figure of a child. Gasps around her proved she wasn't the only one seeing the little... Was it a girl or boy? It was hard to tell, not only due to the dim lighting, but also because half of the child's head was caved in and its old-timey white frock was worn by both sexes. The frock was splattered with crimson stains, like blood from the turn of the century could somehow be fresh.

Guillermo's whisper tickled her ear. "That's a ghost, isn't it?"

"Uh-huh." She stood frozen to the spot, unable to stop staring at the specter. The ghost of the little girl she'd seen in a house downtown hadn't been as vivid as this one.

The specter walked closer to the group. Amelia saw little blue flowers embroidered on the frock and little ruffles around the socks. A girl, then. The child looked up at Mary with large, pleading eyes. "My papa hit me with his hammer and no one wants to play with me anymore."

"That's terrible." Amelia couldn't help responding. She also remembered reading something about this murder.

Mary reached for the girl's hand. "I'll play with you."

"What?" several members of the group whispered in tandem.

Amelia felt her jaw drop as Mary and the ghost walked hand in hand toward the mirrored wall. Dread twisted her gut and squeezed her throat. The previous ghosts she'd seen had been harmless. Some even benign. And although this child who'd been killed by a horrific tragedy looked pitiful, Amelia did not have a good feeling about her.

Mary and the ghost moved like an old stop-motion film, flickering in and out of sight, each reappearance bringing them closer to the wall. Their reflections wavered and blurred, then a sickly green light began to emanate in one concentrated section that began to take the shape of a door.

A door.

"Mary, stop!" Amelia yelled.

"Don't go with it," Alvin pleaded.

"No," Mike shouted.

The rest echoed her protest, chasing after Mary, who walked on like she hadn't heard anything. Amelia ran too, but knew they wouldn't reach her in time. The portal thing glowed brighter. Mary and the ghost girl disappeared into its hungry mouth. The door shrank and winked out of existence like a candle flame blown out. The dusty mirrored wall returned to normal, showing the reflections of eleven shocked people in Halloween costumes.

Miranda was the first to reach the mirrored wall. She placed her palms on the grimy surface, ignoring Cameron shouting that touching the mirror could be dangerous.

"Mary?" she said with a choking sob. "Mary, come back."

Alvin gently pulled Miranda back and held her, stroking her hair. "Maybe she'll come back. Let's wait."

They circled the ballroom, knocking on every part of the mirrored walls and pressing their ears to the cold glass in an attempt to listen for Mary, while calling for her.

Cameron sighed and took off his Randy Savage hat. "She's gone. I think we should get out of here before one of the demons finds us."

As if his words were a portent, a growl sounded behind them, echoing in the cavernous ballroom. They turned to see Susan, Rebecca, and Dave shambling toward them from one of the doorways.

Susan's mouth spread in an unnaturally wide rictus of a smile, her crooked sharp teeth cutting into her cheeks and chin. "Welcome back to the party."

Rebecca licked her lips with a forked tongue and spoke in the same gravelly voice. "The fun is only beginning."

With his throat torn out, Dave's vocal cords were gone, so all he could manage were gurgling noises. The three demons shuffled in a semicircle, ready to attack the living from different sides.

Susan lurched forward first, clawed hands outstretched for Cameron. Cam swung the wood bedpost like a baseball bat. The post struck the side of Susan's head with a sickening crack. The demon crumpled to the floor, legs splayed apart and her cheerleader skirt flipped up to reveal her dark green panties. Her skull was caved in, an indentation from the edge of Susan's forehead to her temple.

Amelia's observation broke as Rebecca and Dave attacked. While Cameron was distracted with Dave, Rebecca jumped on his back. Guillermo and Amelia beat on Rebecca with their makeshift weapons, and between Cameron's shrieks, there was the sharp sound of cracking bone, but the demon continued her attack, clawing ribbons of flesh and hair from Cameron's head. The moment Cameron collapsed, she rolled him over and sank her teeth into his nose. Blood squirted everywhere and Cam's muffled scream resulted in a thunder of footsteps as half the group fled.

Amelia turned and saw Dave collapsing from a blow delivered by Nancy, but not before he'd torn a chunk of flesh off Chuck's cheek.

Guillermo and Alvin managed to drive a bedpost into Rebecca's stomach and black blood poured from the gaping wound. She shrieked as they plunged the makeshift stake harder, slamming her into the mirrored wall. The glass cracked into shards and Rebecca slid to the floor, either dead or unconscious.

Alvin turned around and vomited. Nancy looked almost as green as Miranda's witch face paint.

Guillermo turned to face the survivors of the skirmish, his arms crossed and his chin lifted with determination. "We have to do something with the dead. Rebecca and Dave were dead before they became demons. So there's a good chance Cam will turn into one too. Shit, the ones we killed might rise again."

Amelia did a quick head count. She, Guillermo, Nancy, Alvin, and Miranda remained. Betty, Laura, Mike, and Kevin had run away. Mary had vanished into a sinister portal. Cameron was dead…for now, anyway. Chuck was missing part of his face and was either unconscious or dead. Then she saw Miranda roll Chuck over to reveal a bleeding hole in his back. Dead then. All for a fraternity initiation.

She took a deep breath, suppressing the urge to scream out her grief and horror at all this senseless death. "What should we do with the bodies?"

Guillermo's brow creased and his sensuous lips pouted before he snapped his fingers. "The funeral parlor. We can put them in coffins. Those can't open from the inside. The Alpha Lambdas buried my father in one for his initiation."

Miranda smoothed her long dark hair and hugged herself. Her green face paint was coming off in streaks from tears and sweat. "How are we supposed to find the funeral home when this house keeps turning us around?"

Amelia had the same worry, but she hid it. "We have to try. Besides, the ballroom is on the main floor and so is the funeral parlor, so we have a decent shot at finding it."

Nancy stepped closer to Cam's body and kicked it in the ribs with the pointed toes of her calf-high Wonder Woman boots. "Skeevy bastard."

Amelia put a hand on the mentor's shoulder. "You too?"

Alvin interrupted them. "How are we going to drag the bodies all the way to a room we're not even certain we can reach?"

Guillermo answered. "There are sheets covering furniture everywhere. We can roll the bodies on the sheets, tie them in there like a shroud, and they should slide on these floors fairly easy."

They went into the next room that appeared to serve as a lounge and uncovered a fainting couch, a table and three overstuffed chairs, gaining the five sheets they needed.

Wrapping the five bodies in makeshift shrouds was a tense, macabre task. Everyone jumped at the slightest sound, fearing the body they were covering would open its eyes and attack. Amelia gagged at the foul-smelling fluids that leaked from the corpses: red blood, black ichor, and yellow pus.

Then the five of them dragged the bodies out of the ballroom. The bodies did slide, like Guillermo said, but Amelia finally learned the meaning of the term "dead weight." They took turns carrying their makeshift weapons and dragging bodies. By the time they'd made it around a second corridor, Amelia's back and shoulders were on fire.

When they reached a door with a spray of lilies carved in the thick wood, Guillermo took a bedpost and went ahead of the group to check what lay beyond. While Amelia admired him for his courage and willingness to be the first to put himself in danger, her heart clenched with fear that he'd be killed.

She held her breath as she watched him open the door, crouched low so anything ready to stab or swipe would miss while he could shove his weapon up. He opened the door farther and looked inside. His shoulders visibly relaxed as he turned and gestured them to come. "We found the funeral parlor. And there are still coffins in here."

Somehow, everyone found the strength to haul the five bodies into the funeral parlor. This first room appeared to be the sales floor for the coffins. Nancy opened the first one and jumped back with a shrill yip as something popped out.

Amelia rushed to her with the others, her weapon ready to bash a skull. The thing inside the coffin had a hideous gray face and a mouth full of yellow sharp teeth. Its body was dressed in a long-sleeved shirt, jeans, and beat-up tennis shoes. Aside from popping up to a sitting position when the coffin opened, it remained motionless. That's when Amelia saw the fishing line going from the top of its head to the underside of the lid, where it was affixed by duct tape.

She sighed and pulled the dummy out of the coffin. When it dropped to the floor, the head came off and crumpled newspaper protruded from the neck of the shirt. "We found one of Kirk and Susan's pranks. I wonder where the rest are."

The other three coffins were empty, so Guillermo, Alvin, and Nancy lifted the bodies into the boxes, locking them tight. Since there were only four coffins, they put Susan and Rebecca together in the last one. As soon as their task was complete, they started to head to the door, then froze when the doorknob jiggled.

Guillermo's hand seized Amelia's as he whispered, "Everybody hide."

Miranda, Alvin, and Nancy took his advice and darted after Amelia and Guillermo into the funeral room, grateful that the worn burgundy carpet muffled their steps. Everyone went different directions. Alvin and Miranda dove behind the podium where the eulogies would have been delivered. Amelia, Guillermo, and Nancy found a side door that led to the embalming room.

There were no working lights in this room. The only reason they could tell where they were was because of light from the full moon shining through the window, reflecting off the steel tables and large metal drawers in the walls.

"Is there a lock?" Nancy whispered.

Amelia nodded. "Probably. They wouldn't want just anyone wandering in here during a viewing or funeral service."

She slowly crept back to the door and paused, hearing someone talking. Instead of the dreaded demon growls, she heard familiar voices. Alvin and Miranda's voices joined with Betty's and another guy who sounded familiar, but whom she couldn't place. Since they didn't sound terrified, Amelia opened the door.

Betty jumped and made a little squeak before she recognized Amelia and relaxed. "I'm so sorry we ran away. It was horrible. Tiffany came after us in the study where we'd been hiding. She killed Mike. Then Brandon came out of nowhere and killed Laura. I would have been dead if Gilbert hadn't knocked Brandon out with a fire poker and pulled me out of the room."

Amelia then noticed Kevin standing behind Betty. He nodded, but didn't say anything. She then turned to see the bootleg and drug dealer, Gilbert Curtis, crouched by Alvin, talking to him quietly. He rose and turned his head to meet Amelia's gaze. He'd lost his cowboy hat. "I heard you're the expert on this house and might have some stuff that will work against these things."

"I wouldn't go that far," Amelia told him. "But we put the bodies of some of our group in the coffins so if they turn, they're trapped."

"Good idea. The last time I was in this situation, the bodies stayed dead. We put them in the camp chapel so they wouldn't stink up our holdfast." He fidgeted with the butt of his gun.

Amelia blinked in surprise to see that the gun in his holster was now a real one, not the squirt gun she'd originally spotted. Then Gilbert's words struck a memory. "Oh my *God*. You were there during the Camp Natty Massacre?"

"I was." Gilbert's face contorted into a mask of anguish and relived trauma. "I really don't like talking about it and I was a fucking idiot to agree to come here of all places. I needed the money badly."

Amelia made a sympathetic sound even as she writhed with curiosity about what had happened in that summer camp. "I heard the killer's body was never recovered."

"Yeah, it was buried in a mine shaft when Linnea Langenkamp and Wes Carpenter set off some old dynamite. Those two saved us. I hunkered down with the others in the lodge and provided booze, weed, and moral support. Other than that, I was pretty useless. I sucked at archery and didn't know how to shoot a gun back then, so I couldn't even fire at the thing when it came after us." Again, he stroked the gun in his holster.

His wording intrigued her. "Why do you say 'it'?"

"Because, like the demon versions of these coeds, I don't think the killer was human. I watched Mr. Aripa shoot him close range with a twelve-gauge and it didn't even slow the fucker down." Gilbert ran a hand through dark hair that was sticking up in different directions. "Same with these demons. Earlier from my hiding place, I watched that girl get up after being trampled."

That was not what she wanted to hear. "Shit. That means we probably don't have much time left before the ones we put in the coffins wake up."

"At least they can be put down temporarily. That's meant the difference between life and death for me twice already."

"We need more weapons," Kevin declared in an authoritative voice, as if he hadn't run away during their last skirmish with the demons.

Amelia ignored him and addressed the others. "There's probably some useful stuff in the morgue area we were hiding in."

Guillermo and Kevin lit their Zippos and they scoured the room. They found two big bone saws, a long steel drain tube, a big pump of some sort that Amelia wondered what it could be used for, and a pair of large knives. The scalpels and various pairs of scissors were small but were still better than nothing and easier to carry than the lamp she'd had.

Carefully, they left the funeral parlor and found that the house had changed again. The corridor they entered looked like the one

Amelia and Guillermo had been through during the cleaning expeditions, dusted and vacuumed, with mauve walls and fading reddish-brown carpet. The hall emerged into the kitchen.

Betty rushed to the sink. "Oh, thank heavens. I'm so thirsty."

Amelia grabbed her. "Don't drink the water. If Tiffany got possessed from using face powder from the house, drinking the water could do the same. Hopefully, we can get to the main room where the cooler is."

Luck was on their side for once, and they passed into the dining room where Susan invited the first demon into her body and tore Kirk's head off. A pool of drying blood glistened sickly on the polished wood floor.

Miranda frowned. "Um…where is Kirk's body?"

Alvin shrugged. "Looks like there's a headless corpse wandering around."

"The head's missing too. Along with the body of the girl who was trampled," Guillermo said.

"That was Amy." Nancy's voice was mournful.

They hurried out of the dining room, through the foyer, and sighed in relief when they came into the great room with its decorations, snack table, and coffin-cooler. After grabbing some drinks, the eight survivors sat for the first time in hours.

Gilbert frowned at the undisturbed snack table. "Looks like no one's been in here since the shit hit the fan." He walked back to the doorway and peered over at the entrance to the front parlor where he'd been selling his wares. "My area looks undisturbed too."

Amelia nodded at the accurate assessment. "I wonder why not? This is the only area that has safe food and drink."

While everyone went for beer, Amelia got a Sprite and Guillermo got a root beer. Then they loaded plates with snacks and found seats. For a few moments, the only sounds were of cans opening and thirsty people guzzling drinks.

Kevin broke the silence with a belch. "Maybe Simon and his group found a way out of the house? Who was with him, and who else is unaccounted for?"

After sharing what they knew of each group that had split up and who they remembered attending the party, they determined that in addition to Simon, Paul, Deb, Cheryl, and Valerie, four more hadn't been seen since they'd fled Susan. That made nine people unaccounted for.

Amelia ate some Reese's peanut butter cups, surprised she had an appetite after all the disgusting things she'd seen. She rested her head on Guillermo's shoulder. "Are we still going to try to get the aloe plants?"

Guillermo took a sip of his root beer and nodded. "I was thinking of breaking off a leaf and shredding it, mixing it into water, and filling our squirt guns and maybe this pump we got from the embalming room. Then we can find out if it's the aloe itself, or whether the red string is necessary."

Kevin's eyes narrowed. "Why do you have aloe plants with red string on them?"

"My grandma uses them to ward off evil. I thought I'd try it."

"You're telling me a *Mexican* superstition actually worked?"

Amelia did *not* like the way Kevin had sneered when saying "Mexican." She glared at him. "Who cares where the custom came from? What matters is that it worked. And some of the other things we collected might work too."

Kevin's insolent tone remained. "Why didn't the holy water work?"

"I don't think these demons are of the biblical variety. This property was cursed before the Jesuits came to the area to spread Christianity." Movement from the corner of her eye made Amelia stand up and raise her bone saw. When she saw the approaching man's old-fashioned clothes and, more importantly, how she could see through the clothes, and the man's handlebar mustache, she relaxed slightly at it not being a demon, but remained on edge due to the incident with Mary. "Another ghost. Don't look into its eyes or do anything it asks." Unlike the little girl with the caved-in head, this ghost didn't seem to see them, which was more typical from Amelia's experiences. The man walked past where they all sat. His shoulders were hunched and his face was contorted in grief.

"What the fuck?" Gilbert whispered.

The ghost didn't hear. A rope appeared in his hands and he stepped onto a stool that also wasn't there. He tied the rope around a ceiling beam and made a noose.

Amelia remembered who he was. "Rupert Raimi. The first man to lose the family fortune."

Rupert turned his head and looked at her. She shivered and pressed herself against Guillermo. The ghost put the noose around his neck and stepped off the stool. Even though Rupert was a ghost and what they were seeing happened a hundred years ago, everyone made small sounds of revulsion when they heard Rupert's neck snap and watched his face turn purple and his tongue blacken.

"I don't want to be in this room anymore," Betty said softly.

Gilbert practically bolted from his chair. "Me neither. Let's go get those aloe plants and other supplies."

Although Amelia was reluctant to risk the house changing again and putting them in danger, it was true that they needed something to fend off the demons. Gilbert and Betty left the great room before everyone else.

Guillermo called to them, "Slow down. You don't know where our room was."

Betty looked back over her shoulder. "I do too."

When she looked forward, she screamed. Tiffany, Amy, Brandon, and Simon stood in the foyer, their yellow eyes glowing and sharp teeth shining in feral grins. Amy had the bloody hole in her cheek from when she was trampled to death, but the others looked even more frightening. Simon's left eye was dangling from the socket and Brandon's lips were torn off to reveal jagged yellow teeth.

Gilbert pulled his gun from the holster and fired, putting a hole in Tiffany's chest. Her body jerked from the impact, but she laughed and continued forward. Before Gilbert could fire another shot, Simon and Brandon seized him and spun him around to face Amelia and her petrified companions. While Brandon held the squirming Gilbert, Simon reached into Gilbert's mouth. Cracking sounds tore the air as his jaw dislocated, accompanied by Gilbert's muffled screams and gagging. Simon kept reached into Gilbert's throat until he was almost up to his elbow. There was a loud, wet tearing sound, a sharp snap, and then a gurgle as Simon pulled Gilbert's spine out from his mouth. Blood spurted like a geyser and Gilbert collapsed like a rag doll.

Amelia gagged and stepped backward. She wished she could move faster and get away, but terror held her in place. Tiffany and Amy cornered Betty. The demons clawed the sorority sister's face with nails grown to the size of daggers. Betty screamed and tried to run. Amy seized one of Betty's hands, Tiffany grabbed the other. Together the demons pulled in opposite directions. Amelia heard an ugly pop as Betty's shoulders were pulled from their sockets. Then, her arms were torn from her torso with a squelching, ripping sound that made Alvin double over and vomit.

Guillermo's voice broke the spell that kept Amelia rooted to the spot. "Come on."

She dashed back into the great room with Guillermo, who yanked Alvin back. Miranda and Nancy had already retreated, along with Kevin. She could almost feel the demons' breath on the back of her neck.

A roar of pained rage reverberated behind her. Amelia looked back and saw Tiffany freeze at the threshold of the doorway. Brandon stopped too, looking like a mime pretending to slam into the wall.

Guillermo stopped and watched them. "They can't get in here for some reason."

"What's stopping them?" Miranda asked.

Amelia followed the demon's eye movements, going from the mantel over the fireplace, to the snack table, and back again. She realized what caused their expressions of pain and…was that fear?

"It's the jack-o-lanterns I carved." She shook her head in wonder. "Another old superstition proved real. The Irish carved them from turnips and used them to fend off evil spirits."

Chapter Ten

A small laugh escaped Guillermo at the sight of demons recoiling from carved pumpkins. The situation would have been even funnier if the corpses of their companions hadn't been lying on the foyer's marble floor. But the small bit of mirth at the pumpkins made him think of something.

"Someone, quick. Move the other pumpkins from the DJ table to the other doorway."

"I got it," Alvin said behind him.

The demons hissed and stepped back when Alvin grabbed the third jack-o-lantern. Then, when they saw where he meant to place it, they howled in unmistakable fury.

"How many of these things do we have?" Kevin asked.

Amelia answered. "Five. I carved two, Guillermo carved one, and Miranda and Nancy each carved one. Aside from the pumpkins on the snack table and Dave's DJ setup, there's two on the hearth. There's a sixth in the parlor where Gilbert was selling his stuff, but we can't get to it. No wonder he stayed safe for so long."

"We can make two more," Miranda added. "There are two uncarved pumpkins left over there."

She pulled out the knife from the embalming room and took the uncarved pumpkin from the snack table. She sat and began cutting the top off the pumpkin. Nancy grabbed the other pumpkin and joined her at the DJ table.

"Fuck it," Amelia muttered, and grabbed a wine cooler from the coffin full of drinks.

After she passed Guillermo a beer, they sat in one of the loveseats in the corner. Guillermo took a deep drink of his beer and leaned forward to face the others. "I think we're going to be stuck here for a while. Maybe we can all get to know each other better. Even though I've seen all of you at the frat parties, the music was always too loud to be able to talk." He met Miranda's gaze first, since she looked the most scared. "What's your major? No, don't look at the demons. They can't come in here, and I think it's best for our own sakes if we ignore them."

"Journalism." Miranda pulled out a handful of pumpkin guts and seeds and made a little pile on her side of the table. "My ultimate goal is to be a book reviewer for *The New York Times* or another big magazine, like *USA Today*. If I make it out of here alive, I'm definitely writing about this place."

Everyone but Kevin murmured words of encouragement. Kevin sullenly poked at the logs he'd added to the fireplace. Then Guillermo asked Alvin about his major, computer science. Soon, they were talking about their hopes and dreams for the future as if they weren't trapped in an evil house and surrounded by demons wearing the faces of their fellow university students.

When he met Amelia's eyes, the warmth and gratitude in those pale blue depths heated him all over. Even with her eye makeup smeared and her braid buns falling unevenly, she still looked achingly beautiful. "You know, during all of our research about this house and protective measures, and all our conversations about Stephen King, I never got around to asking about your major."

"Library science." Amelia's voice trilled with delight.

"Wow." *Amelia Craven, dance team champion, most beautiful woman I've ever seen, wants to be a librarian?* "I never would have guessed."

Her lower lip protruded in an adorable pout. "I hope you didn't think I was going for the MRS degree like Tiffany."

"Not at all," Guillermo said quickly. "I'd just assumed you were majoring in English like you did for your associate's and didn't think to ask between the fraternity bullshit and catching you when Tiffany wasn't around to pull you away." He trailed his fingers along her knuckles, enjoying the soft feel of her skin. "Now that I think about it, you'd be an amazing librarian. You're so good about organizing books and doing research and remembering things."

Her cheeks pinkened at his words. Then she threw him a volley, trapping him with those baby blues. "I know you don't want to be majoring in business and you don't want to take over the family construction company, but you never got around to telling me what you *do* want to do."

He looked around to see if anyone else was listening, but the others appeared to be occupied. Alvin was handing beers to Nancy and Miranda while they talked softly, and Kevin was drinking and playing with the fire.

"I want to be a writer." It was the first time he'd said the words aloud. "I've written a few stories and have an idea for a novel. I don't know if I'm any good, though. I'm no Stephen King, that's for sure."

Amelia placed her hand over his, her lips curved in an encouraging smile. "If we make it through this, I'd love to read your work."

Guillermo had *never* let anyone read his stories. He'd been too scared. Yet somehow, the idea of letting Amelia see them didn't unnerve him. He remembered when she'd given him feedback on an English paper back their second year at the community college. She'd been so kind and helpful. Unlike his father, who never wanted to hear about Guillermo's efforts to create stories and declared that writing was a waste of time because it usually didn't pay well.

While his father was right about the low chances of profitability in a writing career, Guillermo was beginning to think some things were worth more than money. "If we get out of this alive, I'm going to stand up to my father and tell him I don't want the business and try to convince him to give it to Maria. My sister *loves* the business. She helps with the books, and the inventory, and will pick up a hammer and help on the job site every chance she gets. She's good at every aspect of building and repairing houses, like she was born to it."

Amelia nodded and stroked his knuckles with her fingertips. "I'll be with you, either physically or in spirit. I don't want to see you be miserable all your life. I l—"

She broke off and Guillermo sucked in a breath. Had she been about to say she loved him? On one hand, that would be too soon since they'd only been dating for a month, and only officially for a few hours. On the other, they'd been friends for two years.

Or maybe it was wishful thinking since he was pretty sure he loved her too.

With his free hand, he reached up and caressed Amelia's soft cheek. "Kiss me," he whispered.

She leaned in and pressed her lush lips to his. Light and teasing at first, then her lips parted and she deepened the kiss. Her fingers slid to the back of his neck, and reached up, as if to plunge into his hair, then moved down again when she encountered the slicked-back stiffness. Guillermo regretted committing so fully to the Gomez costume. He loved when she played with his hair. His hand slipped around her shoulders, pulling her tighter against his body as he fed at her mouth. Memories of the first time they made love flashed before his eyes, and an unbidden groan of arousal escaped him.

"Hey," Kevin's voice pierced his euphoric haze. "Cool it, Gomez."

Amelia and Guillermo broke apart, faces flaming.

If it weren't for these damn demons, we could find a room. Guillermo turned his head to cast the demons a glare and maybe give them the finger. They were gone.

"Hey," he said quietly. "The demons seem to have left us."

"Whoa." Nancy rose from her seat at the DJ table and crept to the doorway, peering out. "Should we stay here or try to get to that room with the protective stuff?"

"I don't know." Amelia looked doubtful. "The candles I put in those pumpkins aren't very large and I don't know if they'll still hold off the demons after they burn out."

"I doubt it," Alvin said. "Since the original jack-o-lanterns were turnips, the important parts are probably the carved faces and the lights."

Miranda held up the pumpkin she carved. "Do we have any more candles left?"

Nancy nodded. "We have several, thanks to the caretaker's warnings about the erratic electricity."

Guillermo pointed to the snack table and the fireplace. "There are a few in here, but the rest are in the kitchen."

Alvin grabbed the three candles that had been on the hearth and stuck a slim candlestick in his back pocket. "I don't think we should risk going in the kitchen unless we have to. I think we should stay here."

"I say we risk going." Kevin held up the iron poker from the fireplace then puffed out his chest as if he were a real cop showing off his badge. "There's still a chance that there's a way out. And if those aloe plants burned one of the demons, maybe there's a way to destroy those things."

They argued back and forth on the merits of staying or going. In the end, since the pumpkins could be carried and used to ward off the demons, they decided to make another attempt to get the protective supplies in Amelia's and Guillermo's room, and after that search for survivors or an exit.

After Nancy lit a candle and put it in her pumpkin and Kevin checked the doorway for signs of the demons, they gathered their weapons and assembled into a square-shaped formation, with people in the corners wielding jack-o-lanterns. They left one pumpkin in the great room in case they needed to return.

Amelia hefted one of the pumpkins she'd carved, like a vampire hunter held up a cross. Guillermo stuck close to her side with his bone saw ready.

Their diminished group made it through the foyer and up the stairs to the second floor. Then they froze as the demon once known as Tiffany floated down the hall toward them, eyes glowing neon yellow and sharp teeth protruding over a new underbite formed in her distorted face. The growls echoed off the suddenly claustrophobic corridor. Guillermo turned and saw Kirk shambling toward them from the other side. He was carrying his head under his arm like it was a football, blood dripping onto the faded blue carpet. Behind Kirk, another of Simon's party approached, Ted Reeves, the fraternity's recruitment chair. Guillermo had no idea where Ted had gone when Susan became possessed, but clearly one of the demons had disemboweled him at some point. His intestines flopped around him like slimy tentacles.

At the bottom of the stairs, Gilbert Curtis slithered along the foyer's marble floor like a snake, his now-spineless body looking oddly deflated. Sharp teeth protruded from his dislocated jaw, and he left a trail of blood behind him. It was an image Guillermo knew would haunt his nightmares forever.

Nancy held out her jack-o-lantern toward Ted and Kirk, while Amelia warded off Tiffany and Gilbert. The demons recoiled like vampires cowered from crosses in the movies. They used the pumpkins to drive the demons back until they reached the supplies room. Gilbert couldn't make it up the stairs. He groaned and slithered back and forth at the foot of the steps.

Guillermo reached back and opened the door and gestured for Alvin to get inside. Then he gently pushed Amelia into the room so she'd have protection in case anything had gone wrong in there. Miranda went in next, followed by Kevin, leaving him and Nancy in the hall. Damn it, he'd hoped Kevin would have stayed out here with his fire poker. Guillermo didn't have a jack-o-lantern, so Kirk and Ted rushed toward him.

Guillermo kicked Kirk away with a boot planted in the belly, then swung the bone saw toward Ted, aiming for his neck. The serrated blade dug in, embedding itself in the muscles and tendons. He began to saw, ignoring Ted's inhuman howls of pain and the blood splattering everywhere, covering his face and arms. Right as Guillermo sawed through the bone, Tiffany jostled him and Nancy, knocking the pumpkin out of Nancy's grip. The jack-o-lantern fell to the floor and split open, tipping over the candle and snuffing its flame.

Nancy jerked the bone saw out of Guillermo's blood-slick grip and shoved him through the door.

"Nancy, no!" he shouted, but the door slammed closed and the last thing he saw was Nancy facing down Tiffany with the bone saw. "She's doomed."

Amelia reached for Guillermo, her other hand frozen over her throat as if trying to stop a lump from forming. "She sacrificed herself for us. She was our mentor, and one of the only sorority sisters who was ever kind to us." Her voice broke off in a sob. "It should have been one of the mean ones, like Deb or Heidi."

"Or Paul," he said aloud. "That guy was a jerk." *And so is Kevin*, he added silently.

Amelia nodded in agreement and her eyes flicked quickly to Kevin, then back to Guillermo as if she'd read his mind. "I need to fix the salt circle. Tiffany broke it before she turned."

Thankfully, the salt container was still on the nightstand by the bed. As Amelia put down fresh trails of salt in all the broken parts of the circle, Guillermo took stock of the aloe plants. Two were knocked over, and three remained in their places. The one on the antique dresser was damaged, one of the thick, leathery leaves were broken, disrupting the careful pattern his grandma had helped him make with the strings.

He bent to pick one up and recoiled as he saw the blood on his hands. "Do you think it's safe for us to wash our hands?"

Amelia paused. "Probably? We touched the tap water a lot when we were cleaning, but I don't think it would be a good idea to drink it. Even if it won't infect us with demons, the pipes could be made of lead."

Miranda heaved an appreciative sigh. "Thank goodness. I'd been dying to get this green witch makeup off my face, and now my hands are covered in pumpkin guts."

Guillermo gave her a mock bow. "Ladies first."

"Wait," Amelia said before she headed to the bathroom. "Let me pour some salt on your hands in case I'm wrong."

She gladly accepted and carefully stepped over the salt circle. Amelia stood guard at the bathroom door.

Alvin kept his ear pressed to the door, listening to the sounds of Nancy's struggles with the demons outside.

"The fight's still going. I hope that soon we'll hear Nancy knock and we can let her in."

"We can't though," Guillermo said quietly. Kevin's and Alvin's heads swiveled to stare at him, but Amelia gave him a resigned nod. "Nancy knows how risky it would be to let her in. We don't know how these demons spread their essence to a person. If Nancy gets a scratch, or inhales their corruption, she'd be like the Trojan Horse, bringing the evil in with her. Hopefully she defeats the ones outside and finds someplace else that's safe to hide and we can find her later."

He met Amelia's eyes and looked down. They both knew how unlikely Nancy's prospects of survival were.

Alvin drew back from the door and slumped on the bed, his face in his hands. "It's hopeless. The more people the demons get, the more demons there are. Before long, it's going to be twenty-four against four. If it's not already that number. I suck at math."

Guillermo blinked at him. "But you're the fraternity treasurer. Why'd they give you the job if you're bad with numbers?"

"My last name is Schwartz."

The deadpan tone told Guillermo the explanation was there, but it took him a second. Then he kicked himself for missing it. How many times had people asked *him* if he could make better tacos? "They stereotyped you."

"Bingo." Alvin sighed and a mocking smile curved his lips. "Of course, they said they gave me the position because no one else wanted it, completely ignoring that I didn't want it either."

"And I don't suppose the frat has enough in the treasury to cover the inevitable lawsuits that will result from this night."

"Nowhere close." Alvin cast a glance at Miranda when she emerged from the bathroom. "I doubt the Pis' treasury has much more."

"With all the kegs you guys bought we probably do have more than the Lambdas, but you're right about it being nowhere near enough to cover the lawsuits. We might have enough to pay for the burial expenses of some…if there are even bodies to bury when this night ends." Miranda set her pumpkin on the dresser and paced the length of the room. "What time is it, anyway?"

Amelia looked over at the fireplace that Kevin was loading up with wood from the little bin on one side. "It doesn't look like that clock on the mantel is working, but my guess is it's around one in the morning. And I don't think sunrise is until seven."

Miranda gaped at her. "You mean we have to stick around for six more hours?"

"At minimum. Because it could be earlier than one AM. The party started at eight, remember? Also, these aren't vampires, so there's not much reason to expect sunlight to harm them. From what I read, some of the tragedies, disappearances, and ghost sightings happened during the day as well as at night."

Amelia sounded so hopeless that Guillermo pulled her into his arms. "From how adamant the caretaker was about us leaving before dark, and the fact that jack-o-lanterns are effective, I still think the demons might leave at sunrise."

Miranda finally sat in one of the overstuffed chairs beside the vanity. "Then all we have to do is stay in here and wait them out. We're safe with the salt and the plants, aren't we?"

Guillermo nodded. "Theoretically, yes. The aloe, at least. Not sure about the salt."

"I believe in the salt," Amelia said. "Remember how I told you I used to hang out with the younger brother of Zelda Shaye-Friedkin, the woman who inherited the Sazerac House?"

Used to date him. "Yeah, I remember."

"Well, Jason told me that shortly after they moved into that house, their eccentric neighbor gave them a loaf of bread and a ridiculous amount of salt as a welcoming gift. Then, after things got progressively spookier in the house, their parents went on vacation together and Jason and his younger sister were sent off to stay the weekend with their uncle, leaving Zelda alone in the house. When the family got back, the house felt peaceful and even though he still saw ghosts, he didn't see or sense the other thing that had been there. He also encountered granules of salt embedded in the rugs and in odd corners of the house. He says he's certain that Zelda, her boyfriend Tobe, and Edith the crazy neighbor lady had done something to drive the evil out of the house."

If anyone except Amelia told such a crazy story, Guillermo would have been skeptical. But he knew by now not to doubt her. Especially because the night Amelia first approached him with her plan for them to research the Raimi House, she *had* started to tell him something about the Sazerac House. The point about the salt might have been it. But that didn't feel like the only thing. He decided not to prod her about the rest, since the others in the room looked like they were regaining their courage. "All right. Now we know salt also works. Let's see what we have left under the bed. I want to be ready in case these monsters do something to drive us out of this room again."

Alvin nodded. "Good point. They're practically guaranteed to pull something."

Together, he and Amelia pulled their backpacks from the closet, then another box out from under the bed. Guillermo immediately took a spool of red yarn and a pair of scissors out of the box the aloe plants had been in. Amelia reached into her backpack, and after pulling out her brown leather bomber jacket, she withdrew a mesh bag holding bulbs of garlic, another container of salt, various bags of herbs—though none of the fun kind—and stones they'd read would protect one from evil. She made a self-deprecating sound when she withdrew a long white nightgown.

"I should have packed a change of clothes so I could get out of this bulky dress." She shoved the nightgown back in her backpack and put her coat on over her Princess Vespa dress.

Guillermo gave her a sympathetic nod, though his inner devil took a moment to imagine her in that nightgown, looking like a gorgeous heroine of a gothic horror film. "I didn't think to pack them either."

He didn't add that he'd hoped to have been naked in bed with her by now. That short time earlier this evening hadn't been enough.

"I still need to use the bathroom, take care of these disastrous braid-buns, and maybe clean up my face. I probably have racoon eyes. Miranda, can you guard the doorway? I agree that we shouldn't close this door, but I don't need Alvin or Kevin peeking in."

Kevin snorted. "Oh, but Guillermo can?"

"Shut the fuck up, Kevin."

While Amelia was using the bathroom and cleaning up, Guillermo unzipped his bag, revealing another jar of useless holy water, some rosary beads, a crucifix, and various items he'd grabbed from the international market in Spokane, including Virgin Mary and Saint Agripinna candles, pendants to ward off the evil eye, more herbs, and woven good luck bracelets. At least he too had a coat, which he shrugged on. Without the heat of the fireplaces downstairs and the warmth generated from running, it was getting cold upstairs. He donned one of the evil eye pendants and tied one of the bracelets around his wrist. The other necklace and bracelet he tucked in his coat pocket for Amelia. Kevin grabbed the crucifix and rosary despite Guillermo's arguments that they probably wouldn't be any help since the holy water had failed.

"Maybe it's your faith that failed," Kevin retorted.

Guillermo considered his words. "Maybe you're right."

But I do believe in something, even if I can't define it as neatly as the bishop at my family's church. He found the spool of red thread. After he fixed the strings on the aloe plants, he passed three of them out to Kevin, Alvin, and Miranda and kept the other two. "Unlike the pumpkins, these don't seem to repel the demons like we'd hoped, but they do burn them."

With that thought, he picked up the leaves from the broken plants and put them in his front pocket. Maybe he could see if aloe juice would do anything on its own.

Amelia emerged from the bathroom, fresh faced and hair loose with gorgeous waves. "If we do have to leave this room, I don't know how much we can take with us. I wish there was a way to test what works."

He wished the same. "To do that, we'd have to trap a demon."

She nodded and accepted the pendant and bracelet he handed her. "But with how strong they are, and how easily they infect others, that would be a dangerous thing to try."

"At least we can bring some things in our backpacks, but I think we need to prioritize weapons." He was grateful for his coat, not only due to the cold of the house, but also for the extra pockets. The pinstripe suit had been sadly lacking, only holding a few small scalpels from the embalming room and no room to hold a drink from downstairs. Also, given the circumstances, he'd felt silly looking like Gomez Addams. If that character had been real, the guy would probably have the demons tamed or locked up in minutes.

Locked up... The thought conjured a ghost of an idea that dissipated when he tried to grasp it.

Alvin and Kevin used the bathroom next, then it was Guillermo's turn.

After making sure the door remained open, he approached the sink and tentatively turned on the hot and cold faucets. He almost reached for the soap, but changed his mind, not wanting to risk using anything that belonged to the house and risk succumbing to Tiffany's fate. Besides, the salt worked like the Borax he and Dad used after working on the old truck.

The blood came off easily enough, but his reflection in the broken mirror seemed wrong, distorted. When his hands were clean, he quickly used the toilet, then checked the mirror once more, wondering if he should rinse out the hair gel. His reflection in the cracked glass disappeared, replaced by a black void. A small shape appeared, growing as if rushing toward him. Guillermo didn't wait to see what it was. He rushed out of the bathroom and slammed the door. "Bathroom's unsafe again."

"What's—" Amelia began, but Miranda cut her off with a startled yelp.

Kevin lurched back and crashed into Guillermo, almost knocking them both over. Something was coming down the chimney. And it wasn't Santa.

Chapter Eleven

Ash fell onto the grate like snow, snuffing the meager flames Kevin had barely got started. A deep growl echoed from the chimney as Amelia reached for the nearest aloe plant and darted to the fireplace. Setting the plant on the grate, she hurried back to the collection of weapons and protective items. She and Guillermo worked to place as many in their backpacks and coat pockets, while Miranda and Alvin took their aloe plants and had them ready.

Kevin paced by the door, the whites of his eyes bulging.

"Don't you dare break the salt circle," Amelia shouted.

But it was too late. A mottled hand reached down from inside the fireplace and Kevin screamed, yanked open the door, and bolted from the room. The salt circle was ruined in one swipe of his shoe.

"God damn it, Kevin," Alvin groaned, and chased after him, wielding a knife and long metal drain tube he'd taken from the embalming room.

Miranda grabbed the fire poker, ready to stab the thing in the eye if the aloe plant didn't drive it back. Guillermo pulled the aloe leaf from his pocket, but also holding a scalpel. Amelia fixed the salt circle, grabbed her pumpkin, and joined him.

Another hand emerged from inside the fireplace, then a head. At first, Amelia didn't recognize the face because it was so distorted with boils, bloody streaks, and distended bones. Then she noticed the hanging mass of filthy brown curls and realized it was Amy, the sorority's pledge recruit chair. There was still a jagged hole in her left cheek from when she'd been trampled to death.

"Pledges," Amy said with a guttural growl, baring sharp yellow teeth. "It's time to swear your souls to us." She reached down and burned her hand on the aloe plant and shrieked so loud Amelia flinched. When Miranda didn't make a move with the poker, Guillermo swiped Amy's arm with his broken leaf and the demon's skin sizzled and reddened.

Amelia considered reaching in her backpack to experiment with some of the herbs or stones they had, but then something ice cold grazed the back of her neck. Her pumpkin slipped from her hands and broke as she whirled around to see a woman in a dress that looked like it came from the thirties, standing only inches from her. A knife wound on her neck gave her a second mouth, bloody and gaping.

The woman's voice came out in alternating gurgles and whistles. It was the most horrifying voice Amelia ever heard. "I'm so sorry."

"What?" Amelia frowned in confusion.

Despite the ghost's grotesque appearance and voice, remorse shone in the woman's hazel eyes. "They made me do it. Now run."

"Made you do wh—" Amelia broke off as she saw the salt circle completely destroyed, the fine grains scattered and spread all over the room.

Footsteps echoed outside. More demons.

Amelia grabbed Guillermo's hand and reached for Miranda. "Let's go."

The hall outside was empty, with no sign of Kevin, Nancy, or Alvin. Growls sounded from the north end of the corridor then a figure rounded the corner. They didn't wait to see who it was and ran in the opposite direction.

Miranda panted beside Amelia. "Let's go to my room. My backpack is there and we can make another salt circle."

"But it didn't work in our room." All along the corridor the lights blinked on and off in a disorienting rhythm, spiking Amelia's fears that they'd be stuck in the dark with demons at their tails.

"Fine, but we still need to hide."

The decision was taken out of their hands when the hall ended at a door. Amelia prayed it wasn't locked as she reached for the knob.

"Oh shit," Guillermo shouted. "They're getting closer. Hurry."

She opened the door and they both went through, but Miranda didn't follow. Instead, she screamed and was thrown backward by an invisible force before the door slammed between them.

"Miranda!." they called together while Guillermo jerked and twisted the knob, but it wouldn't budge.

Amelia pressed her ear to the scarred wood and gestured for him to stop. "I can't hear anything. It's dead quiet out there."

"It's the dead part I'm worried about," he whispered before pressing his ear to the door and listening too. "You're right. I don't even hear the demons. I think the house moved again."

Amelia turned from the door and her heart sank in her belly as she saw a large desk with a meshed glass partition blocking it from the area. An ancient telephone sat on the desk and old filing cabinets lined the walls. "I think I know where we are."

He followed her gaze. "The old asylum?"

"Bingo." She shivered. This part of the house should have been accessible only through a separate staircase. There was no heating or lights here either. The only reason she could see anything was because of the huge glass skylight over the large atrium past the reception desk. Shafts of moonlight painted the sickly green linoleum floor.

After shoving their hands in their coat pockets to stay warm, Amelia and Guillermo carefully moved forward. Though the atrium was half the size of the ballroom, it still made her feel uncomfortably exposed.

The sight of the scarred tables in the center of the room with mismatched chairs, torn couches on one wall, and the open wire cabinet full of dusty toys, board games, and jigsaw puzzles on the opposite wall invoked a strange melancholy. Four steel doors lined the third wall that led to a metal-grated staircase at the end of the chamber.

"Wait." Guillermo paused beside a plush chair that was ripped and showing exposed stuffing and springs. "This was the rec room, but I don't understand how they could have had it here. The patients would be able to easily walk out and get into the main section of the house."

Amelia frowned. He was right. She turned around and looked back at the small hall past the enclosed receptionist station. The hall they'd passed through was easier to see from this angle thanks to the skylight. "Look. It *was* closed off before."

The entryway to the rec room had a metal frame screwed into the wood beams. Twisted iron bars protruded from the frame and more remnants littered the dark green linoleum floor.

"It looks like the gate exploded." Guillermo's dark eyes slowly studied the wreckage around the frame. "Yet there's no scorch marks on the walls or ceiling, or any other clues how it happened."

"*Anything* can happen in this place." Her voice quavered as she caught a glimpse of a transparent figure floating by. "We know that by now."

They turned away from the unnerving sight of the blown-up gate and edged farther into the rec room. Multiple doors and stairwells branched out the rec area in sort of spiderweb configuration, with the upper floors visible, the railings cordoned off with chicken wire from floor to ceiling.

Amelia shivered again, not only from the physical temperature, but also from a different kind of coldness, the chill of the inherent loneliness of this place, where Amteep's wealthy used to abandon their family members to suffer isolation and imprisonment. Those poor inmates had probably been confused as to what they'd done to deserve such punishment.

She kept detecting movement in the corners of her eyes and found herself jerking in each direction to try to see what new threat was approaching. Eventually, her eyes adjusted and as long as she kept her attention on the periphery, she detected wispy figures in bathrobes and hospital gowns, echoes of cries and whimpers of the agonized patients who'd resided here. They could be actual ghosts, but Amelia didn't think so. They were too faint.

If Guillermo saw them too, he didn't give any sign. Instead, he kept with her toward the doorways on the left. He paused to get his flashlight out of his bag before they selected a door at random and stopped at the blackness inside. He turned on the flashlight and Amelia gasped in horror at the illuminated sight before them.

An old examination table dominated the center of the room with all-too-familiar stirrups at one end and a vise and a frightening contraption of straps at the other.

As she shuddered in revulsion, Guillermo's arm wrapped around her, pulling her against his warm strength. "Are you okay?"

She managed a nod and found her voice. "I read that they did horrible things to women in these places to cure them of imagined conditions. Seeing one of the rooms where it happened is worse."

"It's awful." His voice rang with sympathetic understanding. "That table of rusty torture devices is going to give me nightmares. And to think that they did this right beside the area where the others were playing games…"

"Let's try another room." She'd go crazy if she had to look at the torture chamber a minute longer. "Maybe one will mercifully transport us back to the main house, or maybe we'll find something useful."

The other rooms on the first floor were similar chambers of horrors. Exam rooms, operating rooms…even the still-locked-up pharmacy gave off sinister vibes with its glass bottles and vials full of drugs designed to keep people in a helpless stupor.

They left the main floor and went up the stairs to the floor where the patients' rooms were, both subconsciously avoiding touching the scuffed mint green walls with dark green chipped wainscotting. Everything in this place was some sinister shade of green, like the designer had intentionally corrupted a normally vibrant color.

Some of the doors were locked, with only small, wire-reinforced glass windows to show the desolate rooms within. Some of those had tiny windows inside, where shafts of moonlight lay across barren cots and empty bureaus. Others just held blackness.

A deafening boom echoed from the lower level, followed by a growl. The demons had found them.

Guillermo turned off his flashlight. "Shit, we need to hide."

The dust on the linoleum floor muffled their footsteps as they hurried down the corridor, yanking on door handles. Finally, one opened and they dove inside. Amelia lost her footing and fell. Her butt landed on a cushioned surface that sent up a cloud of dust that tickled her throat and brought tears to her eyes. Frantically, she buried her face in the crook of her arm to suppress her coughs.

"A real padded room," Guillermo whispered in awe. "Never thought I'd see one."

Amelia scooted back against the wall beside the door, tugging on Guillermo's hand. He sat beside her and dug in his bag for a weapon. After pulling out a bigger knife, he took his evil eye pendant out of the collar of his coat. Amelia did the same before rummaging in her pack. In fleeing their last safe room, her aloe plant was in sorry shape, dirt spilled in the bag, leaves snapped off. She took a leaf and a knife, ready to fight with either.

Quickly, she made a small salt circle around them and prayed some ghost wouldn't ruin it.

Too soon, they heard shuffling footsteps approaching.

"Ameliaaaaa," Tiffany called in a singsong tone. "I know you're in here. What makes you think that you can keep any of these people safe? Especially since you lost most of them already. You're no leader. You're a follower and always have been. I made you."

A lump of self-doubt grew in Amelia's throat, choking her. Tiffany told the truth. She was crazy to think she could save anyone from this nightmare house full of demons. She'd already failed when Brandon was killed, and every death after was another lead weight of further defeat.

Tiffany continued her taunts. "Without me, you would have remained a chubby loser, laughed at by everyone. Without me, you wouldn't have gone to college. You'd probably be living in a trailer park, married to some slob, pregnant with your second baby with your first one crawling around your ankles."

A small sob escaped Amelia's throat. Guillermo grabbed her hand. "Don't listen to her. She lies. All devils do."

"No," she whispered past the lump in her throat. "You don't understand how right she is. My own father never loved me. I was such a loser, scared of my own shadow, and everyone made fun of me. If Tiffany hadn't befriended me in high school, I'd still be that loser."

"You underestimate yourself." His knuckles caressed her cheek. "If it weren't for you, we'd be dead by now."

"Everyone else is dead." Her voice was as hollow as her heart. "And it's my fault you came to this house in the first place. You were going to drop out. You'd be home now, safe with your family if I hadn't been so stupid and arrogant to believe we could survive this place."

"No." His low voice held a firm, hard edge she'd never heard before. "We've been through this already. You don't get to take credit for my stupidity. Like I told you before, I came here for a chance to spend the night with you. And when I accomplished the mission of turning your fake-dating scheme turn into the real thing, I was determined and *eager* to join you and fend off evil at your side. Our research and the supplies we gathered made me cocky and overconfident. I never imagined that things would get this bad, so I was stupid there. But it's too late to change that. So, let's focus on the fact that some of our protective measures work and we're still alive." He paused, took a deep breath, and fixed his dark eyes intently on hers. "One more thing."

"What?" she breathed.

Guillermo set down the bone saw and took her hands. "I love you, Amelia Craven. I know it's soon to say that, but I don't care, and I'm determined to survive so that we can have a future together."

"I love you too," she whispered, warmth enclosing her, despite the cold, macabre surroundings. "I think I loved you since that first day at the bookstore last month."

He lowered his head and kissed her long and deep. "Funny, that day at the bookstore was when it hit me too, that I was in love. Now let's kill that demon wearing your friend's face."

"How?" Amelia wished she had his confidence. "Kirk was decapitated and he's still up and about."

"We attack fast and without mercy." The hard look in his eyes commanded her to face the truth about Tiffany's fate.

"But what if she's still—" She caught herself and shook her head "No, with all the plastic and glass she swallowed, she's probably gone." It hurt to say the words out loud, but Amelia had to acknowledge the truth that her former best friend was likely already dead. Even if Tiffany lived, the chances of healing the toxicity of their relationship were low, but Amelia had stubbornly clung to that hope until now. It was time to let it go.

Guillermo opened his bag again and snapped a leaf off the aloe plant. He also brought out his packet of basil and bay leaves. Amelia nodded and took out a bulb of garlic. Maybe the aloe wouldn't be the only helpful tool.

The shuffling of Tiffany's footsteps drew nearer along with the unnerving sound of her scraping the walls with her claws. Amelia and Guillermo rose to their feet, holding their weapons poised.

When the door burst open, and Tiffany floated in, Amelia plunged her knife in Tiffany's heart. The demon shrieked and reached for the hilt just as Guillermo stuck an aloe leaf in her mouth.

Amelia pressed the garlic bulb to Tiffany's cheek, gratified at the immediate sizzling flesh. Another thing that worked. She tore a clove from the bulb and tossed it in Tiffany's mouth before Guillermo yanked her back. Tiffany's clawed hand sliced the air an inch in front of Amelia's face.

Then the demon's eyes watered, its face contorting and the body jittering like it was jolted with electricity. Amelia and Guillermo dodged around her and went back out into the hall, slamming the door to the padded room shut.

Amelia spotted a six-inch metal bar hanging from a chain on the door handle and grabbed it while Guillermo pressed his shoulder to the door to keep Tiffany inside.

Amelia slid the bar through the hole in the bracket against the wall, locking the door. "Fuck you, Tiffany." She didn't know if she was cursing her former friend or the demon, but either way, it felt good.

"Holy shit, that's it," Guillermo said, seemingly oblivious to the demon's shrieking and the door shaking from her slamming against it. "I was thinking we could trap the demons. There could be more rooms like this one."

Amelia nodded, half hearing him as she peeked through the small window. Tiffany's howls were deafening even through the steel door. The demon shook so violently that she looked blurry. Then, she exploded. Pink and black goo splattered across the viewing window, making them jump back.

The floor shook below their feet and growls sounded below.

More demons were coming.

Chapter Twelve

As Guillermo huddled with Amelia in the corridor between the patient rooms, listening to scrabbles of claws on the linoleum below, his heart raced. Trapping demons in padded rooms sounded like a good idea a few minutes ago, but now panic clawed his throat. What if the padded room they'd locked Tiffany in was the only one?

Tucking Amelia under his shoulder, he walked them backward, slowly trying the handles of every door they passed.

Shuffling human-sounding footsteps echoed from the stairwell.

"Hey, beaner." Mike Lang's voice was starkly clear for a dead man. Clear, and full of malice. "Do you really think your Mexican superstitions will save you and your little slut from us?"

He came into view, and both Guillermo and Amelia flinched at the sight of the possessed corpse. Deep gouges turned his face into a striped horror of runnels of blood and scraps of dangling flesh. His bloody scalp was bald in some places and showed the white of his skull in others. Guillermo remembered hearing that Mike had been killed by Tiffany and shuddered to think of what had been done to him when he was still alive.

"Speaking of the little slut." Mike's glowing yellow eyes slid sideways as he gave Amelia a disgusting leer. "I'll bet you hate that someone else had her first. I used to watch you checking her out when she was with Cam. Kevin and I laughed at you. And you know what? You're not even good enough for Cameron's sloppy seconds."

Fury coursed through Guillermo's veins, boiling him from the inside in spite of the cold asylum. "Don't talk about her like that, you pig."

He lunged forward in a blind rage, but Amelia grabbed his upper arm. "He's goading you like Tiffany's demon did to me. Don't fall for it."

Her voice broke the spell that had fallen over him. The house must be getting to him. He'd never been the type to resort to violence at mere stupid taunts. Crueler people than Mike had tormented him since preschool.

Yet the Mike demon persisted. "You're definitely not good enough to be an Alpha Lambda. The only reason we let you in is because you're a legacy. The university never should have accepted your kind."

Guillermo blinked at that. The real Mike had been a fellow pledge and sometimes could be a dick when he was trying to show off for the frat bros, but he'd never scorned Guillermo's heritage. That had been Kevin and sometimes Simon. And the sneering tone didn't sound like Mike either.

Instead, it brought back memories of his early school years, when a boy named Gerald Duke had tormented him for years. Gerald's father, Guillermo would later learn, belonged to the Aryan Brotherhood up in Hayden, and so Gerald bleated every slur he'd learned to Guillermo.

Gerald continued to bully Guillermo, and Guillermo did his best to hold his chin high and not let the slurs hurt him. Eventually he made some friends who had his back, and Gerald's torments reduced dramatically. He was only taunted when Gerald caught him alone. The words and the virulent hate behind them still hurt. The ugly flyers the Aryans put on the windshield of his mom's car hurt even worse.

Suddenly, as if feeding on the memories, the Mike demon seemed to morph into Gerald, the bones crunching and the facial features contorting to match the bully's rat-like face.

"Beaner," the demon shouted in Gerald's voice. He stalked closer to Guillermo, shouting a stream of uglier slurs. Each word was like the lash of a whip, filling Guillermo with the old hurt he'd long thought he'd grown immune to. Amelia was shrieking at the demon in angry defiance, yet her words couldn't reach him in the face of Gerald's relentless spewing of degrading words.

Before Guillermo could completely regress into the confused, wounded child he'd been in those days, Amelia wrapped her arms around his shoulders and turned him away from Gerald to face her. "Don't listen to that stupid demon. It's trying to get to you like the Tiffany demon got to me. I listened to you and we defeated her. Listen to me and let's destroy this fucker. I love you."

Those last three words, coupled with the warmth of her embrace and the heat of her breath on his ear, snapped him out of the past and into the now. Gerald's face winced and morphed back to Mike's.

He kissed her quickly, then reached out to touch the next doorknob they'd backed up to. As if Amelia's love had conjured a miracle, the door opened to another padded room.

But before they could maneuver into a position where they could trap the demon, Mike's body lunged for them. Guillermo's palm slapped against the demon's forehead, holding it back from clawing and biting range. For a moment, Guillermo looked like a playground bully, holding a kid out of range, but instead of swinging fists, Mike's claws swiped millimeters from Guillermo's guts.

Amelia's delicate fingers came into Guillermo's view, avoiding Mike's gnashing teeth as she popped a broken aloe leaf into his mouth.

The demon lurched back. Smoke poured from its mouth and blood dripped from its yellow eyes like tears. Guillermo reached into his pocket and found one of the bags of herbs. Without looking to see which ones, he opened the Ziplock, took a small handful of green leaves, and threw them in Mike's face.

Just like with the Tiffany demon, Mike's body jolted and jerked like someone had hooked jumper cables to his ears and hooked them to a hundred-volt battery. Red boils formed on his face and arms, growing bigger and bigger. Smoke trickled from his melting eyes and swelling mouth in greenish plumes.

As the body jerked and spasmed harder, boils swelled to the size of tennis balls and the eyes melted from the sockets in a yellowish stream. Also Guillermo realized that this time they didn't have a door separating them from the demon.

"Run!" he shouted, but before they made it three steps, the demon exploded, and they were pelted with red clots of rubbery flesh and rancid, custard-like goo.

"Eww," Amelia groaned.

Guillermo gagged as he swiped the warm gelatinous pieces of Mike from his face. The growls of more approaching demons neared. "We have to trap these ones."

Amelia nodded then pointed at the bag of herbs he still held. "What did you throw in his face?"

Guillermo looked down and thanked the heavens that the bag had sealed in his grip and had avoided all but the slightest splatters of demon gunk. He opened the Ziplock and sniffed. "Basil. Let's add that to our list of anti-demon weapons."

Their shoes skidded in the mess of goo and guts on the linoleum, but they got the door open and were able to reach in their bags to get more garlic and basil ready.

The first demon came into view. It was Steve, one of the frat brothers who had no official position, so as a result, was kind to pledges, though he'd made up for his lack of cruelty with perversion and obnoxiousness. Guillermo's last memory before this night was of Steve bragging about climbing a tree and watching the Omega Pis getting undressed.

Now Steve floated, his Nike high-tops a foot above the floor, his tux and tails ravaged by gaping tears in his flesh. The black waves of his mullet rippled under an intangible wind. When his yellow eyes lit on Amelia and Guillermo, his fanged mouth curved in a ravenous grin. "Great party, isn't it, lovebirds?"

Behind him, two more demons appeared. One crawled on the walls, defying gravity like a malevolent cockroach. Studying the long brown hair and the remnants of the nurse costume, Guillermo recognized Valerie, one of the coeds who'd gone with Simon when they'd originally split up. Her jaw had been dislocated and her cheeks split open, making her mouth hang open like an insect's mandible. Needle-sharp teeth glinted like stainless steel.

The other demon lurched on a broken ankle, looking like an extra from *Night of the Living Dead*. The teal and yellow Day-Glo windbreaker and neon green headband identified him as James, another frat bro. He'd been a fitness junkie and refused to wear a costume.

"Oh shit." Amelia echoed his thoughts. "How are we going to get three in here?"

"We probably won't." There didn't appear to be a way to get past them either. Guillermo wished he was like one of the heroes in action movies, able to take down multiple bad guys all by himself. Of course, in those movies, the villains conveniently stood still and waited their turn to get beaten. The thought gave him pause. Maybe there *was* a way to take them one at a time.

"We're going to have to fight in the doorway," he told her, hating the quaver in his voice. "That way they have no choice but to attack one at a time."

Amelia nodded and sank into a crouch beside him so that his arms would have full range of motion above her, and she could still attack the demons from the doorway. In one hand she held a knife and a fistful of basil in the other.

He considered using another aloe leaf, then decided against it. There was something else he wanted to try with the aloe, if they survived this skirmish. So he kept a garlic clove and the bag of basil ready and prayed to *Santa Muerte*, as his mother and grandma did when they wanted protection, or feared for their lives. If there was such a saint, surely The Lady of the Dead would disapprove of demons desecrating the bodies of the dead and making them move and attack the living.

Before he could do anything more, Steve reached the doorway, sharp claws extended. Guillermo threw the basil in the demon's face, making Steve immediately scream and cup his hands to his boiling cheeks. There was another shriek and Steve staggered back. Guillermo glanced down to see Amelia gouging Steve's shin with her knife. She thrust her garlic clove in the green, bloody wound and kicked his other shin, making Steve fall on his back, writhing in agony.

Acrid smoke streamed from Steve's leg wound, making Guillermo gag. His eyes burned and filled with tears at the stinging smoke, and he blinked, trying to focus on their next opponent.

At first, watching James shamble toward them like a B-movie zombie, Guillermo was optimistic that he and Amelia would have an easy victory. Valerie, on the other hand... He scanned the ceiling and saw nothing. Where was Valerie?

A piercing shriek echoed in the corridor as Valerie dropped into view, her giant gaping maw of needles inches from Guillermo's arm.

Suddenly, she was jerked back like a fish on a line. James dropped to the floor. Triumphant battle cries rang in his ears before he saw Nancy pulling a fire poker out of Valerie's back, while Paul,

Cheryl, Heidi, and Deb squared off with two more approaching demons.

Amelia sprang out of the doorway and stuffed a clove of garlic in James's mouth before the demon could rise. Guillermo moved to help Nancy, and together, they dragged Valerie and Steve into the padded room and locked the door before the corpse could reanimate once more. Cheryl did the same with James, using the padded room they had used for Tiffany.

Guillermo sucked in a breath, worried that the monster had reformed itself, but from Cheryl's noise of disgust, it seemed all that remained in the room was blobs of goop and gore. With Deb's and Paul's help, they shoved one of the approaching demons into the room and locked the door.

The final demon was dispatched by Amelia, with Heidi's help. After Amelia fried its face with basil, Heidi snuck up behind the demon and drove a knife in a spot right between the center of the neck above the shoulders. The demon collapsed like a puppet whose strings had been cut. Amelia then placed a garlic clove in its mouth and pulled Heidi back to avoid being splattered with demon goo.

Guillermo watched with admiration. His girlfriend was so tough and brave. He sucked in a breath at the realization that she was indeed with him. But *girlfriend* sounded so pedestrian for what they'd been through together this night, and tepid for how he felt about her. *His woman?* He shook his head. *Nah. Too caveman.* Suddenly, he remembered one of the few instances when he'd heard his grandfather speak Spanish under his roof. When he was being affectionate to Grandma, he called her *"mi amor."*

"My love," he whispered under his breath before approaching her and raising his hand for a high five. "That was badass."

"Thanks," Amelia breathed, her palm hot as it made contact with his. Then she turned and hugged Nancy. "We thought you died out there."

Nancy attempted a nonchalant shrug, but the affectation was dampened by the stark lines of trauma in her brown eyes. "I came damn close. But then the weirdest thing happened. I was running toward a door with demons chasing me, and suddenly the whole hallway spun and I ended up in some other part of the house. That's where I found Cheryl and the others. They were huddled up in a large den full of hunting trophies on the walls, fur rugs on the floor, and a fireplace the size of the one in the great room. Then we went to every room with a fireplace and got these pokers. I think iron hurts them, like the legends about it hurting faeries. It doesn't kill them, but they stay down longer."

Guillermo hadn't encountered any room resembling a den and wondered where it could be in relation to the asylum wing. Surely the tortured screams of the inmates would have been distasteful to the Raimi patriarch to listen to. "How did you find us?"

"When we got to the smaller rooms with the tiny fireplaces, we heard someone screaming a bunch of…horrible words that could only be directed at you." Nancy's eyes flashed with a touch of pity that made his face hot. "So, I insisted that we go help you. Who was it? At first, I thought it was that pledge, Mike, but then the voice seemed to change to someone I couldn't recognize."

"The demon used the words of an old grade school bully." Guillermo rolled his eyes as if in smug mockery of the incident, despite the fact that the return of Gerald Duke *had* shaken him. "Before that, Tiffany was taunting Amelia. They want to tear you down, make you insecure so they can feed on your pain and hopelessness."

Nancy nodded. "One of them did that to me too. I don't want to talk about what they said, but it made me feel awful."

Amelia's finger played across her plump lower lip, a sign that indicated she was deep in thought about something important. "Maybe we can—" she broke off, blue eyes widening. "What is that?"

They all turned to follow her gaze. Guillermo's heart jumped up in his throat.

A man in a doctor's white coat with a stethoscope hanging around his neck rounded the corridor. Two nurses in old-fashioned dresses and caps flanked him, pushing a squeaky steel cart.

Unlike other ghosts they'd seen, these ones looked solid. The doctor's eyes glowed white fire and his mouth stretched up in a rictus smile. "Look at these patients out of their rooms. Tsk tsk. And you," he pointed at Paul. "It's time for your lobotomy."

Chapter Thirteen

Amelia shrank back from the approaching asylum spirits. Normally, ghosts weren't supposed to be able to hurt you, but after losing Mary to the ghost of the little boy, she didn't want to risk being anywhere near these ones.

Paul, on the other hand, was oblivious to the danger. "A lobotomy? In your dreams, Casper. One of you asshole ghosts tried taking a swing at me earlier. You can't touch me."

As he stood there with a smug grin, his arms crossed over his chest, Cheryl grabbed his shoulder and tried to pull him back. "I don't think that's a good idea, Paul."

"I'll show you they're harmless. Watch." Paul smirked and strode toward the ghosts, who watched him with savage hunger. Guillermo grabbed Amelia's arm and gently tugged her farther back.

Cheryl's and Deb's warning cries faded to a dull roar in Amelia's ears. She watched with frozen horror as the nurses seized Paul's shoulders and the doctor raised a sharp spike with one hand and a gleaming silver hammer with the other. With a calculated swing, the phantom doctor drove the spike directly into Paul's left eye.

Paul's shriek of startled agony broke through Amelia's panicked torpor. "Oh shit. Run."

As the newly rejoined group darted down the corridor, more ghosts appeared. These were dressed in hospital johnnies or pajamas. Demented laughter poured from their mouths, contradicting the pain and terror in their eyes. Cackling nurses advanced on the group, making them flee back down the stairs. Once Amelia, Guillermo, Heidi, Deb, Cheryl, and Nancy reached the atrium, where the rec room and nurse's station were, Nancy charged to the door where Amelia and Guillermo had been separated from Miranda. Amelia remained near one of the game tables with Guillermo and Cheryl. She had a moment to hope that the door would open, then her spirits sank as Nancy groaned with strain and frustration when tugging at the handle.

More phantom doctors and nurses emerged from the exam room doors bordering the rec room. The ghost patients poured down the stairs after Amelia and her friends. Heidi and Deb edged blindly toward the mesh cabinet full of board games and puzzles. Behind them, Paul slowly descended the staircase, the spike still embedded in one eye and the other eye glowing fiery demonic orange.

With frightening speed, two nurses closed in on Heidi. They seized her arms and pinned her legs by each hooking a leg behind her knees.

A third nurse with a rail-thin figure and a giant hairy mole on her chin stalked toward Heidi with a little paper cup, shaking it to rattle its contents. "Time to take your meds."

The nurses pinned Heidi and pried open her jaws, while a third nurse cackled with maniacal glee and shoved the pills into Heidi's mouth. When she was released, Heidi's eyes turned the dreaded yellow color that indicated demonic infestation.

Deb's fate was worse. While trying to help Heidi, a mob of patients closed in on her like zombies feasting. They clawed at her cheeks and pulled hanks of hair from her scalp as she screamed in agony. Paul made his way to the horde and wrapped his arms around her clumsily, like Frankenstein's monster in a Hammer film. His lips closed over hers, cutting off her screams. Blood trickled down Deb's cheeks as Paul's mouth ground against hers. Was he biting her tongue off?

Amelia shuddered, watching Paul and Deb end their kiss and Deb's eyes change to orangey yellow. The pair of new demons turned to Guillermo and Amelia and stalked toward them, flanked by the multitude of asylum ghosts. Heidi and the phantom nurses approached Cheryl and Nancy.

This was it. Demons and killer ghosts surrounded them, closing in to feast. She could feel the evil within the house humming with carnivorous satisfaction.

Amelia screamed, releasing all her fear, frustration, and grief for everyone who'd suffered and died in this evil place. Her guilt and self-loathing for being the reason Guillermo was here, and her fear of losing the man with whom she'd only just begun to experience the full power of love.

The house seemed to scream with her; high-pitched cracking sounds reverberated through the rec room and atrium above. Guillermo's arms closed around her, pulling her off to the side, near an exam room, and down to the battered green linoleum. A loud, piercing crash tore through the atrium. From under the crook of Guillermo's elbow, she saw giant shattered panes of glass falling.

The newly possessed Heidi and Deb were too clumsy to do more than look up in dead-eyed curiosity before the glass fell on them. Heidi's head was severed in a second, her blood, still red, sprayed everywhere. Amelia shuddered as the hot liquid splattered on her cheek. Another pane fell on Deb, cutting her in half at the waist.

Amelia's choking sob broke as smaller pieces of glass bounced up and rained back down on everyone left alive. Stinging pain screamed against her upper arm and the back of her left hand. Guillermo held her tighter and she felt him flinch as even more pieces of glass struck him.

The silence after was thick enough to crush her ribs.

"What the fuck was that?" Nancy whispered loudly.

Tentatively, Guillermo pulled them both up on their feet. The asylum ghosts had vanished. Cheryl and Nancy held each other, their cheeks and arms bleeding from a multitude of small cuts. Each stared in horror at the carnage left behind by the broken skylight dome. Heidi's head, still adorned with an exercise sweatband, had rolled over to rest against the caged puzzle and game shelves, her hazel eyes staring at nothing. Her body lay near one of the tables, a pool of blood still spreading in a wide tide from the neck of her leotard. Deb's remains were worse off, her intestines spilling out of her severed waist, her spine gleaming wetly in the moonlight from her sliced torso. The pool of blood beneath her soaked the yellow feathered sleeves of her showgirl costume and had spread nearly to where Guillermo and Amelia had huddled.

Guillermo voiced Amelia's horrified realization about the bodies before she could bring herself to speak. "Oh shit, they were alive before the glass came down. The demons bled pink and black, sometimes green. But those two bled like us."

As if to punctuate his point, he wiped a crimson streak of blood from his forehead with the back of his hand.

Amelia watched him bend down and shake his long black curls, tiny pieces of glass falling to the floor with little tinkling sounds. "Does that mean there would have been a chance for them to become unpossessed?" *And does that make me a murderer?*

"I don't know." Guillermo sighed. "For one thing, none of us have an exorcist on hand. For another, your story about what happened the last time the Raimi family tried to exorcise the demons seems to prove that it won't work."

Nancy made a frustrated sound and shifted impatiently on her feet. Or maybe she was just freezing in her Wonder Woman costume. "There has to be a way to get these demons out of people. Even if it's death. I want you all to promise me that if you see my eyes turn yellow, you'll take me out."

"I promise," Cheryl and Guillermo said without hesitation.

Amelia wanted to put Nancy at ease, but she didn't know if she could bear killing someone if there was a chance they could be freed from these demons. A memory about what her ex-boyfriend, Jason Shaye, had told her about the Sazerac House, and the evil entity that had dwelled within, teased her with a hint of revelation. What was it that she'd started to tell Guillermo about what Jason thought had driven the evil from that house?

Then she remembered. "There might be a way…"

A loud boom broke off her words. They all turned to see the main door into the asylum wing had flung open.

"Yes." Guillermo's elated shout echoed through the asylum. "We can get out now. Maybe whatever the hell happened with the atrium glass breaking freed all the doors in this place and we can get out of here."

Amelia frowned. What *had* happened with the glass? She'd done it, but how?

They rushed out the door, Cheryl and Nancy leading the way with their iron fire pokers. Amelia reached into her backpack and grabbed another bag of herbs.

"Miranda," she burst out as the memory of the last trick the house played hit her. "We lost her at this door. I really hope she's alive. Nancy? Cheryl? Did either of you happen to see where Alvin and Kevin went?"

Guilt tugged at her heart for not caring too much about whether Kevin was still alive. Not after the way he talked to Guillermo. But Alvin was a different story. Like Guillermo, he wasn't anything like the usual frat-boy jerk. And Miranda… Amelia swore she'd seen a few sparks kindling between the two.

Nancy interrupted her thoughts. "I saw Alvin chasing Kevin up the stairs toward the servant quarters. Their eyes were normal, but they didn't seem to hear me shouting after them. I started to go after them, but then I heard Paul and Cheryl and the others. And after that, we heard you guys in the asylum."

"Then we'd better try to find them." Amelia took stock of their location, noting that the corridor—what she could see of it anyway—was different than the one where they'd lost Miranda.

Guillermo reached into his bag and got out his flashlight, revealing brown wallpaper decorated with green trees and pastoral hunting scenes. The wall sconces were sturdier than the spindly gold ones in the other hallways. These were practical, thick iron. The masculine décor implied they were probably near the den, the study, and men's guest rooms.

As they cautiously made their way down the hall, Amelia thought about why her scream had brought down the skylight, banished the ghosts, and let them out of the asylum. She'd felt power course through her in that moment that had been fueled by grief and anger. Emotions the house usually fed on and turned against its victims. So why did it recoil from *her* rage and pain? What was different about her feelings than those of the others?

Maybe it wasn't her rage or pain that had broken part of the house. Maybe it was her feelings *behind* them.

She remembered her brief time in the Sazerac House. The tales of that haunted house had been whispered about and appeared in the books about local hauntings for many years before she was born. So, when she finally got a chance to set foot in the old mansion, she was almost disappointed at how different the place was from what she'd expected. There were still ghosts; she'd seen at least one every visit, but there was no sense of spookiness or even the slightest element of danger.

When voicing her disappointments to Jason, he explained that the house used to be full of terrors, starting with his father losing his fingertip by a garbage disposal operating by itself, to making the cleaning lady hang herself in the furnace room.

"Something evil had been here, Mimi," he'd explained, *addressing her by the nickname she hated but was too polite to tell him. "It tormented our family and killed previous residents of this house, but my sister and her husband—boyfriend at the time—drove it out. They never talk about exactly what they did, but I think part of it had to do with love. Even if you can't accept that love can defeat evil because it's the biggest enemy of hate, you at least know that an environment is very influenced by the feelings of the people in it. Even after the evil thing left this house, the ghosts were melancholy. Now they aren't."*

Amelia then remembered some segments of the history of the Raimi House. There had been quiet years, hadn't there? Could it be because Ethel and Samuel Raimi had a loving marriage? Samuel had been the son of Ruth Raimi, and very few ghostly occurrences had been logged during that era. Things had been pretty uneventful during their daughter Rachel Raimi's time too. She'd remained a spinster in definition, but her documented closeness with her lady's companion who'd remained by Miss Raimi's side until her death, a woman only known as Maude, implied Rachel hadn't technically been single.

Amelia then remembered when they'd been talking in the great room, about their hopes and dreams, trying to distract themselves from the demons pacing in the entryway, waiting for an opportunity to get past the protection of the jack-o-lanterns. For a moment, hers and Guillermo's conversation had gotten so intense, the other people sheltering with them seemed to vanish, and for a moment even the demons were forgotten. She remembered how she'd nearly blurted that she loved him then and there, and the way he'd kissed her. After one of the frat brothers broke their cocoon of intimacy, they noticed the demons had stopped lurking. At first, Amelia had assumed they'd went somewhere else to trap them, but now she wondered...

"Hey." She tapped Guillermo's shoulder with her free hand. "I think I know how we could drive the demons out of people. Or at least keep them from claiming us."

"How?" Guillermo asked. His hopeful expression, along with Nancy's and Cheryl's, tugged at her chest.

She opened her mouth to answer, but suddenly, the hallway began to spin and coldness enveloped her. Her stomach lurched and her eyes squeezed shut to hold back the tide of nausea.

When the sense of vertigo dissipated, Amelia opened her eyes to see that she was in a different hallway, at the base of a narrow staircase. She was also alone.

With a choked sob, she sank to her knees.

Guillermo wasn't there.

Chapter Fourteen

Guillermo's heart slammed against his rib cage, threatening to burst. "No," he whispered brokenly, spinning around in search of Amelia.

She'd been right behind him a second ago. She'd tapped him on the shoulder and when he turned to her, the house spun around again, making him close his eyes from dizziness. When he opened his eyes, she was gone.

Everywhere he pointed his flashlight beam the light yielded no sight of her. He checked the closest door, which revealed a spartan, yet still somehow elegant, bedroom. The next one opened to a similar room, and the third revealed a study that could be interesting, but only if Amelia had been with him, ready to open her books to find context in the wealth of papers and books. It took all his remaining practicality not to slam the study door in impotent fury and agony at losing her.

God, he was such an idiot to think this wouldn't happen to him and Amelia. All these times they'd been separated from other people and he'd stupidly assumed they would stay together through this nightmare. With her by his side, they could survive the evil in the house.

Now the Raimi House had cruelly snatched that tiny wisp of hope from his grasp. Tears burned in the back of his eyes, threatening to pour forth in front of Cheryl and Nancy. He wouldn't cry in front of them. Not because he feared they'd think him unmanly, but because if he broke down, their spirits would sink lower. Guillermo knew with his whole being that the house very much wanted his spirit vanquished. His encounter with the Mike demon who put on Gerald Duke's face, and now taking Amelia from him proved its malicious intent. Maybe all it took was inner emptiness, a heart barren of hope, to let the demons in.

There had to be only a few hours left until sunrise. Was the house getting desperate? He *had* to find Amelia.

"Guillermo?" Nancy's voice was tentative. "Should we shout out for her? See if she can hear us?"

He shook his head. "That didn't work for you or Miranda. The house could have put her anywhere. We have other people to find and don't want to attract more demons."

Cheryl gasped. "Don't you care what happened to her?"

A weak sound creaked in his throat as he swallowed a scream. "I care more about her than any of you, to be completely honest. But if I give in to the urge to sit here and wallow in my grief, she'll never forgive me. All I can do is hope that I find her and Miranda and Alvin before the evil in this place devours them."

"And Kevin," Nancy added in a low voice.

"Yeah. Him too."

Cheryl frowned, looking between him and Nancy. "Are those the only ones we know are still alive?"

"I think so."

"God, this is so awful." Cheryl resumed walking, keeping her fire poker at the ready. The tail of her cat costume swayed with every step.

Nancy remained closer to Guillermo, her forehead creased and her mouth moving silently as if she was weighing something to say to him.

When he couldn't stand her tumultuous quiet, he tapped her shoulder. "Is there something wrong?"

"Amelia brought down the glass when she screamed." Nancy's eyes narrowed on him. "Didn't she? And that made the door open so we could escape the asylum."

Guillermo nodded, grasping the significance of her words at last. "I could tell from the look in her eyes that she thought something had happened, but I don't think she did it on purpose. All she seemed to be thinking after that moment was how awful it was that Deb and Heidi had still been alive when the window shattered. That there could have been a chance to save them."

Cheryl clapped a hand over her mouth to muffle a sound. "She must feel so guilty."

"Maybe, but she shouldn't since she saved us. The ghosts vanished and the demons were destroyed before they could rise and turn us into more of them." Guillermo paused, gripping the strap of his backpack. If there had been power in her scream, it seemed to be fueled by emotion, just like the house's powers seemed fueled by despair. "But there was something else. Something more important than that scream. She'd had an idea of how to hold off the evil, I think. That's what she was starting to tell us before the house took her away."

Nancy's eyes widened with comprehension. "That's why we all keep getting separated. You and Amelia have the tools and the knowledge to fight the demons."

Cheryl frowned. "Then why didn't the house separate Amelia and Guillermo right away?"

The answer drifted vaguely through Guillermo's mind, wispy threads teasing him with the promise of the whole tapestry. "I think it has to have been trying. She had an idea about how to drive demons out of people. Or at least keep them from possessing us. The house wouldn't let her speak."

Nancy's mouth flattened to a grim line as she nodded. "And she's probably its prime target now."

An icy chill engulfed Guillermo's heart. What if the house put Amelia in the path of demons? What if the walls themselves reared forward and crushed her to death? What if she was already—no. She had to be alive. He *had* to find her. He didn't think he could bear surviving without her.

For now, maybe he could figure out what her idea was about how to drive out demons. He knew she wasn't religious, but did secular exorcisms exist?

A memory played in his mind like a disjointed dream. Children's movies he'd seen in bits and pieces when his young cousins stayed for the weekend. *The Care Bears* and *Care Bears 2*. One featured an evil talking book, but hadn't the other one had a demon that possessed a kid? Or had that been his imagination? Could kid's movies really be that dark?

Either way, he couldn't shoot rainbows and sunbeams from his belly.

At his unbidden snort of laughter, Nancy raised a brow. "What's so funny?"

He shook his head. "I was thinking about the *Care Bears*."

"The kids' show?"

"More about the movies. It doesn't matter." As they turned a corner, a doorway came into view. "Hey, this part of the house looks familiar. That doorway—"

"Oh, thank God," Cheryl breathed as she rushed forward.

Guillermo followed her and echoed her sigh of relief as he saw that they were back in the room where the party had started. Although there was only one jack-o-lantern left to secure the perimeter, beers and pops awaited in the cooler. A welcome relief for his sandpapery throat.

"Let's get hydrated and then go find Amelia."

Keeping a careful eye out for approaching demons, he reached the coffin cooler and grabbed a beer. The ice had mostly melted, but the water was still cold. He chugged down the first beer so fast that a wave of dizziness made him sway. He stared at the water in the cooler. Had there been a discussion about water earlier in the night?

He took another beer and slumped on the couch beside Nancy, who'd lit a cigarette and was nursing a beer. Cheryl paced around with a can of Coke. Her eyes strayed to Guillermo's backpack as he set it on the floor to check what demon-fighting supplies he had left. "What do you have in there?"

"Stuff Amelia and I collected because our research said it could combat evil spirits. And some things around the house we thought could work as weapons..." And there it was. His fingers fumbled the backpack's zipper as he'd forgotten that the thing was already unzipped. After digging around a bit, he pulled out the large steel tube with a plunger on one end and an IV hose on the other. "Could one of you get me a plastic cup from by the keg and fill it with water from the cooler?"

"Sure." Cheryl set her Coke on the mantel and headed for the keg. "What is that thing and what are you going to do with it?"

Nancy answered for him while he took another drink. "He's going to mix aloe and maybe some other herbs that worked and use this thing we got from the morgue as an improvised squirt gun. It was originally used to pump embalming fluid into dead people."

"You guys saw the morgue?" Cheryl squeaked as she handed Guillermo a plastic cup of water.

Nancy rolled her eyes and dropped her cigarette butt in the beer can. "It was a lot less scary than the shit we've been seeing everywhere else."

Guillermo set the cup between his knees and reached into his backpack. He took one of the few aloe leaves left and first squeezed all the juices possible into the cup. Garlic would be a wonderful addition, but he didn't know how he'd get the juice inside it. What he'd give for a garlic press right now.

In the end, he decided on slicing up a few cloves of garlic and setting them in the water, hoping that some of the juices would seep out and create a marinade. For good measure, he added salt and basil that he crumbled into smaller fragments so it wouldn't clog the device.

After fishing out the garlic pieces and handing them to Cheryl and Nancy, Guillermo put the hose part of the embalming pump into the cup and pulled back the plunger. All the liquid sucked in with a satisfying slurping sound.

"I still wish we had a squirt gun," he said with a regretful sigh. "Amelia and I had some filled with holy water, but I dropped mine when it proved to be useless against the demons."

Cheryl bounced on her heels with a grin. "Gilbert's corner."

Guillermo raised a brow. "The parlor where the guy was selling drugs and bootleg music?"

Cheryl nodded. "I saw that he had more stuff when I bought a joint from him at the beginning of the party."

For the first time since Amelia disappeared, Nancy looked hopeful. "And there's another jack-o-lantern in there."

"Jack-o-lantern?" Cheryl questioned.

Guillermo explained as he got up to get more water. "The old Gaelic myths were right. They do deter evil spirits."

"Wow," Cheryl said after taking another drink of her Coke. "And you and Amelia were researching all this stuff?"

He nodded and began making more garlic and herb liquid to finish filling the pump. "We didn't know about the jack-o-lanterns, but yeah. That's why we were pretending to date in the first place. So Susan and Kirk wouldn't know we were trying to find ways to survive the evil in this house."

Cheryl faced him, a tear spilling down her cheek. "I'm so sorry we decided to hold the initiation here. It was Susan's idea, but as sorority vice president, I should have objected. Now almost everyone is dead and I don't think I'll ever recover from the guilt even if I do get out of here alive." Her eyes suddenly narrowed on Guillermo. "Wait. You and Amelia were only *pretending* to be dating? Because what I saw looked pretty real to me."

"That's because it became real pretty damn fast." As he filled the rest of the embalming pump, a vise crushed Guillermo's heart as he mourned all the time he'd wasted. Years he could have spent with her instead of less than five meager weeks. "We have to find her. I don't think I can survive without her."

Nancy grabbed a wine cooler. "Then we have to get that stuff out of the parlor. Because we can't find the others if we die and become demons."

After filling their pockets and Guillermo's bag with snacks and cans of beer and pop, the three ventured out into the dining room where the mayhem began. Gilbert Curtis's spine lay on the polished hardwood floor, the blood around it now a drying brown sticky mess. The rest of Gilbert was gone, giving Guillermo the mental image of a demon slithering around like a snake, his broken jaw distended like a python eating a mouse. The Ouija board still remained on the dining room table, the planchette a punctuation mark at the end of a scream.

Guillermo paused and put his finger over his lips as he listened for signs of survivors and demons. When only silence answered him, he led the way to the parlor.

The candle had gone out in Gilbert's jack-o-lantern, so he lit it right away before handing the pumpkin to Cheryl. "Use this like people use crosses in the movies."

When he turned his flashlight back on, he was able to see Gil's stashes. One small duffel bag contained rolled joints, baggies of weed, and small bags of cocaine and pills. A bigger bag was filled with cassette tapes and VHS tapes. Another bag held candy bars, whoopie cushions, joy buzzers, water balloons, and sure enough, a pack of cheap squirt guns with one missing. Hadn't Gil had one in the holster of his spaghetti Western costume before he brought out a real one?

Guillermo grabbed the squirt guns and pack of water balloons. He raised a brow as Nancy grabbed the bag of drugs.

"What?" Nancy shot him a look that dared him to challenge her. "I could use a bump to bring up my energy and a toke for later."

They returned to the great room and mixed up more aloe and herb water while Cheryl paced between the doorways with the pumpkin.

After the final squirt gun was loaded, and some water balloons were filled with the garlic and herb mixture from the embalming pump, there were puddles everywhere from the leaked water. Guillermo rubbed at a damp spot on his pinstriped slacks and cursed the fact that the pants would be even more uncomfortable when they left the warmth of the great room.

A loud scream reverberated from up the stairs. It didn't sound like Amelia or Miranda, but it could have been.

Nancy stood and picked up her fire poker with one hand and a squirt gun with the other. "Are we ready to hunt some demons?"

As they followed the screams, Guillermo prayed Amelia hadn't become one.

Chapter Fifteen

Amelia hadn't ever been afraid of the dark, but she was now. The hallway she'd been transported to was freezing, and so dark she might as well be blind. She cursed herself for not packing a flashlight, trusting Guillermo's to be enough for them both. The silence should have been comforting, since it meant there were no demons around, but for some reason, the thick quiet weighed on her like a lead shroud.

Her heart cried out in longing to feel Guillermo's arms around her again. Her mind shrieked in panic that she'd never see him again because one or both of them would be killed.

She cursed the Raimi House for taking her away from the man she loved. Why did it have to be now? She'd been on the verge of telling him that love could help drive back the evil when she was sent to this cold dark part of the house.

"Holy shit," she whispered to the house to combat the oppressive silence. "This means I'm probably right. You moved me to keep me and Guillermo from fighting you and your demons, you fucking hellhole."

It was bad enough she'd been sitting here in the dark, hunched over in despair for hell knew how long, letting the house drag her down in despair. It was time to stand on her feet and not let the evil take her so easily. After some rummaging in her backpack, she found a candle and her lighter. She scolded herself for letting her panic prevent her from remembering that she had a light source.

When the weak, flickering flame illuminated the area, her heart sank to see surroundings she didn't recognize. The walls were covered with dingy, peeling brown wallpaper. The floor was bare pine boards that were scuffed and dull. A small door with a plain, tarnished brass knob was ahead of her on the right.

The narrow hall was so cold that Amelia had to resist the urge to hold the candle closer to her body to seek the meager warmth from the tiny flame. The last thing she needed was to set her hair on fire.

A drop of something cold and wet hit her forehead, making her jump with an embarrassing yip. Dreading the worst, she wiped at the droplet and brought the candle to the back of her free hand. Just water. She sighed with relief when she heard the soft patter of rain above. The roof had a leak in this part of the house.

As she approached the narrow door and turned the knob, a fresh chill greeted her. There was also a stale odor, as if this room had been sealed for decades. The sound of raindrops striking a window that wasn't boarded was preferable to the heavy silence that had overtaken her for those panicked moments in the dark. A quick perusal of the narrow cot, scant shelves, and unadorned bureau made Amelia figured out where she was. The servant's quarters. Wait, hadn't Nancy mentioned seeing Alvin and Kevin run this way?

Sudden movement by the window caught her eye. The narrow cot was no longer empty. The ghost of a woman was there, straining to free herself from the ropes that tied her wrists to the iron bars in the headboard. Her belly beneath the linen cloth of her nightgown was rounded from early pregnancy. The woman disappeared from view and Amelia saw a man dressed in a crimson velvet smoking jacket and silk pants standing over the bed.

"Lucy, my beautiful, stupid girl, I told you to get rid of the inconvenience, and you defied me. Did you really think I'd permit the presence of a bastard to dishonor my wife and the Raimi name?" The man's voice had an odd, tinny echo, as if Amelia was listening to him through an empty can. Lucy shook her head and tried to plead with him, but her mouth was gagged with a dirty strip of cloth.

The man untied the sash of his smoking jacket and reached for his pants, and Amelia shuddered, realizing what he was about to do. When both figures vanished from her sight, she couldn't help being relieved. But the house didn't spare her psyche so easily. The bed shook and its frame slammed against the wall in a familiar rhythmic motion.

When the bed stopped moving, the man and woman came back into view. The man had pulled his pants back up and was tying the sash closed on his smoking jacket. Lucy was motionless, eyes staring into oblivion. Amelia bet money that if the room had more light, she'd see bruises around the woman's neck.

Remembering something she'd read in the Raimi history about the cousin who inherited the mansion after Rachel Raimi had died, Amelia realized she knew who this was.

She watched Randall Raimi untie the maid's lifeless wrists and lift the body from the bed. The history said Randall had thrown out the maid in the middle of the night because she'd gotten pregnant out of wedlock. His wife, Corrine Raimi, suspected the maid had been Randall's mistress.

"But I wasn't thrown out, was I?" A voice made Amelia jump. Even though she could still see Randall carrying the maid's corpse, Lucy now stood beside her. "You need to get to the attic fast."

Amelia refused to tremble as she stared down the ghost. "The last ghosts I saw killed a man. And before that, one blew away our salt circle at the command of demons. Why should I trust you?"

"Because I'm one of those who the Raimi family and this house destroyed. If I can stop them from claiming even one of the lives of you fools who came here, I'll do it. I may be trapped here, but they have no power over me." Lucy held something out and Amelia gasped as she recognized it as Miranda's witch hat.

Lucy shoved her. "Now hurry down the hall to the right. The last door leads to the attic stairs."

Amelia needed no more encouragement. She started for the door, then paused. "Corrine killed Randall a year after you were murdered."

Lucy beamed, looking breathtakingly beautiful. "Thank you for telling me. That does warm whatever semblance of a heart I have left. Be careful. As you've observed, other ghosts are under the house's power."

Suddenly, a blinding beam of light appeared over Lucy. "I'm free," she gasped seconds before disappearing.

Although she was reeling from shock at what had just happened—did Lucy just cross over into the afterlife?—Amelia had to save Miranda from whatever danger the maid had warned about. She dashed down the hall, found the door at the end, but the knob refused to turn. So Amelia poured forth her hope and determination in a silent scream of defiance, and the doorknob yielded, turning like an oiled bearing.

She ran up the stairs, handfuls of garlic and basil ready. The attic was a vast chamber of covered furniture, stacked with dusty boxes and chests, and illuminated by a huge octagonal window that also wasn't boarded up. The wallpaper was stained and peeling, the air was redolent with the smell of mothballs and mouse droppings, and the full moon was partially obscured by clouds. Rainwater leaked from multiple parts of the roof. After a droplet fell on her head, Amelia darted to the side, scanning the area in confusion. Could Miranda be hiding in one of those big trunks? Or maybe under one of the sheets covering the furniture? Looking down at the wood floor, Amelia saw that the dust was thick enough to show footprints. Only hers were visible.

She noticed an uncovered cot in the corner and remembered Claudia and other Raimi women had been imprisoned up here for long periods of time back when the medical community believed that too much stimulation of the mind made women hysterical. She shuddered at the thought of being locked in a gloomy attic for months at a time, forbidden to read, write, or even converse with another human being. Had some of the women truly been visited by ghosts, as some of them had claimed? Or had their loneliness spawned vivid imaginings as a way to cope with their isolation?

A figure appeared in the doorway, breaking her thoughts. It was too large to be Miranda, and when the figure shambled into the beam of moonlight, Amelia's heart sank. It was Paul. Damn it, she'd hoped he'd been vanquished in the asylum. The pick from his lobotomy was still embedded in his left eye socket, blood and ichor running down his face. His sport coat was shredded from when the ghost doctors and nurses restrained him, and his white shirt beneath was soaked with blood.. Shards of glass protruded from his face and body, glimmering in the moonlight.

He leered at her, his eyes glowing a molten yellow orange. "Well, if it isn't the bitch who cockblocked Cam last month."

Amelia threw the basil at him and Paul howled in agony as the bits of the herb that reached him made his face boil with angry red blisters.

Amelia tried to pop a garlic clove in his mouth, but his hand closed around hers, squeezing it painfully until the garlic dropped from her grasp. Paul laughed, licking his blistered lips. "I could turn you into one of us with just a scratch, but Paul holds a grudge on what you did to Cam. He's also wanted to have the ice princess for himself, and I'm happy to oblige."

His free hand squeezed her breast and Amelia yelped in enraged fury. His other hand released hers to grope her further. She immediately jumped back and kicked him the balls. The demon groaned and clutched his wounded manhood, giving her a chance to get farther away. But when she tried to dodge around him, his fist swung out and punched her hip, making her stumble and fall to the floor.

Before he could launch himself on top of her, Amelia scrabbled back toward the big window. She'd rather jump through it and die than be possessed and possibly kill Guillermo or the others.

Paul stalked toward her, his leer splitting the corners of his mouth and tearing his cheeks, revealing long, sharp yellow teeth. His gore-splattered dress shirt and sport coat made him look somehow even more obscene.

She grabbed the window ledge and started to pull herself up. Maybe she could take Paul down with her.

Drool dribbled down from Paul's enlarged fanged mouth as he came nearer. "I'm going to have a lot of fun with you, ice princess. So much fu—"

Suddenly, Paul lurched forward and a woman yelled, "Duck."

Amelia reflexively obeyed, sinking down to a turtle-like huddle. Paul's shins slammed into her side before there was a loud crash of breaking glass and a demonic roar of mingled fear and fury.

When Amelia opened her eyes, she saw Miranda standing in front of her, grinning in triumph. Then, the light died from Miranda's eyes and her lower lip trembled before she collapsed on her knees and sobbed.

Amelia rushed to Miranda and threw her arms around her. "Are you okay?" A derisive laugh escaped her lips. "I mean, I know none of us are really okay, but are you at least unhurt?"

"I'm not injured, if that's what you mean. But I'm not okay." Miranda clung to her so tight it was hard to breathe. "The ghosts are so much worse that I was relieved to encounter one of these demons. And that made me feel like a monster because I just shoved Paul out of a fourth-story window and I'm happy about it."

Amelia squeezed her tighter. "It wasn't Paul anymore."

"I know, but it's hard to stay convinced of that when that thing wore his face and he's not coming back again."

"Then why were the ghosts worse?" Amelia drew back but kept her gentle grip on Miranda's shoulders, willing her to make eye contact. "They aren't anyone you knew and most can't do any damage." She paused, shivering as she remembered the asylum ghosts. Oh hell, were there more like those ones floating around?

"It's because of what they said and how they tricked me." Miranda hiccupped and wiped her streaming eyes. "They almost convinced me to kill myself. I was about to do it when I heard you scream."

"Holy shit," Amelia whispered. The house, ghosts, and demons had been tormenting her with her darkest fears and insecurities too, but none of them had tried *that* with her. Why hadn't they? Maybe because she wanted to live so badly. To die after she'd finally found the courage to live life on *her* terms and stood up to Tiffany? After at last being with the man she'd admired and desired for years? It was too unbearable to think about.

Once more, it all came back to love. Love for herself and love for Guillermo.

She straightened her spine. "We shouldn't stay in here. Alvin and Nancy and Guillermo have to be searching for us. If we make them come up here, they could be in danger."

"But what if we encounter more demons and get ourselves killed?" Miranda paused, her brown eyes lighting up. "Wait. Did you say Alvin? Have you seen him after he ran after dumbass Kevin? Is he still alive?"

"I don't know," Amelia answered honestly. "But I didn't see him among the other demons who attacked Guillermo and me in the asylum wing. So, there's hope. The evil in this house *hates* hope, which gives us more reason to hold on to it."

Miranda reached out and clasped her hands. "Finding you already restored a lot of my hope. But hearing you tell me there's a chance Alvin could still be alive? It's funny. I never really paid him much notice before, but tonight I was blown away at how brave and sweet he is. And I know this sounds completely ridiculous in these circumstances, but I'm beginning to like him a lot."

"Amelia," an aching familiar voice called from below. "Are you up here?"

The sound of Guillermo's voice made her choke back a sob of relief. She resisted the urge to run down the attic stairs and fly into his arms and instead shushed Miranda. As much as she couldn't bear to think of it, Guillermo and the others they heard could be demons now, trying to lure them out so they could claim their lives and souls.

They crept out of their hiding place, fists clenched around handfuls of basil and garlic. When they crept down the stairs and emerged on the second-floor hall, with its rose cabbage wallpaper and polished balcony rails, Amelia's shoulders slumped with relief when those brown eyes that looked back at her with joy and love were Guillermo's.

He ran to her, picking her up and spinning her in a wide circle.

"I thought I lost you," he murmured before bending down and covering her lips with his.

The nightmares momentarily vanished as she melted in his warm embrace and returned his kiss with hunger to have all of him to herself.

Someone coughed behind them and Amelia reluctantly loosened her arms around Guillermo's waist. But it took a sharp gasp from Miranda for her to fully disengage from Guillermo's embrace and turn to see what was approaching.

Alvin and Kevin stood in the hall, looking bedraggled, but still themselves. Miranda launched herself into Alvin's arms, nearly knocking him over. Amelia had to cover her mouth to hold back a giggle at how gobsmacked Alvin looked at having a gorgeous woman in his arms. Kevin scowled at the pair, perhaps feeling left out. When Cheryl told them both she was glad to see them alive, he looked placated.

Nancy didn't bother with niceties. "Did either of you happen to reach a door that leads outside?"

Kevin nodded. "We found what looked like a rear exit, but we couldn't get it to budge. We even tried to pry the boards off the windows, but it was like they were welded to the walls." He extended his fists forward, showing off his bloody knuckles.

Alvin chuckled bitterly. "Finally, you admit it. The asshole was trying to blame me. Called me a weakling. I'm no jock, but it became obvious pretty quick that the house wasn't going to allow those boards to come off."

Amelia gasped as a memory struck her. "The window in the embalming room."

Kevin's sneering gaze shifted from Alvin to her. "What about it?"

"That window wasn't boarded up. Maybe we can get out that way."

Nancy nodded. "It's worth a try."

"Yes," Guillermo's voice was infused with hope. "And at least the demons there are trapped in coffins." Before they could head toward the staircase, he held up a hand and reached into his backpack. "Before we head down there, I got something for all of you."

Amelia blinked when he handed her a squirt gun. "Is that what I think it is?"

"Yup," he answered as he handed squirt guns to Miranda, Alvin, and Paul. "Cheryl found a ten-pack of them in Gilbert's stash of goods to sell. We mixed the water with aloe and garlic juice and crumbled some sage and basil in there for good measure. We also have some water balloons."

Nancy passed them out. Amelia silently thanked the fates that more squirt guns had been found. Somewhere in the chaos, her holy water squirt gun had been cracked from either the weight of the potted aloe plant or one of the weapons from the embalming room.

She grinned up at Guillermo, studying his gorgeous features, trying to commit them to memory in case they were separated again. Her heart felt like it could burst from the intensity of her love. "You really are brilliant, you know that?"

On the way down the stairs, they encountered one demon, Kirk, who shambled toward them, carrying his severed head. He growled out a combination of gibberish and obscenities until Cheryl held him off with a jack-o-lantern and Nancy dispatched him with a water balloon, melting part of his torso into a mess of pink and greenish gunk. The head rolled away, gibbering obscenities.

The rest of the trip was uneventful as they passed through the foyer, the dining room, kitchen, and finally they entered the funeral home section of the house. Amelia eyed the coffins warily. Even though the caskets remained still and silent, she couldn't hold back a tide of unease, expecting the demons they'd trapped to burst out of the lids and attack.

When they reached the embalming room, Guillermo made a triumphant sound as he saw the window Amelia mentioned. Sure enough, the glass wasn't boarded up. The window was small, though, only about two feet wide and one foot tall. Squeezing through would be tough, but possible, and that was all that mattered.

Miranda and Cheryl wheeled a gurney below the window so they could reach it, and used a fire poker to break the glass. Nancy climbed up and used a rag she'd found in the room to pry out the remaining sharp pieces of glass from the frame.

Cheryl was the first to go, getting a boost from Nancy. Alvin offered to help her up next, but she shook her head, reaching for Miranda's hand to boost her up. Alvin wouldn't have that, and instead, he helped Miranda through the window.

Just as Amelia was hoping they'd have a smooth escape, a loud boom and sharp crack echoed from the funeral parlor, followed by roars of rage. The demons were breaking out of the coffins.

Kevin pushed past Guillermo. "Oh shit. Let me through."

Guillermo grabbed his arm and flung him back. "Fuck off, you cowardly *pendejo*. The ladies go first. Lock the door and be ready to soak those evil *hijos de putas* with the water balloons and our squirt guns."

Amelia's eyes widened. She'd never seen Guillermo so furious, nor heard him curse in Spanish. Though she'd heard him speak the language fluently when he was with his family, he'd always been so careful to speak nothing but crisp American English around his classmates and fraternity brothers.

Loud growls and pounding at the door pulled her from these thoughts she had no time to be pondering.

Kevin's eyes darted to Guillermo and his voice squeaked with terror. "We need to hurry on getting the chicks out, Romero, or we're gonna regret this chivalry bullshit."

Alvin helped Nancy out, despite her protests that she'd be better at guarding their flanks than Kevin, and while Amelia agreed, they didn't have time to argue, either. Alvin started to turn, probably to help her next, but his arms were seized by both Nancy, and another pair of hands that had to be Miranda's. In spite of her fear, Miranda smiled. There was no way Miranda was going to let her newly discovered crush out of her sight.

Then it was Amelia's turn. After she tossed her backpack out the window, Guillermo boosted her up and she squirmed through the window, wriggling like a kid finding a tight spot in a game of hide-and-seek. Her Princess Vespa gown kept catching and snagging. She winced every time she heard the fabric tear on the remnants of the glass that Nancy had missed. Guillermo's warm, strong hands grasped her thighs, helping to guide her through. She felt a tingle of pleasure at his touch and vowed that if they survived this, she'd tear off his clothes and ride him like a succubus.

How the hell could she be horny at a time like this? Maybe it was the fact that she was so close to danger and death. Some form of her mortality crying out in a primal language. The demons roared and she heard the sound of splitting wood as they broke through the door.

Then she was out in the icy October night. Rain sprinkled on her hair and clothes in a freezing shower. Mist blanketed the overgrown grass and obscured the carriage house and grounds in a thick veil. She scrambled to her feet and turned, hoping to see Guillermo's face appear next in the window. But instead, it was Kevin. Her fists clenched with fury. If his selfishness caused the death of the man she loved, she'd be tempted to kill Kevin herself. Although she considered letting him struggle his beefy form through the small space by himself, she needed him out of the way for Guillermo.

Before she could reach for him, Alvin and Miranda seized Kevin's arms and tugged him out with an ungracious hurry. Amelia darted around his prone, panting body to try to see what was happening in the embalming room, but it was too dark from outside. She heard the something in there crash to the floor and an agonized roar that hopefully meant Guillermo had incapacitated them with his herb water.

Then Guillermo's backpack thudded on the wet grass at her feet before his head emerged through the window. She crouched and offered her hand in case he needed help. Her heart pounded in terror that the demons would pull him out and tear him to pieces. But he made it all the way through and took her hand and pulled them both to their feet. He gave her a heart-stopping smile and raised her hand to his lips, kissing the back of her hand and her wrists like he truly was Gomez Addams.

For the first time since the chaos began, Amelia felt her lips curve up in a smile. Warmth flooded her panicked heart and a profound thought temporarily blanketed her awareness of the terror and carnage of the night. *It's really happened. I've fallen in love with this man.*

Love. Its previously unrealized importance for this situation came back to her in an insistent rush. She'd have to tell Guillermo what she'd discovered about the power of love against evil. Power they could have used if they'd remained trapped in the house and without other weapons.

But now they were outside and mere steps from freedom. She could tell him about love later.

And show him.

Chapter Sixteen

Guillermo clung to Amelia, warmth filling him not only from her very welcome body heat, but also from the intensity of his love for her. They'd succeeded. *Together*, they'd defeated the evil of the Raimi House and escaped its hungry clutches.

Kevin clapped Guillermo's back so hard, that not only did it hurt, but it also nearly made him slip on the wet grass and take Amelia down with him.

Oblivious to Guillermo's furious glare, Kevin grinned at them. "You two can make out in the back of Simon's van when we get past the gate. Now, let's get the hell out of here."

Much as he hated to admit it, Kevin was right—except for the part about Simon's van. He and Amelia would be going home in his own truck. As for the making out, maybe, but really, all he wanted to do right now was lie down in a safe room and hold her for the next eight hours. Reluctantly, he released Amelia and scanned their surroundings. With everything being obscured by rain and thick fog, it was impossible to see where they were, much less where the gate stood.

He turned to Amelia. "Do you know where the front of the house would be in relation to the morgue window?"

Amelia closed her eyes, a line between her eyebrows formed and her nose scrunched a little like she always did when deep in thought. She looked so cute he could kiss her again. Then her shoulders slumped and she opened her eyes. "Since it was on the north wing of the house, we'll either have to go left or right, but from here, I can't remember. We didn't even get the best tour of the house."

She looked so dejected that Guillermo tucked her under his arm again. "The worst that can happen is we'll have to double back. Now let's have a vote. Left or right?"

Amelia and Guillermo voted left, but were outnumbered by the others. Guillermo wondered if there was some truth to people instinctively preferring to follow their dominant hand.

They stayed close to the house, not wanting to get lost in the fog, but not too close in case the demons found their way out. The side of the mansion seemed endless and the chill of the rain made them burrow their necks in the collars of their coats like turtles. The only good thing was the water washed some of the demon goop and blood from their clothes. After at least five minutes of walking, they had yet to find the edge of the north wing.

"Do you think we can drink some of the herb water?" Kevin asked. "I'm gonna die of thirst."

Guilt suffused Guillermo. He'd completely forgotten to tell Amelia and the other reunited survivors that he, Cheryl, and Nancy had gotten snacks and drinks. All four of them had to be hungry and parched. And no one except Kevin had voiced a complaint.

"We need to save the water for the next demons we encounter," Guillermo told him. "But I got some beer or pop instead."

"You have beer in that backpack?" The fraternity standards officer stared at him, incredulous. "I take back everything I said about you. Except you're a bastard for not telling us sooner."

Guillermo shrugged and got a can of Coors out of his backpack for Kevin and a wine cooler for Amelia. "I didn't have time to think about it, since our main focus was getting out of that evil house."

"That's understandable." Kevin cracked the can open and slurped eagerly at the foam.

Amelia opened her wine cooler with a deep frown, and pointed at the barely visible arrangement of hedges off in the distance. "The evil isn't restricted to the house. The entire property is cursed. That area with those hedges has been everything from a croquet lawn to a topiary to a maze, and finally a giant rose garden. Bad things happened in almost every incarnation from what I've read."

That put a damper on everyone's relief. Amelia looked like she felt guilty for telling them. Guillermo took her free hand to reassure her. Further disappointment awaited when they finally reached the end corner of the north wing. When they turned the corner, sidestepping a giant puddle of mud made from rainwater pouring out of a cracked clay gutter pipe, it was obvious to all that they'd come to the back of the house, not the front. Barely visible through the fog stood a forest of pine trees. Amelia explained how these had been replanted by Claudia Raimi in an attempt to appease the spirits of the tribespeople whose sacred burial grounds and forest had been stolen then clear-cut by the Army to build their accursed fort.

Nancy made a snide sound as they turned back around to head to the front of the house. "They definitely weren't appeased."

Amelia sighed. "Nor are the spirits of the army troops who vanished from here."

Cheryl whimpered. "Can you *please* stop telling us these creepy stories? I'm scared enough as it is."

"Sure." Amelia squeezed Guillermo's hand. "I'm sorry."

They walked in silence for the rest of the way. Guillermo was dying to know where Amelia had gone when the house took her away, how she'd found Miranda, and if she'd suffered during the time they'd been separated.

As they rounded the corner of the house and saw the pillars of the covered porch, he sighed in relief. From this direction, it should be a straight shot to the gate and then their vehicles.

"Why were you planning to take Simon's van, anyway?" he asked Kevin. "Doesn't he still have the keys? And what about your truck?"

"I figured we can fit more people in the van. As for Simon..." Kevin shook his head, a rare expression of grief flashing across his normally cold features. "I overheard Paul saying he didn't want Kirk or Susan taking off with his keys again, so he stuck 'em in the visor. Man, when we get out of here, I'm gonna take us straight to Denny's, get a Triple Grand Slam breakfast to go."

Cheryl cleared her throat. "I'll buy breakfast for *all* of us. And after that, we can flip coins for who gets a shower first."

Miranda spoke up in a shaky voice. "Aren't we going to have to talk to the police first?"

Nancy sighed. "Yeah, we probably should. But I don't know if they'll believe us about what happened."

"I think they might." Amelia released Guillermo's hand to wipe raindrops from her forehead. "Or at least, the old-timers will."

"They came by the Alpha and Pi houses to talk to Susan and Kirk," Cheryl said matter-of-factly, as if that settled the argument. "To try to talk them out of having the party there."

Guillermo blinked at her. *The cops had paid a visit in advance?* "When was that?"

"Right after that opinion piece in the paper ran about us renting the place." She looked down at the wet grass, her voice abashed. "They warned them that they'd had an entire file cabinet full of homicides and unsolved deaths and disappearances and that if anything happened to any of us, there probably wasn't anything they could do about it."

He gaped at her in astonished disbelief. It was one thing for Kirk and Susan to have heard stories about the Raimi House being a scary place, but for the police department to warn them in person about how dangerous the place was known to be was an entirely different matter. "And they *still* went through with this disaster of an initiation?"

"Hey," Alvin interrupted their argument. "I think I see the gate."

Sure enough, Guillermo could see the rusted black bars ahead. He could barely make them out through the thick fog, but they were *there*. Elation sped up his steps, and before he knew it, everyone was jogging toward the gate.

But the closer they got, the farther away it seemed. Then the view changed, and they seemed to be approaching something larger, with more mass. Something about it filled him with growing dread.

Amelia recognized what they were nearing before he did and skidded to a stop. "Oh no."

Guillermo almost slipped on the wet grass as he tried to halt beside her. He cursed his dress shoes.

Somehow, they'd been jogging back toward the Raimi House. The fog parted, and so did the clouds, to reveal the un-boarded windows of the upper floors reflecting the moonlight, making them look like eyes staring at them with wicked avarice. The front door under the shadowed porch resembled a gaping mouth waiting to devour them.

"What the fuck?" Kevin yelled. "How'd you losers get us turned around?"

They turned back and tried to get to the gate instead, but every time the gate began to come into view, the fog would part and they'd find themselves nearing the house again.

"It's the house," Amelia explained to Kevin like he was five. "It's not going to let us leave."

"So that's it then?" Alvin panted with breathless frustration. "We just go back in and feed ourselves to it?"

"Fuck no," Amelia growled. "Maybe all the property isn't gated. We might find a way through the forest to a road, or find a point far enough from the house that its influence can't turn us back around."

Nancy shot Amelia a grateful look and patted her arm. "I'm glad you think there's still options. Even if they don't work, there's no way I'm setting foot back in that house."

"I agree," Guillermo told her. "Let's try the woods. There's supposed to be a road back there. If the physics of this place actually followed the rules, it should be only fifty feet from where we are. Of course, we already know it won't, but we have to reach the road sometime."

They followed the north end of the house for the third time, this attempt purposefully aiming for the forest behind the house. The fog remained thick, and Guillermo silently prayed that the edges of the trees wouldn't turn into a view of the rear of the house. Though the back doors had refused to open from the inside, he was certain they'd open from the outside. And once inside, they'd never be let out again.

As they neared the edges of the trees, hope tightened his chest, and when they made it under the shelter of the boughs of the Douglas firs and white pines, he heard audible sighs of relief from everyone aside from Amelia. Her shoulders remained tense, her eyes vigilantly darting all around, surveying the forest for any hints of a threat.

Guillermo's relief abated when he heard what sounded like sinister whispering all above them. Before he could wonder if it was his imagination, Miranda edged closer to Amelia. "Do you guys hear that? It sounded like someone's laughing at us."

"I hear it too," Cheryl said, while Nancy nodded.

Kevin scoffed and swept them with derisive glares. "You all are acting like a bunch of pansies. The noise is just the wind through the trees. Anyone who's ever camped would know that."

Guillermo shook his head. He'd been in Scouts and camped plenty. Never had he heard trees making such sounds. He opened his mouth to say so, but then Kevin yelped and was jerked backward.

At first, everyone was frozen, baffled. No demons were in view, so what grabbed Kevin? Then, a wooden groan answered the question right before Guillermo's flashlight beam found what held Kevin in its clutches.

A tree branch?

No, several tree branches. The little green needles of the fir looked like feathers, partially obscuring the reddish-brown bark that now defied physics, twisting around Kevin's waist and his right leg. Kevin was screaming now, but this stopped when another branch thrust into his mouth. The muffled gags and wails of pain made Guillermo flinch.

Amelia's voice pulled him from his paralyzed stupor. "Get away from the trees!"

Guillermo lunged backward just as a branch slithered across his cheek like a monstrous snake. A woman screamed behind him, and he twisted back to help Miranda, who'd been seized by the silvery limbs of a white pine. Pulling out his squirt gun, he fired the aloe and garlic water, but it did nothing. With Amelia's and Alvin's help, they worked Miranda free. Her black witch robe tore from the branches they'd pulled her from and the raw scrapes on her arm looked like road rash.

They ran out of reach of the grasping branches, gasping in terror. There was nothing to be done for Kevin, though once they were out of danger, Guillermo and the others all stood in a line and watched, as if their consciences demanded they bear witness.

Kevin continued to kick and flail until branches coiled around his arms and free leg. His muffled cries intensified, then abruptly ceased as the trees tore him apart, splitting him like firewood. The sound was a horrific wet rip with shotgun cracks as his bones snapped. Blood burst out in every direction, making a crimson rain patter down on the nearby trees. The moss and pine needle-carpeted forest floor drank down the blood like the marble floor of the Raimi House.

A drop of the hot liquid landed on Guillermo's right eyelashes. For a moment, his vision was consumed in a haze of fiery red. Although he'd been splattered with demon blood and guts, the heat and sticky wetness of the little red droplet made him want to fall to his knees and scream.

Only the warm, hard grip of Amelia's hand tugging on him made him wipe his eye and run with her and the others.

When they got back to the house's back lawn, Guillermo looked up at the cloudy sky. Was the horizon starting to turn gray to the east, or was that only the still-bright full moon reflecting off the clouds? It felt like the nightmare had begun twenty hours ago. But what if time worked different here? What if it had only been four hours? No, it had to be longer than that. At least it had stopped raining sometime during their futile attempts to reach the gate.

"I don't suppose any of you have a watch?" He felt like an idiot for not asking sooner. At least now was the perfect time to bring up something that had been plaguing his mind for hours. Best to talk about anything other than what happened to Kevin.

Alvin spoke up in a grateful tone, extending his arm to show a fancy gold watch on a leather band. "I do, but it stopped working sometime after eight tonight. Could be the house, or it could be that I forgot to wind it."

"It's the house," Miranda said with full confidence. "Don't you remember when you pledges had cleaning duty for the first floor and those couple bedrooms? Rebecca told me that even though there were two clocks in the great room, one in the foyer, one in the dining room, and one in the kitchen, not a single one of them worked. I thought that was creepy as hell, just hearing about it. Don't you or Amelia remember?"

Guillermo hadn't noticed, even when he'd dusted the clock on top of the mantel in the great room. Someone else had been responsible for the huge grandfather clocks in the dining room and the foyer.

Amelia, on the other hand, nodded with a gleam of remembrance. "I did think it was odd that it was so quiet in the house. And while I cleaned the kitchen clocks myself, it didn't even occur to me that I'd expected to hear them ticking. I guess I figured the caretaker hadn't bothered to wind them."

Cheryl interrupted them impatiently. "Are you guys trying to figure out when the sun's supposed to come up?"

Guillermo nodded. "If the legends are true that Halloween is the one night evil spirits can roam freely, then maybe at dawn the power of this place will be reduced enough that we can get out of here. At the very least, we hope it means the demons will be gone."

Amelia stopped him with a gentle touch on his wrist. "Look, it's the guest-house."

Miranda started to head toward the dilapidated Victorian cottage with a sagging covered porch and boarded-up windows. "Do you think it will be safe for us to hide out in until sunrise?"

"I don't think anywhere is safe. I read about some tragedies in the guesthouse too, so even if there aren't any demons, which is a big if, there are most definitely some angry ghosts." Amelia's voice was sullen and tired. "But if we don't find a way off these grounds, it could be our best option."

For some reason, Cheryl and the others looked to Guillermo as if expecting him to have final say. He gave Amelia a brisk nod. "I say we avoid the house for now. The last thing we want is to set foot in another trap."

They continued on, moving southwest and close to the edges of the mist.

When they managed to walk farther without being obscured by the fog, a seed of hope sprouted in his being. Was there a weakness in the evil barrier? A familiar sound reached his ears, making his heart beat faster in spite of the sound's normally soothing rhythm. "Stop for a sec. Listen."

With the halting of their footsteps, he was able to hear the sound better; longing filled him, along with a long-missed sense of direction.

Amelia's small gasp of delight gave him a pleasant shiver. "Is that the lake?"

"I think so." Guillermo's voice sped up with excitement. "Bodies of water were mentioned a lot in those occult books we read. Things needing to be cleansed in a lake or stream, vampires and other creatures being unable to cross running water. Maybe the lake is exuding its own power that interferes with the barrier of the Raimi land."

He and Amelia started toward the sound until Nancy's shout stopped them.

"Wait. If we're on the part of the property that faces the lake, that means we're headed toward a cliff."

Guillermo slowed his steps, disappointment creeping in to wage war with his hope. She was right. That's why there wasn't a gate here. After a few more steps, the fog completely dissipated.

And that's when he saw that the tips of his shoes were inches from the precipice. His stomach dropped, but he resisted the urge to step back. He'd spent hours on tall ladders, scaffolds, and roofs of lake houses, where one stumble would have him falling down to break his skull on wave-swept rocks below.

This cliff wasn't straight above Lake Skeetshue, though. If it had been, he'd be tempted to take a running jump and hope to land in water deep enough not to kill him. No, instead what lay below was the black asphalt of Lakeview Drive, limned in silvery moonlight. The Raimis' private beach and rotting dock across the road were somewhat obscured by tall pines, but from this height, he could see the glittering waves of the lake, and even lights off in the distance from possibly a boat or houses across the lake.

Amelia's hopeful voice broke through his study of the refreshing, tempting view of the outside world. "Do you think we can climb down?"

"I'm not sure yet." He sank to a crouch and pulled his flashlight from his backpack. Then he lay down on his stomach, wincing as the wetness from the grass seeped into his coat and Gomez suit. The rain earlier had rinsed out his hair gel, making his long, damp curls fall into his face. He leaned his head over the edge and shined his flashlight across the cliffside, examining the mixture of mossy rock and straight, angular basalt columns that framed the road below. Every surface looked slick with few handholds that looked precarious as hell. There were some exposed tree roots a few yards to his right, where some trees framed the cemetery, and even a few intrepid bushes sprouting out of the earthier sections between the basalt, but he wasn't optimistic.

He scrambled back up to feet. "I don't think we should risk it. That's at least a seventy-foot drop—maybe even a hundred—that could easily have one or all of us splattered onto the road. It's probably best to wait it out until sunrise."

"Hey." Miranda stepped forward with an oddly optimistic tone in the face of his fatalistic analysis of the situation. "What if we shout for help? Someone might be out on a boat on the lake, and sound carries over it well. Or maybe a car or morning jogger comes down the road."

Cheryl gave a pessimistic shake of her head. "It's still pitch black out, with the moon high, and it's freezing out here. I doubt even the biggest fitness junkies like James Bonner would be jogging out here at this hour."

Amelia gave her a sympathetic look, acknowledging the pain in her voice when she brought up James. "It's still worth a try."

They yelled together for what felt like an hour, first together in a chorus, then in shifts, taking turns while the others recovered their voices. Then they soothed their sore throats with Guillermo's dwindling supply of beer and pop. They were freezing from standing in range of the chill wind blowing from the lake and their throats too raw to keep yelling.

"It's hopeless," Alvin croaked, his voice hoarse. "We're going to have to get out of this wind and start moving again to warm up. It would be incredibly shitty if we died of hypothermia."

Guillermo nodded, rubbing his hands together to keep his fingers from going numb. They backed away from the cliff and circled back to heading northward. Guillermo put his arm around Amelia's waist, pulling her against him to warm her. It made walking more awkward and slow, but he noticed Miranda and Alvin had done the same, keeping pace with them. Cheryl and Nancy exchanged shy glances before slipping into the same walking embrace.

Soon, they were walking in a huddle to gain body heat.

Alvin managed a genuine laugh, his breath puffing out in clouds of steam in the chill air. "I feel like we're a herd of penguins."

"Wouldn't that be a flock?" Miranda asked.

"I don't think so. They can't fly." Alvin shrugged. "I guess I don't know what term is used for a group of penguins."

Cheryl laughed next. "They're called a waddle. I remember that from zoology class."

Amelia chuckled. "Like we're pretty much doing now."

Everyone had a good giggle over that fitting trivia, until they reached the Raimi cemetery. The laughter died as quickly as new blooms after a frost.

Miranda groaned. "The last place I want to be right now is in a graveyard."

Nancy scoffed. "It's the safest place we could be. Everyone here is dead and buried."

"That's a good point." Guillermo spoke in a calm tone to remind them all that they were on the same side. "But it sucks that we've almost come full circle."

Nancy nodded. "Maybe we'll be fine walking the perimeter until sunup. As long as we stay away from those killer trees in the back."

Suddenly, the ground trembled under their feet. Guillermo shifted his weight and pulled Amelia tighter against him, steadying her before she could stumble.

"What the fuck?" Amelia growled, then broke off as a scream pierced the night.

A skeletal hand was curled around Cheryl's ankle. Nancy pulled her free, but the earth continued to rumble as bodies and skeletons of the dead crawled out of their graves.

Chapter Seventeen

Amelia stared in horror as the animated corpses emerged from their earthen beds and turned their malicious eye sockets toward them. "Oh shit, run!"

But everyone else was already ahead of her, fleeing from the cemetery. When Amelia caught up with Guillermo, Miranda, and Alvin, she almost ran into their backs as the trio halted abruptly with startled yelps. Nancy and Cheryl charged over to join the fray. Amelia looked over Miranda's shoulder and saw the source of their terror: Paul, the demon Miranda had shoved out of the attic window, was shambling toward them, his head resting on his shoulder and his leg bent oddly, making him limp. His caved-in face still managed a leer as his remaining glowing eye raked over Amelia and Miranda.

"You can't keep a good man down," he rasped as black blood trickled down his chin like drool.

The group turned away from him, only to see that the zombies had fanned out behind them, closing in. Nancy aimed a squirt gun at Paul, spraying him in rapid, but ever-weakening bursts. The demon winced and growled in pain, but he kept coming. She continued spraying him, and Alvin and Guillermo joined in, but the meager spray did little to slow Paul down.

Amelia turned to spray the skeletal corpses. Her eyes watered at the ripe rot of the ones with scraps of flesh remaining on their bones, but she still saw clearly that the herb and garlic water seemed to have even less of an effect, barely making them cringe.

A cry made her turn around to see Cheryl struggling against Paul's hold on her wrist. Guillermo tossed a balloon of herb water on the demon, making him yelp. Cheryl slipped out of Paul's grasp, but her momentum propelled her right into the zombies. They fell on her like a pack of ravenous vultures, biting and tearing into her exposed skin. Her screams were muffled as blood and chunks of flesh flew out in different directions, leaving no hope for her survival.

Paul remained undefeated, though the uncrushed half of his face appeared to be melting. Flesh bubbled and slid down his forehead and left cheek to expose stark white bone. He lunged for Guillermo, but Amelia shoved Paul away with all her strength. Searing pain sliced through her upper arm, as the demon's claws grazed her before he fell on his back.

She saw Nancy, Alvin, and Miranda being surrounded by zombies with bits of Cheryl's skin and hair dangling from their teeth and fingernails. They were corralling them back into the house. Amelia tried to call out a warning, but Guillermo grabbed her and pulled her in the opposite direction toward the guesthouse.

"We can't leave them," she protested.

Guillermo shook his head brusquely and kept tugging her away. "Paul and the zombies block us from reaching them. And I'm not about to lose you. Not even at the cost of their lives. Besides, Nancy is tough. She'll be able to keep Alvin and Miranda safe. Hell, those two have been good enough at surviving on their own."

His words made her feel a little better, but still, guilt roiled in her stomach for not making more of an effort to help her friends.

Friends. The word echoed profoundly in her mind. In one night, Nancy, Miranda, Alvin, and even Cheryl had listened to her more than Tiffany ever had. Tiffany's so-called help was only for shallow things, like making Amelia popular in school, getting her on the dance team, and into a sorority she never wanted to join in the first place. And all the things Tiffany had done for Amelia came with a price. That price almost always being things Amelia didn't want to do.

Too bad such clarity in what friendship really was, and what it was like to truly not be lonely had come to her so late in her life.

When they reached the decrepit cottage, the stairs groaned and the porch felt spongy beneath her feet. Amelia half expected the front door to be locked, but its rusted hinges and swollen frame opened with only a little bit of straining from Guillermo.

Guillermo swept the area with the beam of his flashlight in search of demons or ghouls lying in wait. Only an empty foyer leading into a dining room with a sheet-covered table and chairs greeted their initial inspection. The scent of mildew and mothballs hung heavy in the stale air. Meager light streamed in between the cracks of a boarded-up picture window straight ahead.

As Amelia stood shivering in the little foyer, Guillermo placed his hand on her shoulder, making her jump. "I'm going to check the gaps between the boards on the windows and see if Paul or those walking corpses are coming this way. We should probably barricade ourselves in too."

Confused at her reaction to his touch, Amelia struggled to think straight. "What if Nancy and the others make it here?"

"Then we'll remove the barricade and hope there's enough time for them to be able to get inside."

She rubbed her arms, flinching at the sting on her right bicep where Paul had scratched her, barely able to make her legs move to follow him into the cozy living room. Why did she feel so cold and numb? It had to be a few degrees warmer in here than outside, given that the house created a shelter from the chill wind.

And why did her legs feel so leaden? Sure, she'd done a lot of running from demons this night, but something about the way her muscles were refusing to cooperate made her feel there was more to her body's protests.

The sound of Guillermo's voice comforted her even before she processed his words. "I don't see anyone coming near the house. Let's move the kitchen table to block the door and then—" He broke off as he noticed her trembling. "Okay, first we need to warm you up. Let's get you settled on the loveseat and I'll make a fire."

He yanked the sheet off the loveseat and shook off the dust. After a couple sharp sneezes, he took the knitted afghan off the threadbare gray cushions and walked over to Amelia, his eyes full of caring concern. As he settled the little blanket over her shoulders and kissed her forehead, her heart warmed with love at his affection and consideration. And yet, something inside recoiled.

Watching Guillermo take wood from the box beside the hearth and stack them in the fireplace, Amelia's heart warred with her gut. She loved him so much, but some unidentified fury surged from her belly. An uncomfortable tingling sensation began to crawl over her, making her skin feel like it was covered with insects.

She opened her mouth, needing to fill the hollow silence before she went insane. "Remember how Mike turned into an old school bully of yours?"

"Gerald Duke." Guillermo spat the name and struck his lighter to the kindling. "His dad was one of the leaders of the Aryan Brotherhood, and by high school, he followed in his dad's footsteps. The guy had bullied me on and off from grade school to high school. And one day in eighth grade, he and a bunch of older Aryan kids from the high school waited for me at the bus stop that was a mile from my house."

"Over by the base of Northrup Mountain," Amelia said, *seeing* the area clear in her mind, even though she'd only been there a couple times. "Where it's wooded and marshy."

"Yeah." He gave her an odd look before turning his attention back to the fire. "They hoped to chase me into the woods and hang me with the rope one of them carried, or maybe beat me to death with one of the bats the others had, but I ran toward the houses instead. It wasn't a long chase, and I made it to a neighbor's, but I was still afraid because they really meant to kill me. They meant it with every ounce of their being. I got rides from my parents or friends from then until I got my own car."

Amelia had a vision of Guillermo's parents shouting at a police officer on their doorstep; the cop smirked and shrugged as he doodled on the pad where he pretended to take notes. His little sister had told him about the doodling later on. "And the cops didn't do anything about them?"

"Nope." Her outraged tone made him turn back around. "But how did you know my parents called the cops? And where my bus stop was?"

Before she could answer, she was overcome by a barrage of Guillermo's memories. Of him being little and putting on a brave face as Gerald Duke taunted him for the color of his skin, of crying in his mother's arms when he was safe from the world seeing him. His parents giving him conflicting advice. Mom telling him to be proud of his heritage. Dad telling him to hide it and act like he belonged.

"Bigoted bullies like Gerald aren't the ones you have to worry about. At least you know where you stand with them. It's the people

who smile and act nice to your face and then say those words behind your back and hold you back from opportunities..."

Some horrific thing inside her tried to speak through her, tell him that he would never belong, that he would never be good enough, and that if he ever acted on his secret dream of meeting his relatives in Mexico, they'd slam the door in his face.

The voice reminded her of Tiffany.

By the time Guillermo had the logs burning in the fireplace and warmth filling the room, Amelia was writhing in agony. What was happening to her? When her arm began to burn with acidic fury, she knew the answer.

"Guillermo," her voice emerged a pitiful whimper. "You need to get out of here."

He turned to her, mouth gaping in wounded shock. "Why?"

"Because of this." She removed her suede coat and showed him the long, ugly scratch on her arm. Its edges puckered an ugly red as if the wound was infected. Wait. It *was* infected. And no antibiotics could fight this infection. "Paul scratched me. That means I'm going to turn into one of them. I..." her voice broke with a hitching sob, "I can already feel the evil inside me, trying to take me over, trying to make me say hateful things to you. Soon it will make me hurt you."

Instead of running away like a smart man should, Guillermo sat on the loveseat beside her. "I am not leaving you. We're going to banish this evil before it takes root." He cupped her cheek with his hand, warm from the fire. "You're the one who knew the answer."

"I had a theory," she started, then her throat closed, making her wheeze for breath. The sensations of ants crawling all over and biting her intensified.

He took her hand and leaned forward; his voice was soft as velvet. "Love is the key, isn't it?"

The demon roared and seemed to strangle her from the inside.. Somehow, she forced the words out. "The Sazerac house had an evil spirit inside it that was removed. Jason Shaye is pretty sure that the love his sister had for her boyfriend had something to do with the banishment. That, and cats."

"Cats?" he echoed skeptically.

Her voice held the demon's edge of scorn, but at least she could still control her words. "Yeah, which does us no good because we don't have any. And I really wish the books and diary I read would have mentioned if any of the Raimi family members ever had cats."

Oh shit. Did the demon let her keep talking to make her stall Guillermo, or distract him from using his love to save her?

"Give me a piece of garlic." Her demand emerged in choking bursts.

"What if you explode?"

"I'm still me, barely, so I think we'll be okay."

Guillermo eyed her warily as he dug into his backpack. "I'm down to my last clove."

After he brushed off some fuzz that had stuck to the garlic, Amelia seized it from him and popped it in her mouth before the demon could stop her. She used its fury to chomp up the piece, her tongue burning and her eyes watering, as if he'd given her a habanero instead.

But the demon didn't go away so easily. Her stomach lurched with nausea, and she gagged, but shook her head, refusing to let the garlic come back up. Her back bowed as she contorted in agony, fighting the demon's will to control her.

Guillermo gasped, edging farther away from her. "Your eyes, they keep flashing green and yellow."

"Get more garlic from my bag," she growled, then winced at the underlay of the demon's voice beneath her own.

"Not yet." He shook his head and reached into his bag instead. "I want to try something else first."

He pulled out two of his saint candles and lit both. St. Agrippina and *Santa Muerte.* Amelia remembered him saying that Agrippina was supposed to protect against evil spirits, but had forgotten why the Lady of Death would be useful.

"I thought religious icons were *uselessss,*" she said, wincing as her voice changed to a hiss. Did that mean the demon was wary of the candles?

"I'm not lighting these for religious reasons. I'm lighting them in honor of my grandma. To feel closer to her. Any time my family and I was sick or she thought we were in danger, she lit candles for Agrippina to drive away any evil spirits, and candles for *Santa Muerte* to keep death from stealing a life before its time." He glared at Amelia, no, at the demon, and continued. "I may not believe in God or saints, but I do believe in the power of my grandma's love—

" his gaze changed so Amelia could feel his contact with her— "which I extend to you."

After placing the candles on the dusty end tables, Guillermo returned to the loveseat and pulled Amelia into his arms.

"I love you," he murmured into her hair, making her scalp tingle pleasurably. "And I know you love me. Say it, Amelia."

The demon's growl rumbled in her throat. Her nerves twitched with the urge to curl her fingers into claws. Amelia looked at Guillermo's grandma's candle, then closed her eyes and focused on the feel of his arms around her, the firmness of his chest. She soaked in the warmth of his embrace and fought for control of her voice.

"I love you," her voice rasped, and it was *hers*, not the demon's. Its voice was still inside her; she could hear it screaming, but the sound seemed farther away. She tried to repeat those three magical words, but her throat closed again and she whimpered.

"It's okay." Guillermo kissed the top of her head and rocked her. "Concentrate on us. Know that I loved you even before we first made love and that—"

"*No.*" The demon shoved him back, but deceptively used Amelia's voice as she shrank in dread. "You only wanted to get in my pants. And since I went to bed with you so fast, the thrill and the challenge is gone for you and you've lost all respect. The only reason you're trying to help me now is because you feel guilty for your puppy-love dying off the second you made me cum. Now you think I'm a slut. Admit it."

Guillermo's hand clenched in a fist, and Amelia heard the demon cackle in silent triumph. Then he grabbed a crocheted doily from one of the end tables and, keeping a steady eye on her, bent down and got the embalming fluid pump from his backpack. He squirted some water from the pump and reached toward her.

Amelia's demon tried to scramble away, but the loveseat was small and her back slammed into its arm while Guillermo straddled her. Seeing his heated expression and feeling him pinning her made her body stir with arousal. Weirdly, the lust put her back on top in her battle with the demon. Before she could reach up to touch him, or arch her hips beneath him, anything to get closer to him, he spoke in a soft tone that soothed the prickling sensation on her skin.

"I know that's the demon talking, not you." With gentle care, he pressed the damp doily to her forehead, like he was tending a fever.

She detected the scent of aloe, along with more garlic, and other herbs. Her skin stopped burning, but the demon recoiled within, not ready to give up.

Guillermo continued to stroke her forehead and her cheeks with the cool cloth. He spoke softly, but with conviction that forbade her or the demon to dispute. "I don't think anything less of you after we made love. And it *didn't* happen too soon. For one thing, think about how long you've known me, how long we've been friends, and know that I would have done *anything* for you if you'd ever asked. And while I can't say there wasn't a time that I *didn't* want you in my bed, I swear on my grandmother's soul that the first thing that always matters to me is your happiness." He lowered his head, his damp curls stroking her cheeks. "The love we share is real. When love is real, nothing is ever too soon."

Then he sealed his words with a kiss that sent poignant warmth cascading through her body, drowning the demon with tenderness and passion. She kissed him back, her love for him pouring forth, breaking the dam the evil tried to build inside her.

"Make love to me," she whispered, ignoring the demon's roar of protest. "I need to feel you close."

"Are you sure that's a good idea?" His full pouting lips and the quirk of worry in his brows made him look all the more desirable.

She pulled him down on top of her, needing to feel him in her arms, his body against hers. "I love you, Guillermo Romero. So much that the intensity of my love is too powerful and too large to leave any room in my heart and mind for this pathetic demon. And it knows it."

The demon raged within her again, but she beat it further back by kissing Guillermo again, focusing her mind on the years of deep yearning she'd felt every time she was around him, but had been unable to voice. Then she reveled in the bliss she felt at their first kiss, bliss that transformed to irrepressible joy at learning that he felt the same about her. The joy now mingled with potent desire as she felt his hardness pressing to her hot center between the fabric of their costumes.

When she slipped her hand between their chests to reach for the buttons on his suit jacket, Guillermo seized her fingers and raised her hand to kiss her knuckles before shaking his head. "We should keep our clothes on in case..."

Then he sat up and unzipped his pants, and with some maneuvering, brought out his impressive erection. Amelia became hyperaware of her own arousal as she lifted the skirt and petticoat under her dress before straddling him. A sigh escaped her lips at how right he felt between her thighs.

Too late, she realized she'd forgotten to remove her underwear. Her little awkward laugh made the demon recoil. *Interesting.* Did any expression of happiness or humor repel these things?

"What's funny?" Guillermo asked, his voice husky with desire.

Amelia reveled in his wanting her and giggled again. "I forgot to take off my panties."

"Oh?" Now his voice sounded seductive. He gave her an equally sensuous smile before reaching under her dress and stroking her across the thin, hot satin barrier.

She gasped at the delicious sensation and arched her pelvis against his hand.

Guillermo's lips caressed her ear as he whispered, "God, you are *so* wet." Then his fingers moved her panties to the side and she felt the core of her arousal come into contact with his firm heat. "I love you, Amelia Craven," he whispered before guiding his tip to her entrance.

Amelia moaned in ecstasy as she slowly sank down, taking him inside her inch by breathtaking inch. For the moment, the rest of the world vanished and she felt like she and Guillermo were the only ones in this room. She rode him in a slow, hypnotic rhythm that sent her senses spiraling with growing bliss.

Suddenly, her insides burned and prickled again before the demon roared from her mouth. "No. The slut is mine."

Amelia shook her head, struggling for control as the evil within tried to disengage her from her lover's embrace. Weak whimpers escaped her. She took deep breaths and battled to remain with Guillermo, fought to keep her sense of self.

Thankfully, he didn't mistake her struggles for wanting to end their lovemaking. His hands stopped their teasing caresses and moved to steady her, securing their joined embrace.

"Stay with me, Amelia." Guillermo held her tight against him with one arm around her waist, and the other tangled in her hair, holding her so they were face-to-face. "Feel our bodies becoming one. The demon can't have you. You're mine."

"Yes," she gasped as she clung to him, her hips bucking against his, taking him in harder and deeper. "I love you," she repeated over and over, only stopping the mantra to kiss him again and again.

He echoed those magical, heartfelt words back to her as he matched her rhythm, moving in tandem with her in an eternal dance.

The demon's flame was quenched by the inferno of pleasure, the fires of Amelia's passion purifying her from the inside, then melding her to Guillermo until she truly felt like their joined bodies had become one sublime being.

She writhed against him as her ecstasy climbed higher, ascending an impossible peak. Guillermo matched her frenetic, seeking pace, thrusting into her harder, bringing electric pulses of pleasure that made her cry out in primal satisfaction.

Her orgasm multiplied, making black and white spots dance in her vision. She felt like she was touching heaven; no moment could be as cataclysmic as this. As her climax reached its highest peak and tumbled over the precipice in deep, shuddering waves, Amelia screamed in ecstasy.

The demon screamed in agony as it left her body, banished by the power of the love she and Guillermo shared.

Amelia could still feel the throbbing pulses of tapering pleasure when Guillermo lifted her from his lap and laid her on the loveseat. Then the world went dark.

Chapter Eighteen

Guillermo breathed a sigh of relief that he remembered to pull out. Although expressing their love physically seemed to repel the demon, and hopefully drove it out, he didn't want to get Amelia pregnant. Aside from neither of them being ready for such a thing in normal circumstances, he had a gut feeling it'd be a bad idea for a woman to conceive a child anywhere near the Raimi estate.

After using another doily to clean up, he glanced over at Amelia. At first, it looked like she was basking in the afterglow, but when her eyes didn't open, his heart clenched with worry. Had the demon decided if it couldn't have her, no one could? Had the power used to expel the demon been too much and killed her?

Tentatively, he placed his hand above her breasts and felt a strong heartbeat beneath his palm, as well as the gentle rise and fall of her breath.

He opened his mouth to speak her name, but then she made a soft murmur and her eyelashes fluttered, on the verge of waking.

Guillermo froze in panic. Would those eyes be blue or yellow?

Amelia's beautiful long lashes fluttered and lifted to frame the pale sapphire eyes that never failed to steal his breath. Guillermo's heart leaped in joy as he bent and scooped her up in his arms.

"How do you feel?" he asked as he rocked her gently. "Are you...you know...*you* again?"

Her voice came out husky, probably from the combination of battling the demon and their cataclysmic lovemaking. "I think so. The only thing I'm sure of is that we need to get out of here and off this property."

"We tried that. There is no way off the property." Hopelessness threatened to crush him as he struggled to keep speaking. "You saw how it turned out. We lost two, maybe four more people and the only benefit we got was finding this guesthouse. Why *can't* we stay here until sunrise?"

"Because I feel like the demon can come back and get inside me again if we don't get past the barrier soon. And aside from that, the main house isn't the only place where terrible things have happened. I remember reading about the time that Helen Raimi's Uncle Bill lived here and they found out that he'd been bringing prostitutes from Wallace up here to torture and kill them. I can feel the remnants of that evil still staining the walls of this place." Amelia reached for his hand as she continued. "And there is a way out of here. We need to get down the cliff. I know it's fucking dangerous, but it's our only chance."

Looking at her bright eyes, full of hope, Guillermo found it nearly impossible to reiterate the painful truth. "Amelia, the cliff is too sheer. There aren't enough handholds. It's impossible for us to climb down."

"Not if we have a rope."

A flicker of hope lit within, then died. "We don't have any rope. Come to think of it, we were kinda dumb not to pack any. Rope is always useful."

Amelia smiled and lifted the corner of the sheet covering the loveseat. "We can make one. There are sheets everywhere in this place."

"God, you're so smart. I love you." He kissed her deeply before reluctantly releasing her and getting off the sofa to get to work.

Together, they went through the house, pulling sheets from tables, wardrobes, beds, and dressers. The furniture they uncovered was more scarred and threadbare than in the main house. The whole place was in a state of rot that made him nervous about the structural integrity. Black mold creeped down the corners of some ceilings and coated the bathroom. In one room mushrooms grew out of the walls. They also found rusty shackles bolted to the walls above a bed with a stained mattress. They put that sheet back over the creepy bed, unable to handle the idea of using it to make their rope.

Constructing the rope wasn't that difficult, but it was monotonous to twist each sheet and tie knots at regular intervals. The biggest challenge was connecting each sheet-rope to the other. Guillermo did his best to make sure those knots were tight and silently prayed they'd hold.

Amelia worked beside him, twisting and knotting. "My mouth still tastes like garlic. How could you stand kissing me while we...you know...?"

He chuckled at her sudden shyness. "I love garlic. The added basil flavor made you even more delicious. And anyway, it really didn't register, given the circumstances. What I can't believe is that we drove a demon out of you by having sex."

Her blush was visible even in the firelight when she giggled. "We could call it a sexorcism."

"Sounds like a good band name." Guillermo shook his head at how crazy this night had been. "What happened wasn't exactly what I had in mind to get that thing out of you, but it worked and I can't say I didn't enjoy it. There was something different about it from our first time. Like...it had a sense of power to it." Now his face felt hot. He shut up and went back to tying another knot.

"I know what you mean. It was...transcendental," Amelia breathed. She quieted a moment to tie another knot before looking back up at him. "What *did* you have in mind for driving out the demon?"

He lifted a brow and forced a warning tone. "Promise not to laugh."

"I promise." She put her hand over her heart to emphasize her sincerity.

"I'd been thinking of the *Care Bears* movies my younger cousins love to watch when they visit for sleepovers with *Abuela*." He sneaked a glance at Amelia to make sure she wasn't on the verge of laughter. "In several scenes, they drove off evil spirits, and even did a sort of exorcism by joining hands and chanting that they cared. And though I can't shoot rainbows or beams of light from my belly, I could hold you and tell you how much I love you."

Instead of mocking him, she scooted closer and put her hands on his shoulders. "That *was* effective, the demon was in agony every time you said it and every time we kissed. But it also didn't like when I got turned on by you being on top of me, so I figured if we went further..." She trailed off and leaned toward him, her lips still plump and reddened from his kisses.

He accepted her silent invitation and covered her lips with his, closing his eyes in bliss at how wonderful her mouth felt moving with his. He didn't think that would ever get less magical.

Even though it was the last thing he wanted to do, he broke the kiss. "We should get back to work."

While their rope increased in length, they talked to keep their minds from the evils they'd encountered and the impossible challenge they faced to escape. They conversed about what books they had on their reading list for winter break, and about what it would be like if Stephen King and Peter Straub wrote a sequel to *The Talisman*. There was a sense of defiance in their conversation, a vow that the Raimi House wouldn't claim them, that they'd live to read all those books, both existing and hypothetical.

By the time they'd constructed a rope that looked like it would be long enough to reach the road below the cliff, Guillermo's hands and wrists ached. More pain would come when they used the rope. Now, the big worry was getting back to the cliffside without being caught by zombies or demons.

Amelia shouldered her backpack and started coiling the rope. "Let's do this."

"Wait. I'm going to make sure there's not a trap waiting outside."

He went to each window and checked for signs of anything approaching the house. The coast seemed clear, but he remained uneasy as he took the rope from Amelia and put the coil around his shoulder like when carrying electrical wiring on a job site.

Slowly, they opened the rear door of the guesthouse, looking out both ways in case a demon or shambling corpse lay in wait. Guillermo took a deep breath and readied his flashlight and bag of basil, frowning at how little was left. He put it back and grabbed the embalming pump. The squirt guns had been too weak. At least this thing would have heavier spray and, when it was empty, he could use it to bludgeon the enemy.

Amelia took out a water balloon that had miraculously survived along with the last three aloe leaves. "Shouldn't we try to find the others?"

Guillermo's gut twisted with remorse as he shook his head. "Too risky. Especially if they did go back into the house." He looked up at the sky and his heart sank to see it was still black. And had the moon even moved at all? What if the evil power of the Raimi House and grounds had the ability to mess with time? If that was the case, there was zero hope of making it to see a sunrise that would never come. "Maybe when we get the rope secured, we can call out to them in case they're still outside."

If Amelia heard the doubt in his voice at the last, she did a good job ignoring it. "Okay. And maybe if they don't hear us, they'll spot the rope."

They slowly walked toward the cliff, constantly checking to make sure they weren't being followed. The spot between Guillermo's shoulder blades itched with the feeling of being watched. Maybe the evil in the land could sense that they were at the verge of escaping its clutches.

When they walked through the thin barrier of fog, he half expected for them to suddenly be turned around, walking toward either the guesthouse or, worse, the demon-infested main house.

Instead, the sound of gentle lapping waves greeted him, followed by a view of the lake and its tree-lined beach lit by the full moon hanging over the mountains across the water. A measure of Guillermo's tension relaxed, not only from making it back to the cliff, but also that his fear of time being held captive by the Raimi property appeared to be untrue. Though it was still dark out, the moon had moved. They were facing west, so there was no way to tell if the sky was growing lighter, but his heart told him it had to be.

Amelia's voice broke through his study of the horizon. "We need to find somewhere to secure the rope."

"A tree would be best," Guillermo began before a horrific memory of Kevin being pulled apart by a tree like a pork roast made him shiver and run a hand through his hair. "Oh shit. What if we get killed for trying that?"

"We have to try." Her voice, though raspy, was strong as iron. "If we don't, we're stuck. But maybe if we throw some salt at the tree or squirt it with the garlic water, we'll be able to tell if it's normal or evil."

"Another good idea." He looked at the nearest trees. "Let's try that white pine past the spruce. It's closest to the edge." Also, because the pine's branches were thinner and hopefully less able to tear someone apart.

They approached the tree without any sight or sound of demons and when Amelia salted and sprayed the tree without it reacting, he thanked whatever forces for good existed in this universe.

The damp ground soaked his slacks when he knelt and tied one end of the rope around the tree's shiny silver trunk. A little bit of sap got on his hands. At first Guillermo was irritated, then he realized the stickiness could help his grip on the sheets. He tied a first knot, looped the roped around the tree, and tied another, then another. After three, he backed up parallel to the cliff, uncoiling the rope a few more feet, then leaned back on his heels until the rope took all his weight. The rope went taut, but stayed strong. The tree trunk didn't so much as creak.

"Amelia, come here and hold on to me."

"Gladly." The eagerness in her voice made him smile. She could always make him smile. She put her water balloon and aloe back in her coat pocket and wrapped her arms around his waist.

"Let the rope take our weight. I need to see if it's strong enough to hold both of us." *Please don't let it break, please*, he chanted inwardly while trying to sound calm. "I plan to have us go one at a time, but it's better to be prepared, just in case."

He took a second to enjoy her warmth and closeness before he tipped them backwards. This time, there was a small creaking noise, but he couldn't tell if it came from the tree or the rope. He let the rope hold their weight a little longer, waiting. Nothing snapped and the tree didn't groan.

He steadied his voice so she wouldn't know he'd been scared shitless that the rope would tear. "Okay. Our rope can hold two, thank God. Should we try to call for the others?"

Amelia nodded and cupped her hands around her mouth. Guillermo stopped her with a hand on her shoulder. "Let me. Your throat has to be killing you."

He turned in the direction of the house, took a deep breath, and immediately choked in startled fear.

Susan Acuff walked toward them, Cameron Dane beside her. Susan's forehead was partly caved in from when Cam had knocked her out with a bedpost before Rebecca had shredded his face and bitten off his nose. Neither appeared to notice their injuries.

Susan pointed at them, her gravelly voice still ringing with the authority she had as sorority president. "Where do you think you're going, pledges? You're not allowed to leave until your initiation is over."

Chapter Nineteen

"Screw your initiation," Amelia yelled, hating how raspy her voice sounded. "And screw your stupid fucking sorority."

As ridiculous as her words should have sounded, the demon flinched, as if there was still some vestige of the real Susan still in there.

The Cameron demon laughed. His voice distorted from his missing nose. "Sorry, Guillermo, Mimi is gonna get back together with me. We're meant to be together, forev—"

The demon's taunt waned as a blast of water from Guillermo's embalming pump sprayed Cam's face, blistering and melting the mutilated flesh. Amelia threw the water balloon at Susan, making her gray mottled skin turn an angry, boiling red, but when she saw more demons emerging from the fog, she grabbed Guillermo's hand.

"Come on, let's climb down."

Her heart pounded as Guillermo bent to grab the rope and they darted under the tree. Amelia hoped the widespread branches would get in the clumsy demons' way and slow them down at least a little.

Guillermo dropped to his belly and propped himself up with his elbows. "I'll start down first so if the rope breaks, I can break your fall."

"You shouldn't—"

"No time to argue." He clung to the rope with both hands and scooted over the cliff's edge. "When I say go, follow me down. I'll direct you to what footholds I can find."

When the last black curl on his head disappeared off the cliff, Amelia's heart lodged in the throat. What if he slipped and fell? What if—

"Go," his voice echoed off the walls of the cliff.

Amelia took the rope in both hands and lowered herself to start the climb. As she began to scoot back, something thudded on the ground and rolled in front of her.

Kirk's severed head grinned at her, his mouth full of gleaming fangs and greenish drool. They were nearly eye to eye. "Not so fast, pledge."

And like a scene in the movie *The Thing*, little tentacles sprouted from Kirk's neck. The head started to slither over to her, its eyes glowing traffic-light yellow.

Amelia couldn't bear to look at the hideous thing a second longer, much less risk having her fingers bitten off. She scooched back even faster, her legs hanging in midair for a second, untangling themselves from the skirts of her wedding dress, before her shoes found tenuous purchase on the basalt cliff edge. The head tried to follow, then stopped suddenly, inches from the edge.

Susan's voice called out in that same grating tone Amelia heard on the first day in the Omega Pi house. A singsong cadence that was somehow always tyrannical. "Oh, Amelia, you know deep down that you were never worthy of being an Omega Pi sister. The only reason I gave you a chance is because Tiffany Henreid had enough class for the both of you. Your true colors showed tonight when you abandoned Tiffany to die in this house. How could you do that to your best friend? Betray her for a construction worker with an inferior bloodline? It's not too late to repent." The saccharine tone bled from Susan's voice, leaving only the commanding voice of a dictator. "Climb back up here, pledge. Join our sisterhood and make up with your best friend. *Now*, or your pitiful body will be splattered on that road below."

Amelia paused on the cliff face and frowned in confusion. Was the Susan demon unaware that Tiffany had exploded? Or had that splattered mess of gunk and goo somehow re-formed and made Tiffany whole again? It didn't matter. Amelia had been bossed around and mocked by a bigger bitch than Susan. One who'd pretended to be her friend.

"You think I give a fuck about Tiffany?" she yelled back in defiance. Her sweaty hands slipped on the makeshift rope and her stomach plummeted as she slid down in a free fall that was only about a foot but felt like ten.

Guillermo's voice calmed her panicked scream. "Ignore them and hold on, Amelia. There's an outcropping a few inches to the right of your left foot. Work your way down, steady yourself, and take a few deep breaths. I'm only two feet below you now."

Amelia followed his advice, shifting her foot until she felt a ledge of solid stone beneath her shoe. After allowing the majority of her weight to rest on the rock, the strain in her shoulders eased a bit and she followed Guillermo's advice, closing her eyes and willing herself to deeply inhale and exhale.

The demons couldn't reach her. Guillermo was with her. They *would not* fall.

More noises and growls came from above. She opened her eyes and looked up to see Rebecca peering over the edge, grinning at her with malevolent eyes. She could hear other demons above, the sound of them pacing and shambling across the grass filling Amelia with a mixture of elation that they couldn't reach her and Guillermo, and dread that one or more of them could be Nancy, Miranda, or Alvin.

Reluctantly, Amelia shifted her hands down the rope another few inches. "I'm going to keep climbing down."

"Okay," Guillermo's voice remained calm and encouraging. "A few feet down, there will be an outcropping with moss and a thick root to your left. I'm at it now."

She removed her foot from the rock and resumed relying on her upper body strength and her knees to keep hold of the rope as she guided herself down. The wind from the lake increased the chill in the air and stiffened her fingers. Soon, her hands would be numb. But she tried not to think about that.

Suddenly, she felt vibrations from the rope. Possible creaks too, though it was harder to hear beneath the sound of the winds and the lapping waves from the lake. The vibrations were stronger. Amelia looked up to see if one of the knots were breaking, but it was hard to see in the shadows. Then the cliffside lit up with a yellow beam from Guillermo's flashlight.

The knots looked fine, but when the sound of the demons laughing reached her ears, her blood went cold. The demons were trying to untie the rope. The memory of Kirk's head slithering toward her, its mouth full of fangs, made her heart sink in dread. Those teeth could chew through knotted sheets easily.

"We have to hurry!" Amelia shouted. "They're breaking the rope."

She felt a tug below her as he followed suit, shimmying down. She tried to maintain her hold with her knees as she loosened her grip on the rope, letting the fabric slide through her hands. Her hands burned with the friction, and her wrists jolted painfully with every knot they bumped into.

By the time she'd made it down another ten feet, she couldn't feel Guillermo's movements on the rope anymore. But she hadn't heard him fall, so he had to still be with her.

The rope jolted above her, as part of it had been broken. Amelia shimmied down another foot before a sharp ripping sound reached her ears as the last bit of fabric tore. Guillermo's hand closed around her right wrist, giving her a millisecond of security. Then they both dropped. Demon laughter echoed above. Her free hand scrabbled across the slick basalt surface as she sought for purchase. Her stomach plummeted to her feet; her breath forced from her lungs. After she slapped what felt like a bush, her fingers wrapped around one of the roots Guillermo was talking about back when he'd first surveyed the cliffside. Back when Cheryl had still been alive and Miranda, Alvin, and Nancy had been with them. An eternity ago.

Guillermo's weight pulled her arm for a moment as he found something to further brace himself. Panting with terror, Amelia glanced down at him. His free hand grasped several thin branches of a bush growing from the meager dirt that accumulated between the cracks and atop the outcroppings of the basalt columns. Before Amelia could look around and see if there was some way for him to find another safe path down, the bush Guillermo held tore from the dirt, its thin roots unable to support his mass.

He dropped down, his full weight jerking on her arm. She heard the ugly popping noise of her shoulder tearing from its socket before a scalding wave of agonizing pain forced the breath from her body in a sound that was part gasp and part scream. Still, her numb fingers weakly tried to keep their grip around Guillermo's wrist.

She sucked in a breath through gritted teeth, trying to fight to cling to consciousness and see through the black and white spots blurring her vision.

"Don't let go." She forced the words out in a whimper while the demons continued to laugh. Their voices were too faint for her to understand their taunts.

At first it seemed that he'd follow her plea. Her shoulder burned with hellish fire, the pain intensifying as he worked one strap of his backpack off, then switched hands gripping her wrist, so he could work off the other strap and let the backpack fall. Between cringes at the jolts of agony his movements caused, she also winced at the faraway thump when the backpack hit the pavement below. They were still too far from the bottom. She wondered why he dropped the pack, until she felt the root in her grasp rise a fraction. He was trying to reduce their weight.

And now that the echoes of her screams faded, she heard the root groan.

"Can...you...get my backpack off?" she managed to gasp between sunbursts of pain. It hurt even worse to crane her neck to the side, downward, and back as far as humanly possible to be able to meet his eyes.

"No." Guillermo's voice held a flat resignation as he continued. "You can't switch hands to get the other strap off even when I let go of you. Not with your shoulder torn from your socket."

While she absorbed the painful truth that her right hand was now useless, it took a second to process the worst thing he'd said. *When I let go.*

"*No,*" she sobbed, still holding his gaze in spite of the added pain to her neck. That discomfort was small potatoes compared to the agony of her shoulder. "You can't let go. Maybe someone will come. Maybe you can find something else to hold on to."

"I'll definitely try on the way down." His eyes remained fixed intently on hers. "But I can't stay with you. That root can't support both our weight. It's about to crack." The root groaned again in agreement. "If I don't survive the trip down, never forget that I love you. Hang on as long as you can. Promise me."

"I..." she stumbled. How could he ask her to live without him? Especially since she didn't think she could maintain her grip for very much longer, and it was exceedingly likely that the root would break anyway. Why not die with him?

"Promise me!" he demanded. The root groaned again. Louder this time.

"I promise," she managed through the lump in her throat. He became a blur through the tears she could no longer hold back.

"I love you," he repeated as his fingers released her wrist.

She screamed again as she watched him fall, his hands still extended upward like he'd changed his mind and was reaching for her too late. His black curls, rinsed free of the gel, rippled in the wind of his momentum. He looked like an angel plummeting from heaven.

The loud thud of him hitting the pavement stole her breath before she moaned in dread. The pain in her shoulder had dulled slightly, either from loss of strain from holding Guillermo's weight, or because she was going into shock. She didn't care either way. She wanted to know if Guillermo had survived.

Ignoring the returning spikes of pain when she moved, Amelia swung awkwardly to the left, trying to find something to brace her foot so she'd be able to look down. After some awkward flailing and lifting her knee, running the toe of her shoe along the cliffside in blind exploration, Amelia found the slightest protrusion of rock. She braced part of her weight on it, reducing the burden of the root slightly, and positioned herself in an awkward diagonal position across the cliff face that allowed her to see Guillermo lying on the side of the road.

His right leg was bent in an unnatural angle that made her wince. The lower part was definitely broken, which would make it harder for them to make it to the nearest place that would have help and even more impossible to get up the steep, winding road back to Guillermo's truck, which was parked at the gate. Then she remembered Simon had parked his van behind them, blocking them in. But Kevin said Simon had left his keys in the visor of the van.

If she could make it down, then maybe she could pull Guillermo off the road and go up to get the van herself.

Her hope began to die when Guillermo remained silent. Was he breathing? She couldn't tell. His eyes weren't visible in the meager moonlight.

"Guillermo?" she called shakily. "Are you okay?"

Oh God, that was a stupid question. His leg was broken. He had to be in agony. But if he was, wouldn't he make a sound? Unless he was knocked out.

"Guillermo." Her voice was a hysterical sob. No. He couldn't be dead. *He couldn't be.*

Lights appeared in the distance, growing larger and brighter as they rounded the corner of the road.

Headlights. A car was heading north, back toward town from heaven knew where at this hour. Aside from more lake houses and a very expensive steak house out in Wolf Lodge fifteen miles away, nothing much existed past the Raimi House for at least a hundred miles.

The beams of the headlights revealed Guillermo's motionless body in stark detail. Amelia sucked in a breath. His eyes were closed, all the color in his face had drained away, and it didn't look like he was breathing.

And if Guillermo was still alive, he wouldn't be much longer because the car was heading right for him, the left tires lined up in a path to crush his head.

Amelia screamed.

Chapter Twenty

Guillermo woke to the sound of Amelia screaming and the stink of asphalt and exhaust. The ground vibrated beneath him, and lightning bolts of pain shot through his left leg along with waves of nausea at how *wrong* his right leg felt. He opened his eyes, but all he could see was blinding bright lights. Head spinning in confusion, it took a moment to figure out what he was doing: lying on a road with his body battered, leg fucked up.

Then his mind answered with vivid flashbacks of climbing down the cliffside with demons taunting him and Amelia. The rope breaking, him clinging to Amelia's wrist, painfully pulling her shoulder from its socket. His guilt not having a chance to sink in because the root she held couldn't support their weight. The cool acceptance he'd let go, even if it meant dying to ensure the woman he loved would survive.

Well, at least he hadn't died. But with his leg and the saints knew what else broken, he doubted he'd be any use to her.

"Oh *fuck*," he gasped, still mostly out of breath from having the wind knocked out of his body from the fall. Fear prickled up and down his spine at the sound of Amelia screaming. Had she fallen too?

He tore his gaze away from the light and his eyes strained to look up at the cliffside, seeking out Amelia. If not for the white dress, he wasn't sure he'd be able to see her up there. Not with spots flaring in his vision from the lights—and his possible concussion.

"Guillermo," Amelia yelled down at him, thankfully still clinging to the root. "There's a car coming."

Too late, he realized what those bright lights were, and the car was about to run him over. His muscles felt like broken lead as he raised his arm, which thankfully didn't seem to be broken, and struggled to wave.

"Hey," he wheezed, instead of the loud yell he'd intended.

Yet miraculously, the car slowed and then stopped with a good six feet between his head and the thick black tires. The brighter headlights turned off, easing his blindness and revealing an older muscle car. Guillermo squinted above the dual headlights of the black car, and saw "*Plymouth*" in silver letters spaced below the line of the hood. He couldn't see any higher than that. The smell of exhaust was stronger, but he welcomed the faint bit of warmth that reached him from the car's engine. Beneath stabs and thuds of pain, he felt the biting cold.

Amelia's relieved sigh could be heard even through the guttural idling of the engine. "Oh thank goodness."

He swallowed, and managed to speak a little louder than a whisper. "Hang on, Amelia. Just a little bit longer."

Now that he was no longer in danger of being run over, he tried to scoot closer to the warmth—and immediately cried out as his broken leg protested any movement. The car door opened and Guillermo tensed with a mix of hope and trepidation as the driver's footsteps approached him.

A tall man who looked to be in his mid- to late twenties crouched beside him. He had straight black hair pulled tight in a ponytail and green eyes that were bright in contrast to his pale, square face that seemed to reflect the light from his car.

"Are ye all right?" he asked in an accent that sounded familiar, but Guillermo couldn't place.

"Fuck no," Guillermo croaked in reflexive response to the inanity of the man's question in the face of all he'd been through. He took a deep breath and adjusted his tone. "I'm sorry. I mean that my girlfriend and I escaped the Raimi House. We came down the cliff, but our rope broke and I fell. My girlfriend is up there, clinging to a root." He looked up at Amelia, his heart threatening to claw itself out of his chest at the sight of her dangling and vulnerable. "*Please*, help her. She has a dislocated shoulder and I don't know how much longer she can hang on."

Even as he asked that question, he looked back up at Amelia to see how close she was to the ground. She was about thirty feet up. Guillermo looked back at the man, who was looking up at Amelia, and his heart sank with doubt at the sight of the guy's tailored black slacks, fancy button-up shirt, and even fancier black peacoat. He'd expected someone driving a sixties muscle car to be a badass, not this guy who looked like some executive who went to cocktail parties. Hell, that's probably where he came from. A guy like that wouldn't want to get his hands dirty, much less climb up a cliff and rescue a woman.

But maybe the guy could drive him down to the hotel they'd passed on their way up to the Raimi House. Then he could call 9-1-1.

Before Guillermo could make the suggestion, the man was shrugging out of his peacoat. He put it over Guillermo like a blanket. "Don't move, lad. I'll get her for ye."

If he wasn't in shock that the guy was actually going to try to climb the cliff, Guillermo would have been tempted to pop off a smart-ass remark. Where the hell was he going to go with a busted leg and probably plenty of other injuries? Not only that, but the man's accented voice held a note of command reserved for only the most powerful people. And that accent... Was it Scottish or Irish?

Instead, Guillermo nodded obediently, enjoying the warmth of the coat. As the man found the first handholds and pulled himself up the cliff, Guillermo noticed that he'd misjudged the guy in other ways. There were no shoulder pads in the coat. The man's shoulders truly were that broad. And he was muscular. Guillermo stared at the flex of muscles beneath that silky shirt with a combination of envy and contrition for misjudging the guy.

The mystery rescuer scaled the cliffside with a quickness that made him wonder if he was a professional rock climber. When he reached Amelia, he carefully wrapped his arm around her waist and managed to carry her down one-handed. Guillermo's envy surged. Was this hero secretly Spider-Man?

Because what he'd asked of the man should have been impossible.

Since Amelia would be unable to hold on to him with both arms, he had to climb down with one hand. Guillermo felt a pang of worry for Amelia's safety, not at the odds of the man losing his grip on her or the cliff, but at the possibility that he could pose a danger to her.

The strange feelings were buried with sorrow at the cries and whimpers of pain she fought to suppress on the journey down. No matter how carefully she was being carried, any movement had to be hurting her. The man murmured something too quiet to hear and she visibly relaxed.

At about ten feet from the bottom, the man let go of the cliff and dropped smoothly to the ground, only jarring Amelia a little. Surprisingly, she didn't cry out. Then Guillermo got nervous again when he set Amelia on her feet, but didn't immediately release her. Instead, he grasped her shoulders and bent down so they were face-to-face. How far he had to bend showed how tall he really was.

"Is it ye at last?" the man asked in a soft tone that Guillermo *did not* like. Then he shook his head, and a look of profound sadness cut into his features. "No. Your eyes are blue."

Finally, he removed his hands from Amelia's shoulders and stepped away from her. Guillermo let out his pent-up breath, then sucked in another when the man stalked over to him, looking dangerous all over again. Amelia held on to her dislocated shoulder and rushed over to Guillermo's side, ignoring the man.

She sank to her knees, placed her hands on his face, and kissed him repeatedly. "When you fell, I thought you were dead. How bad are you hurt?"

"I don't know yet." Only then did he become aware of the awkward shapes poking at his head, neck, and shoulders. "Holy shit, I partly landed on my backpack. No wonder my head feels wet. Water balloons and a few cans of beer were in there. I thought my head was bleeding."

The man cleared his throat and interrupted. "It still might be from falling from as high as the lass was. Now, I'm sorry to interrupt your joyous reunion, but I think it best if I get you out of the road and over to some medics."

Guillermo nodded. The guy was right. He struggled to a sitting position, hissing in pain as his leg and other parts protested with blasts of pain. Amelia tucked her good arm under his and the man took his other arm. Together, they slowly pulled him up while he tried to keep his leg off the ground.

As they guided him to the car, a Barracuda, Guillermo observed when he saw the emblem on the fender, the man scolded him, his accent—now unmistakably Scottish—thicker than before. "What in the name of all that is holy were ye two thinkin' goin' to tha' evil house?"

Amelia hung her head. "It was an initiation for the fraternity and sorority. We were supposed to spend the night there."

The Scotsman made a tsk sound and continued his rant. "An' I 'spose ye were curious about the tales of the ghosties and ghoulies that house is infamous for. In most cases I couldna' blame ye. Not all creatures of the night are bad, but everything in that accursed place certainly is, an' ye should know that. A pair o' numpty radges, ye are. Even if ye both have good taste in costumes. I love *Spaceballs* and the *Addams Family*."

While Guillermo gaped at the Scotsman in surprise, the guy pinched the bridge of his nose and took a deep breath as if trying to compose himself. For a moment, it looked like his eyes were glowing bright green, but that had to be a trick of light from the headlights reflecting off the pavement.

When they got to the passenger side of the car, the Scotsman had Amelia help Guillermo lean against the fender so he could open the door and adjust the seat to accommodate his broken leg. He didn't speak again until everyone was settled in the car, Guillermo mostly lying down in the front seat, covered once more with the Scotsman's coat, and Amelia safely tucked in the back.

Then the man turned to look at Guillermo, his eyes barely visible in the darkness and certainly not glowing. When he next spoke, his voice was gentle, and his accent once more subtle. "How many died up there?"

"Almost everyone." Guillermo's heart clenched with sorrow at the brutal deaths he'd witnessed, and the knowledge that Nancy, Miranda, and Alvin might not have made it. "We had three friends left with us, but we got separated. They might still be alive."

"I pray they are. You'll find out soon, I suppose." The car began to move.

After not barely a minute had passed, Amelia grabbed the driver's seat and leaned forward. "What are you doing? This road goes back to the Raimi House."

Guillermo gasped in horror. He knew there was something off about this man. "You can't take us back there."

"I have to," the man explained calmly. "That's where the ambulances and rescue team are."

Sure enough, when Guillermo managed to raise his head high enough to see out the windshield, he saw red and blue flashing lights at the top of the hill.

When the car made it up to the area near the gates of the Raimi House, Guillermo saw tons of new cars, two ambulances, two cop cars, and a crowd of people gathered by the wrought-iron gates. The house was invisible past the gate, still obscured by fog.

"Holy shit." Amelia's breath tickled his ear. "Do you think they were there this whole time, or did we simply miss them when we were hiding in the guesthouse?"

"I don't know." *But he did, didn't he?* "I guess we'll find out."

A police officer saw their rescuer's car and waved for them to stop with one hand, the other resting on his gun holster.

The Scotsman rolled down his window and gave a terse explanation of discovering Amelia and Guillermo on the road below the cliff and that he was simply bringing them up here for medical care. "The boy has a broken leg and possible other injuries. The girl in the backseat has a dislocated shoulder. They are in a lot of pain. Please hurry."

Guillermo cringed at being called a boy and wondered why the man omitted the part where Amelia had been rescued from the side of the cliff, not the bottom. Then things got weirder.

After the cop called for the medics, he turned back to the Scotsman. "Thank you for helping find more survivors. I'd like you to stay and answer more questions."

Instead of agreeing, the Scotsman's tone switched to one that was low, rhythmic, and somehow heavy with authority. "You do not need to ask me anything. The sun will be up soon. I must go."

"I don't need to ask you anything," the cop droned like he was under hypnosis.

The Scot continued. "You will not remember me."

"I will not remember you."

The Scot turned to face Guillermo, his eyes glowing neon green. "You—"

The passenger door opened so suddenly that Guillermo nearly fell out.

"Careful, son," another man said gently. "Just relax and let us help you."

After Guillermo was pulled out of the car and carried to a stretcher, he watched the medics slide the front seat forward and help Amelia get out of the back. Her face was stark white and lined with pain as she clutched her arm. He glanced back at their weird rescuer and saw him momentarily slump in the driver's seat and press his forehead to the steering wheel in a classic display of frustration before putting his car in reverse and backing out of the driveway and turning smoothly back to the road down. Too late, Guillermo realized he still had the man's coat draped over him.

Amelia's warm fingertips brushed his, taking his attention from the Barracuda's taillights to her beautiful, beloved face. He gripped her hand, and refused to let go when the medics tried to wheel him away.

Amelia looked up at them with pleading eyes and a trembling lower lip. "Please let me hold his hand while you set his leg."

In the end, they allowed it. On their way to the ambulance, they passed another, where Alvin and Miranda sat on the open tailgate, wrapped in blankets and holding steaming mugs with bandaged hands. When they noticed Guillermo and Amelia, they cheered and tried to follow them to the other ambulance, but were held back.

"We'll talk soon," Guillermo shouted to them. His heart surged with joy at seeing his friends alive.

As soon as they were settled in the back of the ambulance, both he and Amelia were given shots of some sort of painkiller that kicked in almost immediately. Still, he couldn't hold back an embarrassingly loud cry of agony when the medics straightened his leg before they splinted and wrapped it. He was surprised he didn't break Amelia's fingers.

She nearly broke his when he returned the favor and held her hand while they popped her shoulder back in its socket. After they put her arm in a sling, she was free to leave the ambulance and get some hot soup and water.

Guillermo was escorted to a camp chair set up by one of the outdoor cookstoves that volunteers had set up to keep warm. The police tried to question him about what had happened inside the house, but he followed the advice of one of the medics, who'd told him to request a delay to making a statement due to being in shock and on pain medication.

The officer reluctantly agreed and gave him his card so they could set up an appointment to come to the station when he was released from the hospital. Guillermo hid his relief and huddled in the blanket he'd been given. And the Scotsman's coat. The weapons he and Amelia had collected in their backpacks could make them suspects for murder.

Wait, where was his backpack? He didn't remember seeing it in the ambulance. It must still be in that weird Scottish guy's car.

Amelia sat in the empty camping chair he'd requested to be reserved for her. She handed him a cup of soup. Her cup was safely secured in her sling. "I got a delay from questioning by the cops, did you?"

He nodded, taking the plastic spoon she'd tucked in her sling. "That guy who saved you and drove us up here has our backpacks. I was freaking out about what they'd think about some of the things we had in them."

"Damn. That means he has my copy of Claudia Raimi's diary and Ellen Raimi's autobiography." She took her cup of soup from the sling and tucked it between her knees while she fished for the spoon. "But I don't know if I care about them anymore. I've had more than my fill of the place." She leaned closer to him and whispered, "I think that guy was a vampire."

His eyes widened and he leaned over farther until the camping chair threatened to tip over. "When I saw the way he moved up that cliff and carried you down one-handed, I started to think there was something off about him. Then when he did that Jedi mind trick with the cop and his eyes glowed, I was pretty sure he wasn't human. But a vampire? I'm not so sure."

Amelia gave him a sideways smirk. "If demons and ghosts exist, then why wouldn't vampires? And come on, you heard him say he was in a hurry because the sun was coming up soon. That spells vampire in my book."

"Okay, you have a point." Guillermo shivered at the thought of being in a car with a vampire. The memory of the way he held Amelia and bent down so he was close enough to kiss her took on a sinister context. "What did he say to you when he was getting you down the cliff??"

"He did his 'Jedi mind trick' so I was calm and my pain vanished for a little bit." Amelia didn't look freaked out about that; instead, she looked wistful. "Then when we got down, he acted like I was someone he knew and was looking for. When he said my eyes were the wrong color, he looked like he was about to cry. It reminded me of the movie *Blacula*, where he encountered the reincarnation of his lost love. Maybe this vampire is looking for his."

"Well, I'm glad it wasn't you." How the hell could he compete with a good-looking, clearly rich, immortal being who could hypnotize people to his will?

"Me too." She put her hand over his, a little awkwardly with the spoon's handle tucked between her fingers. "From now on, I only want to encounter the supernatural in books."

A voice interrupted them. "Amelia? *You* were at that party?"

Guillermo saw a tall guy with dark red hair peeking out from the hood of a gray parka approaching them.

"Hi, Jason." Amelia sounded abashed. "You can berate me later. Is Zelda here?"

"Yeah. She and Tobe are at the gates with their cats, along with our neighbor, Edith." He pointed toward the wrought-iron barrier. "They're the ones who helped the other two survivors climb over the gate, since no one out here could get it open."

Guillermo looked over at the group gathered by the fence. Sure enough, there was a couple who each had a cat on a leash, a blue-haired old woman with four. The six felines sat up straight and regal, like statues of the goddess Bastet. The fog in front of them was thin enough to make out a sliver of the grounds and even the Raimi House off in the distance. He'd thought the demon inside Amelia had been lying about cats helping fight evil spirits. But it had been Amelia telling the truth.

Before he could ask about that, Alvin and Miranda joined them. Miranda carefully hugged Amelia while Alvin patted Guillermo's shoulder. "I'm so happy you two are alive. How'd you get out?"

"We made a rope and went down the cliff. The demons broke it before we made it all the way down."

"That explains the broken leg," Alvin said. "We found a gap in the fog and climbed the fence. The sharp points got us in a couple places. And to think there was a whole rescue team outside the whole time. They couldn't get in and we couldn't get out."

"What about Nancy?" Amelia asked softly.

Miranda shook her head. "The house changed and we got separated again."

Alvin tucked Miranda under his arm. "It's almost dawn, so there's still hope."

Everyone maintained their vigil, eyes peeled on the fence and gate as the sky turned gray and the fog beyond the gates began to dissipate. Birds started chirping in the distance. When the lake turned pink and gold, Guillermo's heart began to sink.

Miranda sighed ruefully. "There were so many demons in there. I don't know how she could have survived."

"She was so strong." Amelia's voice broke in a sob. "She fought *so hard*."

The paramedics approached their little group and one put a hand on Guillermo's shoulder. "Come on. It's way past time we get you four to the hospital."

"Wait!" Amelia shouted. "*Look*."

They followed the direction she pointed to the locked gates. Nancy staggered toward them like one of the demons. Blood and black and pink demon goo covered her from head to toe. But the reason for her awkward shamble was because she had a body of a woman over her shoulder. A mass of blood-soaked blonde hair obscured her face, but the Cinderella costume looked familiar.

Amelia gasped. "It's Laura Hayward. I thought Brandon killed her."

Nancy laid Laura's unconscious form down on the dewy grass and blinked in surprise before putting her hands on her hips and glaring at the crowd. "Can one of you make yourselves useful and open this gate?"

One of the firemen brought out his ax. "We tried to break the lock earlier, but it wouldn't work. Maybe now it will."

"Wait," Guillermo said. "There should be a key in the visor of that van. I saw Kirk put it on Simon's keyring the first time we came here."

After the gate was unlocked, Nancy lifted Laura again and carried her out of the Raimi grounds. Laura's lashes fluttered before her eyes opened. "Nancy? What happened?"

Nancy kissed Laura's forehead. "I'll tell you later."

Applause rang out around them. And Guillermo and Amelia exchanged grins with Nancy before they turned their attention back to each other.

Guillermo cupped Amelia's cheek in his hand, his heart swelling with adoration. "I know what happened."

"What?" she breathed, leaning closer.

"Love defeated evil."

He enfolded her in his arms and kissed her while cheers rang out around them.

Epilogue

Zihuatanejo, Mexico
Five years later

Amelia thanked *Tia* Salma and *Tio* Renzo for the fourth time for the lovely dinner, still embarrassed at how awkward her Spanish was. Guillermo kissed his aunt and uncle on their cheeks again and swept Amelia out the door.

"Well," Guillermo said with a broad grin as they got in their rental car to drive back to the resort where they'd been celebrating their honeymoon. "So much for our intentions to get back in time for another scuba diving lesson."

"I don't mind," Amelia assured him, putting her hand over his on the gearshift. Her moonstone and sapphire ring gleamed in the golden light of the setting sun. "What do you think of their offer for us to extend the honeymoon for another week?"

"I'm tempted, but I don't think it would be a good idea for you to miss more work when you got the job only eight months ago."

"That's what I was thinking too." She looked out the window, taking in the view of the ocean and white sandy beaches, before looking back at him with a smile. "But you look so happy with your newfound family members."

And seeing him happy made her heart swell with joy.

"I *am* happy." Guillermo grinned at her. "That's why I told them we'd try to visit once a year. Or, if my next book deal pans out with better royalties, maybe I can pay for their flights to come visit us."

"Those will have to be huge royalties. You have so much family here. All these aunts, uncles, great-aunts, and so many cousins I couldn't count them all." Watching Guillermo connect with them had been bittersweet. While she was happy to see him find the family his father and grandfather had abandoned, she couldn't help the pang of loneliness at knowing she had no way of finding any of her relatives. And even if she did, it was doubtful they'd be as welcoming.

"They're your family now too," Guillermo said, brushing her knuckles with his thumb.

Tears brimmed beneath her eyes as she realized his words were true. Cousin Xochitl had immediately embraced Amelia, called her *prima,* and planned to take her on a big shopping trip tomorrow.

When they got to the resort, Guillermo lifted her and carried her all the way to their room and gently laid her on the bed. They took their time undressing each other and made love even more slowly, something they hadn't been able to do often back in their college dorm rooms, and had only begun to appreciate when they got their own apartment after graduation.

He'd proposed three years ago on graduation night, and while Amelia's father had made a gruff pronouncement that he thought she was too young, Guillermo's family had welcomed her with open arms. Though, back when they'd first began dating, they had reservations about her. His father blamed her when Guillermo immediately dropped out of the fraternity—which only had one surviving member—and changed his major from business management, to getting an MFA in creative writing. Guillermo's mother had briefly tried to blame Amelia for them being at the Raimi House that horrific Halloween night, but Guillermo quashed that quickly by pointing out how insistent his father had been he join a fraternity and take part in any initiation required to do so.

After that, Guillermo's father received the brunt of his wife's and mother's wrath while Amelia was vindicated and showered with kindness. Guillermo then convinced his father that Guillermo's sister, Maria, should become the heiress to Romero Construction. And, after North Idaho University made a rule that all fraternity and sorority initiations had to get approval from the dean, Guillermo's little brother, Antonio, assured his father he'd join the Alpha Lambdas when he graduated from the community college. Antonio fulfilled that promise last year, pursuing an engineering degree.

Amelia was so proud of both of them, beginning to feel like they were her little sister and brother too. Along with their brother, they took on the task of helping her learn to speak Spanish. They'd thrown her a surprise party when she'd gotten her dream job at the Amteep Public Library, and took her to a nice dinner when she'd been inducted into the Amteep Historical Society. Maria had been Amelia's only stable source of sanity when planning and preparing for the wedding.

But most importantly, they'd defended their older brother fiercely when their father got frustrated with Guillermo's mission to be a writer.

The smug way they'd grinned when Guillermo had gotten his first book deal for his historical novel about the Aztecs before the Spanish conquest... Oh, how Amelia wished she'd gotten a picture. She did get a Polaroid of Guillermo's father hugging him with the book contract in his hand.

Now here they were in Mexico, fulfilling his dream of connecting with his extended family and spending languorous hours in an oceanside paradise.

After they made love, Guillermo held Amelia in his arms. "*Mi amor*, I am so happy. All of our dreams have come true. Well, almost all."

She rested her head on his chest, listening to his heartbeat gradually slowing from its rapid pace from their lovemaking. Amelia knew what he meant by *almost*. "The nightmares will go away. They're already happening less often."

After Amelia and Guillermo escaped the Raimi House, they'd quickly discovered that parts of themselves hadn't really escaped after all. Nightmares haunted them both. Sometimes separately, and one would wake the other and comfort them until they felt secure enough to go back to sleep. Other times, they'd both awaken, screaming and trembling from experiencing the horrors of that night all over again. On those nights, they were both too shaken to go back to sleep, so Amelia would make tea and they'd either cuddle in bed and read books together, head to the couch for movies, or simply hold hands and talk, either about Guillermo's novel or Amelia's homework.

Guillermo's parents paid for him to see a good therapist, and he was still seeing the same one. Amelia had to utilize low-income services to seek counseling and had been through three before she found a counselor she clicked with. The first few were too fixated on Amelia's chilly relationship with her father and the codependent relationship she'd had with Tiffany, which were necessary issues to work on, but not the source of her nightmares and panic attacks. They didn't want to talk about the Raimi House. Amelia couldn't blame them, but she needed someone who'd help her deal with the horrors that were embedded in her psyche. Someone who believed in the existence of evil.

Alvin and Miranda had the same issue, so they referred Amelia to their therapist and now the three of them finally felt like they were making progress. As for Nancy and Laura, both had left Amteep the summer after that fateful Halloween. Sometimes they wrote. Laura had blocked most of that night from her memory, and Nancy was terse, not wanting to talk about it.

As for the house itself, the owners had allowed the bank to foreclose on it after paying out settlements to the parents of those who'd died there. The house had remained property of the bank ever since. Amelia wished the place would be demolished, even though that wouldn't lift the curse from the place. The evil was embedded too deeply in the soil.

Police and a neighborhood watch had maintained patrols ever since that night. More as a deterrent to keep people from entering those unholy gates rather than to help anyone escape. And every Halloween, a group of townspeople kept a special watch. Amelia, Guillermo, Alvin, and Miranda often took turns organizing or joining those watches.

"Amelia." Guillermo's voice brought her back to the present.

She stiffened, immediately wary. She knew that tone.

"I've been talking with my therapist about my next book," he began nervously.

"Oh?" She lifted her head and met his rich brown eyes. "The one you didn't want to talk to me about?"

"It's a horror novel." He made it sound like a sinful confession. "I think it's my way of processing what happened that night. If you don't want to read it, I understand, but I thought you should know. I didn't like keeping it secret."

He tensed beneath her, as if waiting for her to be angry. Instead, she sighed with sublime relief and snuggled against him. "I should probably tell you I've been secretly reading horror novels on my breaks at work and when you're not home. I don't know if it's because I always loved the genre and nothing would stop that, or if it's my way of dealing with the Raimi House. But either way, I better get to read your book first when it's done."

"I love you so much." He kissed the top of her head. "But there's something else. Someone bought the place."

Her heart leapt into her throat. "Who?"

"Another anonymous buyer." Scorn and dread dripped from his voice.

"Oh shit." She rolled off his chest and leaned up on her elbow. "It's going to happen again, isn't it? Either some dumb family is going to settle down in that place, or they're going to be stupid and rent it out to the next batch of idiots who want to throw a party."

"I'm afraid so." Guillermo sighed in defeat. "We're going to have to do our best to find out who owns the place and warn them not to set foot inside."

But Amelia knew they'd fail. What was the saying?

The house always wins.

ABOUT THE AUTHOR

Formerly an auto-mechanic, Brooklyn Ann thrives on writing romance featuring unconventional heroines and the heroes who adore them. Author of historical paranormal romance in her critically acclaimed Scandals with Bite series, urban fantasy in the cult favorite, Brides of Prophecy novels, and the New Adult winner of the 2016 Reader's Choice Award Hearts of Metal series, she provides love for the broken and strange.

She lives in Coeur d'Alene, Idaho with her son, miscellaneous horror memorabilia, and a 1980 Datsun 210.

She can be found online at http://brooklynannauthor.com as well as on Twitter, Instagram, and Facebook.

For exclusive updates, sneak peeks, and giveaways, sign up for Brooklyn Ann's Newsletter.

Connect with Brooklyn Ann:

twitter.com/@brooklyn_ann
facebook.com/brooklyn.ann.7
instagram.com/@brooklynann_author

www.BOROUGHSPUBLISHINGGROUP.com

If you enjoyed this book, please write a review. Our authors appreciate the feedback, and it helps future readers find books they love. We welcome your comments and invite you to send them to info@boroughspublishinggroup.com.

Follow us on Facebook, Twitter and Instagram, and be sure to sign up for our newsletter for surprises and new releases from your favorite authors.

Are you an aspiring writer? Check out www.boroughspublishinggroup.com/submit and see if we can help you make your dreams come true.

Love podcasts? Enjoy ours at www.boroughspublishinggroup.com/podcast

www.ingramcontent.com/pod-product-compliance
Lightning Source LLC
Chambersburg PA
CBHW031337170626
46807CB00002B/744